Also by Piper J. Drake

Mythwoven

Wings Once Cursed & Bound

Fangs So Bright & Deadly

FANGS SO BRIGHT AND DEADLY

PIPER J. DRAKE

Published by Sourcebooks Casablanca, an imprint of Sourcebooks
P.O. Box 4410, Naperville, Illinois 60567-4410
(630) 961-3900
sourcebooks.com

Cataloging-in-Publication Data is on file with the Library of Congress.

Printed and bound in Canada.
MBP 10 9 8 7 6 5 4 3 2 1

To the readers who make Why Choose? *an approach to life.*

ONE

Marie

First impressions are established within the first seven seconds of an encounter.

Marie Xiao had learned this from her father as a child entering grade school. All she'd wanted to do back then was fit in with the rest of the kids in class, be a part of the games on the playground. Back then, those lessons in how to blend in had been about having fun and making friends. They'd been a foundation for a lifetime of survival, building a life as a successful woman and a witch.

Three decades later, she'd refined her understanding of what an impression actually was. She'd also become much more intentional about what kind of impression she wanted to give, adjusting for timing and circumstance. There hadn't been a whole lot she could control in the early parts of her life, but she was making up for it now.

She strode into the grand foyer of the brand-new high-rise, projecting confidence with every step. Her custom-tailored two-piece suit was a conservative cut blazer over a fitted sheath dress. The hem hit two inches below her knees, allowing her to maintain the standards of even the stuffiest propriety when she sat. It was the color and fabric that caught the eye.

The Thai silk had been a gift from her new friend Peeraphan, otherwise known as Punch. The fabric held color the way few other materials could, wrapping her in the deepest iridescent blue, almost indigo, the color of the night sky just before dawn.

Paired with nude stiletto heels, the outfit made Marie feel powerful without being ostentatious. Eye-catching without being gaudy. It gave her the confidence she needed to accomplish anything she set her mind to.

Perfect for today.

The young guard at the security desk blushed slightly as they greeted her and asked who she was there to meet.

She gave them a serene smile. “Rosemary Xiao, consultant. Here to meet with Tobias Mancini.”

Minutes later a bear of a man—not literally, but she’d encountered those too—came barreling out of the elevators and headed straight for her. He was still a dozen steps away as he held his arms open and greeted her in a booming voice, “Miss Ex-igh-o! Let’s take a walk.”

The man continued to hold his arms out, like he was herding her forward. She turned toward him and caught his right hand in her own, giving it a single, firm shake. “It’s a pleasure to meet you, Mr. Mancini.”

Brown eyes flickered with surprise, then narrowed as the man smiled. “Of course.” His right hand tightened around hers. “Call me Toby.”

She kept her smile, but brought her left hand to join her right in their handshake and returned the pressure of his grip with her own. “You’re too kind. My family name is pronounced a bit more like sh-ih-ow. I appreciate you making the effort.”

He laughed and the sound came out in a series of barks, like a sea lion making himself heard. She just continued to smile until he eased his grip on her hand and she let the handshake drop on her own terms.

When he swept his left hand out ahead of them, indicating the direction in which he intended for them to walk, she fell into step beside him. He did not place his hand at the small of her back as he'd initially tried to do, before she'd maneuvered him into acknowledging her with that pointed handshake.

It was all posturing, and in those few seconds, they'd both established their impressions of each other. She knew exactly how to handle him, and he was aware she wouldn't be the kind of business associate he could steamroll into doing whatever he wanted.

So far, so good, as far as she was concerned.

He led her to the far end of the foyer, where a set of stairs curved up to the second floor. The building had an airy, open design, and a portion of the second floor looked out over the foyer below.

"As you can see, Miss Xiao," he began with slightly improved pronunciation, "our building is a recently completed construction. We had plans to enhance certain areas with greenery, but we weren't happy with the designs proposed by the original builder. We heard you're the best in the Pacific Northwest, so when we decided to contract for the job, you were at the top of our list."

Well, at least he was making some effort to respect her, and she wasn't immune to compliments, especially when they were in regard to her expertise and not her looks. She could probably work with this person.

"Many top employers around the world recognize the benefits of gardens in the workplace. They become places to provide a bit of respite, build camaraderie, encourage collaboration, and improve morale." This part of the discussion flowed easily for Marie, mostly because she believed in what she was saying. "Designed properly, people love where they work, even if the work they do is challenging. Environment could make the difference between high-performing employees flourishing and unhappy workers burning out."

Toby nodded, grinning broadly. "Exactly. Yes. What you said. Glad we're on the same page. We need our people at the top of their game. We're not just making potato chips here."

He laughed and she gave him a brighter smile so he'd feel she appreciated the joke. Personally, she placed a lot of value on the people who were a part of the process of making potato chips. Trying new flavors from across the globe was a hobby of hers. She had a snack-size bag in her shoulder bag of Thai miang kham–flavored chips, her favorite. Maybe she should offer him some.

They continued walking as he showed her the common spaces she would be including in her design. They took the elevators to a few different floors, as well as the roof, then returned to a different set of elevators to reach the subterranean floors.

"This area is where our research and development happens." He led her out of the elevators to a security checkpoint. "The original builder left a lot of plants in one of the storage rooms down here to be used in the greenery design. Waste not, and all that."

She nodded, offering her visitor badge to the camera as she stepped into the revolving door. It locked in place as she stepped in, holding her while security confirmed her identity and visitor status. While she waited, she glanced around, mildly entertaining herself with calculating the chances she might catch sight of an umbrella logo. Really, they could do anything to her in here—gas, lasers, flooding. The possibilities were disturbing.

After a moment, a voice sounded from somewhere above her. "Please step through."

The revolving door turned, letting her out on the other side. She'd done freelance consulting for a lot of companies, and only one or two big pharmaceutical companies had this kind of extra security inside the building.

"It's a fuss, I know," Toby said as he joined her, tugging at his shirt cuffs. "But the storage room has lights and all, so it's a good place to keep the plants alive until you're ready to move them to the rest of the building."

"It's no problem." Or at least, it wouldn't be so long as security had the appropriate notification to allow her to come and go as needed.

Toby reached for a door. "Here we go. We've also got diagrams and blueprints you'll need for the areas of the building we want you to set up with garden things. If you have additional recommendations beyond those, we're open to your proposals, but we'll want estimates on budget and time required. We'll need to approve your designs as well, before you get started."

Marie didn't step into the room, taking in the rows upon rows of cuttings under plant lights. Some specimens were in buckets of water and others were in seedling pots. The life energy of these plants was faint, yet there was a determination there, in the way nature tended to persist. She could help these plants flourish. Would enjoy it. It was one of the reasons her mundane day job complemented the not-quite normal aspects of who she truly was.

"There are some unusual specimens here." She let a little awe creep into her voice.

Toby's chest puffed out with pride. "Of course. Can't have those glass balls over on Seventh Avenue be the gold standard for innovative urban workspaces. We want you to be sure to incorporate these plants into your designs."

Marie stared at one plant, then looked around at several others. None of these were native to the Pacific Northwest, but one or two of these in particular had no business in this part of the world. Even more interesting, at least one was mislabeled. An easy mistake to make, but she didn't think it was by accident.

She turned to Toby. "If you have an inventory list of what's in here, I'll be sure to include all of these in my designs."

"Ah. Ahem." Toby cleared his throat, handing her a flash drive. "I don't know if there's an inventory list in there, but the diagrams you'll require are. If you need to, you can come back to do an inventory yourself after you show us your first draft."

Obviously, he hadn't put whatever files were on the flash drive there himself, or he'd have known if they included an inventory list. Not a surprise. People as high-placed on an org chart as Tobias Mancini tended to focus on strategy rather than tactical details. He'd probably left the task to an administrative assistant. It wasn't a particularly good or bad sign. She ought to avoid making him feel awkward about such things in the future, though. Independent consultants got the best repeat contracts from clients who felt comfortable working with them.

"Of course." It cost her nothing to be agreeable.

This particular contract gave her plenty of time to confirm exactly what varieties those plants were. Besides, she needed to figure out if anyone at this company knew what they might have down here in their storage room. Because at least one of those plants could induce a mental state that was absolutely not what would be considered safe for work.

"I'll look forward to it," she murmured, and it was true. This contract had suddenly gotten a lot more interesting.

If no one at this company realized what they had, she could always propose to swap the plant samples out for something that looked similar and cost less. Clients usually agreed, and she had peace of mind that her designs incorporated plants with far less potential danger to anyone or anything coming in contact with them. Too often, people underestimated plants, choosing them for appearance or scent without understanding what a plant was capable of.

They returned to the hallway. Toby shut the door to the storage room and turned to her, opening his mouth. Before he could say anything, someone came through the security check and brushed past them.

Marie stepped back quickly, managing to avoid both the man in the lab coat and Toby.

Toby, on the other hand, let out a disgruntled huff and called after the man. "You. Who is your supervisor?"

The man kept walking.

Toby followed after him, catching up in two or three ground-eating strides, and grabbed the man's arm. "I asked you who your supervisor is."

The man turned, blinking down at Toby's grip on his upper arm and then up at Toby, his gaze resting finally on Toby's employee badge.

"Oh." The man removed an earbud from his ear. "I'm sorry. I didn't hear you."

"That doesn't explain why you just blew by us in the hallway," Toby snapped. He proceeded to give the man an earful about common courtesy and recognizing the executives in the company anywhere, anytime.

Marie let most of it wash over her, since it wasn't directed toward her anyway. The man's lab coat opened wider, and a flash of gold caught her attention.

The man was wearing a serious piece of jewelry, intricately carved with accents of blue and green and yellow. The central stone was an unusual green-tinged yellow, carved into the shape of a beetle. Maybe a scarab? It definitely had an Egyptian feel to it.

She had several friends and acquaintances who wore amulets and carved pendants, either for fashion or for faith. This was possibly the biggest she'd ever seen, though, as big as her open hand with fingers spread wide. It seemed large enough in height and width to be impractical for someone working in a lab—more like a chest plate. But then, who was she to say what someone ought to wear? Fashion choices weren't her business.

The amulet had her attention for reasons other than fashion.

The man extracted his arm from Toby's grip and straightened his lab coat, hiding the amulet from view. He glared at her, and she kept her features schooled to an expression of polite curiosity. She might have even widened her eyes a little to lean into the cute, clueless appearance.

"I'll be having a word with your manager," Toby was finishing up. "Be glad I don't speak with HR about your attitude."

Honestly, she wondered how often HR got feedback about Toby. The man was too tactile in general. She had avoided it today, but she thought the way he'd stopped this employee was crossing a line.

She made a mental note to include it in her feedback at the end of this contract. She didn't want to walk away from this project yet.

After another minute or so of listening to Toby, the man in the lab coat was able to go on about his business.

Marie made sure to study his features, his build, even the way he walked. She wanted to be able to recognize him again, even if she couldn't see his face right away.

"Sorry you had to witness that." Toby didn't sound at all apologetic. "People don't have common decency these days. Rudeness in the workplace is just not acceptable. Doesn't make for good team building. I see behavior like that, and it's like waving a red flag in front of a bull."

She only offered a pleasant smile in response and allowed him to usher her back up to the grand foyer. As she left, she assured him she would be in touch by the first draft deadline or before. Then she left the building at a brisk pace, her heels clicking across the floor in a staccato beat.

She had research to do. There were plants in that room that

shouldn't be allowed anywhere outside Egypt, and there'd been power coming from that amulet. Old magic. Either one would have warranted her returning to deal with them.

The presence of both? Probably not a coincidence.

TWO

KURO

Yamamoto Kuro sat on a bench with a boba tea in hand, enjoying the sun as it burned away the morning mist hanging over the city. People were going to start emerging from the high-rises around him soon, off to early lunches. This was as good a place as any to people watch, especially the employees emerging from the shiny new Socrates Industries building.

"Why is it that I get the rooftop view and you get the boba tea?" His lover's tenor voice sounded in his earbud.

No one in this part of town would glance twice at Kuro having a conversation with air. There were so many people wearing various types of audio devices, stationary or on the move, he was just another person immersed in technology.

"I can pick up a boba tea for you later," Kuro murmured, amused.

"But I have to watch you suck balls into your mouth now, and I can't do anything fun about it," Joe responded, laughter in his voice.

Kuro sighed. "You've got the intellectual maturity of a twelve-year-old."

Joe laughed. "Only when I'm hungry."

Kuro sobered slightly. "You should have gone hunting, then."

Kuro scowled. Neither of them should go too long without

feeding. The moon would be waning over the next week or so as well. Neither of them would be at their strongest, and they didn't usually hunt together. It got too complicated. But he could make an exception if it kept Joe in good health.

"We can go barhopping or clubbing tonight. I don't mind playing wingman," he offered.

They worked well as a team, and shared many things in their lives, even lovers, but they never shared prey. Their means for gaining sustenance was one of the major differences in their natures. But he could support his partner in a hunt, then go off in search of his own prey a different night.

"It's not something to worry about." Joe still sounded unconcerned. "I'd rather not miss anything important and waste the time we've invested in this project. It'd be a shame for this many hours of boredom to be for nothing."

They'd been taking note of the coming and going of several employees, systematically learning routines and habits. It was tedious at best. They didn't have to be so thorough in their research for a quick job, but they had no information about what went on inside Socrates Industries's latest R&D facility. They couldn't be sure they would be able to acquire their target in one go. So it made more sense to gather as much information as they could about multiple employees to give them more personas to work with.

"*Hello*. I see a familiar face." Joe's tone had brightened. "Exiting the front entrance. She should walk right by you. Tell me if she smells as good as I remember."

Kuro wasn't as susceptible to distractions as Joe was, but his curiosity was piqued as the sweet scent of lemon blossoms reached him, intertwined with rosemary and earthy sandalwood, warmed with the personal essence of a woman he'd met once before. They'd met this witch in the woods under awkward circumstances. They'd pulled her out of a difficult situation, and she'd been a delight to spend a few moments with.

Kuro only hummed an affirmative to his lover. She did smell good.

"She cleans up impressive," Joe murmured with a generous dose of appreciation in his tone.

Indeed she did. Kuro also liked the sure strides she took in those elegant heels. Her head was held high, her posture erect, and there was a natural sway to her hips that was doing terrible things to his heart rate. "What business do you think she had inside Socrates Industries?"

He had thought the probability of crossing paths with the witch from the Darke Consortium was at least fifty-fifty, but he hadn't anticipated it would be so soon.

"Whatever business she had, I think she left a trail of broken hearts and devastation in her wake," said Joe.

Kuro rolled his eyes. "Dramatic."

"Not at all." Joe chuckled.

"I didn't go through every employee record, but something tells me she doesn't work here." Kuro considered the possibility as he watched her, the cadence of her steps brisk as they carried her past him.

"How's that?" Joe asked.

"Every person who goes through those front doors wears corporate clothing," Kuro said. "They wear black or gray or navy blue. Once in a while you see a beige or olive green. The fabric is usually wool or linen, maybe some polyester blend. She's dressed sharp. That is a power color, without going with an aggressive red that might put people on the defensive."

Excellent choice. He personally enjoyed meeting people who knew how to make this kind of play in corporate environments. And then there was her scent. She smelled of herb gardens and lemon trees, an interesting counterpoint to her obvious competence in this glass and steel and concrete high-rise environment.

"You're intrigued; I can tell." Joe sounded delighted by the prospect.

Kuro frowned, even as he watched her ponytail sway with her steps as she continued onward. A pair of young people walking in the opposite direction openly stared at her for a few beats, until they both blundered into a pack of tiny dogs leashed to an equally distracted dog walker. Kuro snorted.

Joe's unrestrained laughter filled his ears. "Enjoy your boba tea and keep eyes on the building, will you? I'll be right back."

"What? Wait." Kuro sat forward, glancing up at the glass building and searching the reflection for Joe's vantage point.

It probably wouldn't have mattered if Kuro had given away Joe's perch because his lover was gone. Scowling, Kuro shifted in his seat and sucked on his straw, drawing up a few boba and chewing them in frustration.

"If I'm going to be the responsible one and stay to maintain surveillance on our target," Kuro muttered over their connection, "you had better—"

"Woo the witch," Joe interjected gleefully. "I'm on it."

Kuro sighed. There was no way this could end badly.

Joe

Joseph Choe enjoyed playing all sorts of games, but anything that required days of waiting and watching got old quick for him. Sure, he'd agreed to this particular job. And he'd get back to his post. He would. As soon as he indulged in this little break from the tedium.

After all, all work and no play made Joe a boring partner.

He rushed down the stairwell to the ground floor and emerged on the street, then walked at a brisk pace up a few blocks. If the witch continued on the path she'd been on, with luck, he'd already be at the corner as she passed. Better, he thought, than him trailing behind her and chasing her to catch up. That could be creepy.

He reached the street corner he had in mind and deliberately leaned against the pole supporting the streetlight. She was easy to spot approaching, rocking that gorgeous suit and walking at an easy pace, her heels making a decisive *click-click* on the pavement. Her gaze was directed straight ahead, but he caught the slight movements as she noted anyone and anything to the sides of her. She gave off a distinct person-with-things-to-do-and-places-to-be vibe, which was smart in any city environment. When her glance swept over him, he gave her his brightest, sauciest grin.

Eye contact achieved.

She gave him her full, undivided attention. The force of her personality sent a jolt through him, traveling through his center and straight to his groin. Now *that* was chemistry.

If she felt the same—surely she must feel something—she didn't show it. Her gaze swept smoothly away from him as she continued forward as if she hadn't stared at him for the space of an endless moment in time. She didn't even slow her pace. So he decided to help fate, just a little. He sent a pulse of his magic through the pole at his back, changing the traffic signal and pedestrian crossing so she'd need to pause.

And she did, coming to a stop a step or two short of him, just out of arm's reach.

"Hello, again," he greeted her cheerfully.

He continued to lean against the pole, not wanting to move toward her too soon. That could be interpreted as aggressive. He was going for open and friendly.

Hopefully not too eager, but hey, he kind of was. He could own it.

The force of her gaze landed on him again. A pang of doubt hit him in the chest. She might not remember him, especially without Kuro. It'd been dark that night, at least for human eyes. Her expression now was a sort of pleasant neutral. No frown, nothing to indicate any negative sentiment. But also, no sign she was happy to see him, either.

"I know you." Her voice was low and rich, a decadent contralto that flowed over his skin.

He wanted to roll over and invite her to pet his belly, but he was in human form and it was a little too soon to be asking for that. Or maybe not too soon, just a little too public. Kuro would scowl over it.

Instead, he nodded and let himself push away from the pole to stand a little closer to her. Close enough to fill his nose with her scent. "You remember me."

She had to tilt her face up to keep eye contact. "You and your partner."

He almost bounced on the balls of his feet as elation bubbled up inside him. Sure, she might be using the word in the context of a working arrangement, but Kuro was his partner in every way, and hearing it from the lips of another person never got old.

Wait. He shook himself slightly and took a deep breath. He normally didn't let himself get this carried away on the happy feels with anyone but Kuro, even someone as interesting as this witch was.

"I'm Joe," he offered. "We didn't get the chance to exchange names last time."

He thought one of the corners of her mouth quirked up, just a little. "You can call me Marie."

"Okay, Marie." He let his voice drop a little into his deeper register.

Neither of them was offering a full name yet, and that wasn't a bad thing. Certain people could wield all sorts of power with one's full, true name. Even if you didn't take into account the supernatural considerations of her being a witch and him being a gumiho, humans were cautious with how much personal information they gave out, too.

"Did you just happen to catch sight of me out here in the streets of Seattle?" Marie asked. "Or were you playing another game of hide-and-seek?"

Joe grinned at the reference. Their initial meeting had been spur of the moment, and all of them had been in a place they weren't particularly welcome. Evading the perimeter security patrols had been easy for him and Kuro, but stealth wasn't one of the witch's strengths apparently. So they'd decided to help her out.

They'd owed her friend anyway, which was a longer story and not as interesting to ponder as the witch in front of him now.

"While the game was very fun," he drawled, "I think you prefer honesty, so I'll admit I caught sight of you. But I did rush over here to make sure our paths crossed."

She smiled again, her lips curving upward just a bit. He was going to have to work harder.

"And what are your intentions now?" There was amusement in her voice, and a touch of curiosity.

Good. He liked both of those things in a person.

"That is a good question." He hadn't really thought about what to do after he caught up to her.

All he knew was that things were finally not boring. Time with Kuro when Joe could have his undivided attention was always great. But there were too many things the two of them had to do that meant they were out and about and not wrapped up in each other. And Kuro was the responsible one who kept them on task. Even when the tasks were dull.

She shifted her weight slightly. The movement was minute, but still, he'd kept her standing a while now. Then he lost whatever he'd intended to say because she stepped closer, into his space, and every part of him warmed to her proximity. Every part.

"You can let the traffic lights get back on cycle," she said quietly. She quirked an eyebrow at him. "I'll stay long enough to hear you out."

"Oh. Yeah." He chuckled. He released the bit of magic he'd been maintaining and the traffic—both motor vehicle and pedestrian—resumed around them. "Thanks for the reminder."

"You're not worried about subtlety?" she asked, stepping back.

He followed, not reaching for her, but wanting to maintain the closeness she'd established. She tipped her head to one side, but didn't move away.

Good.

She'd asked a fair question. Not many humans were aware of the supernaturals living among them. It wasn't wise to do things to spook humans. But he didn't want that to be their first real conversation.

"Could I interest you in a boba tea?" He jerked his chin back toward the way she'd come and where Kuro was. "I have a craving."

He let his gaze fall to her lips for a full second before he focused back on her eyes. Her cheeks flushed a very lovely shade of pink.

"All right," she said slowly.

His veins with her acceptance of his invitation, and he thought his grin might split his face. He started back in the direction she'd come, and she fell in beside him. Conscious of his longer legs, he adjusted his pace to hers. It was nice, walking with her out in the sun.

Minutes later, Kuro came into view. As the other man caught sight of them, he rose from his seat on the bench and crossed the distance to meet them halfway. Kuro was a good-looking man under any circumstance, but Joe particularly enjoyed Kuro in motion. His posture was upright, his shoulders were squared, and his stride was sure. He had a rangy build, maybe a little broader and with a little more muscle through the upper body than most Japanese diaspora had in general, but that was a quirk of mixed genetics. Kuro moved all that muscle efficiently and smoothly and with an economy of energy. He made everything look effortless.

As Kuro approached, Joe cheerfully announced, "We're going to get some boba tea."

He watched Kuro carefully. His lover tended to project a serious expression to the world, but just the fact that Kuro had immediately gotten to his feet when they'd come into view and come to meet them indicated how eager he had been to connect with the witch again, too.

Kuro looked at Joe, giving him a slow blink, then transferred his attention to Marie. "We meet again."

"Indeed." Marie gave Kuro a smile as small as the one she'd offered Joe. "I'm told this was by chance."

Joe pouted. "I said it was."

Her lips curved upward further, and amusement danced in her eyes. She was teasing him, and he wasn't even going to try to pretend he didn't like it.

"It was a coincidence," Kuro confirmed. His voice was deeper than Joe's, and he was delighted as the pink bloomed fresh over her cheeks.

Yeah, Joe could relate. Kuro's voice had an effect on him, too.

They all stood there, considering each other. It was one of those moments when the world faded into background noise. A frisson of attraction was building between the three of them, filling their shared space. Kuro finally lifted his gaze from Marie's to meet Joe's, and Joe swallowed hard at the heat he saw in Kuro's eyes.

It wasn't often they were both attracted to the same person, but when it happened, the potential could be mind-blowing.

"I don't want to get in the way of anything," Marie said abruptly. She was already stepping back, straining the bubble of potential forming around them.

"You're not," both of them said equally as quickly.

She seemed like a straightforward kind of person. Joe figured it might be worth it to be up front about his and Kuro's shared interest in her. It might also be moving too fast, but better to get it out in the open than for her to withdraw in possible misunderstanding.

He started to give it a go. "The invitation was from both—"

Someone walked right through the three of them, cutting between him and Marie so she stumbled to the side. As she fell into Kuro, he caught her around the waist, steadying her.

Marie stared after the middle-aged man wearing a lab coat. "He's not..."

Joe shifted closer to her and Kuro, his shoulder brushing hers. "No, he's not."

"No heartbeat." On her other side, Kuro leaned in close, his arm still around her waist. He spoke low to the both of them. "That was a dead man walking. Literally."

Joe was incredibly curious. Beside him, Marie was practically vibrating with energy, and he wondered if she would leave them behind. He was honestly torn. He didn't want to separate from her, but there was also a dead body walking through the streets of downtown Seattle in broad daylight. Marie took a few steps forward, then hesitated. She turned back to the two of them.

"Excuse me, while I—"

"We'll go with you," Kuro interjected.

Joe grinned. Excellent. Yes. Conflicting emotions resolved. "Okay then, let's follow the dead man."

"This really isn't the sort of thing I investigate with anyone outside..." She trailed off, biting her lower lip.

Joe let his eyebrows raise and he placed a hand over his chest. "Outside what? Are we not allowed to come with you because we're not part of the cool kids' consortium?"

Okay, that had been a little rude. But was she really hesitating to go off on an adventure with them because they weren't one of the stuffy academics in her precious consortium? Her expression hardened, and she glared at him.

"And coming with me wouldn't be some kind of conflict of interest for you and—what was it called? Babel?"

They were still speaking in lowered voices, but the heat between them had evolved into simmering temper. Joe wasn't any less turned on by it, though.

"Let's talk this out later," Kuro suggested, sounding completely unperturbed. "There's a person of interest we all want to follow. We're all headed in the same direction, regardless."

Joe closed his mouth, swallowing what he would have said next, and Marie seemed to have also paused the momentum they had been picking up. She would be fun in a debate, he just knew it.

Marie rolled her shoulders and addressed Kuro. "Good point. Casual stroll in whatever direction he went?"

Kuro nodded.

They started off, walking three across. That worked for about a block, but Seattle's sidewalks weren't empty in the middle of the day, and it wasn't exactly subtle to be the group forcing others to go around them. Eventually, Joe and Kuro starting taking turns falling back to bring up the rear as they passed others headed in the opposite direction. Their quarry didn't turn back to look at them, or even pause except when everyone did for pedestrian traffic signals.

"If I didn't know better," Marie said in a conversational tone, "I would think he was just someone headed somewhere absentmindedly. He seems preoccupied or distracted." She paused. "Not so different from how he acted when he was alive less than an hour ago."

Joe shot a glance her way. That was unexpected.

"You know him?" Kuro prompted.

She lifted one shoulder in a half shrug. "No. I encountered him during a client consult, but I wasn't the one interacting with him. Before you ask, he didn't seem unwell. The only notable thing about him was his interesting choice in accessories."

Joe tried to remember what the man had been wearing. It had been a fleeting impression, since Joe had been focused on Marie and Kuro. He mostly only remembered the lab coat. It was also the thing about their person of interest that made him so easy to follow at a distance. Joe glanced at Kuro over Marie's head.

His partner was unobtrusively sniffing, scenting the air as they went. Both of them had a heightened sense of smell as compared to humans, but Kuro hunted by scent more often than Joe did.

Joe looked from his companions to their target and back to his companions again. "What exactly are we going to do once we follow him to wherever he's going?"

"He needs to be separated from the human populace," Kuro responded immediately.

Marie waited until a few tourists had passed them before adding her thoughts. "Agreed. Any instance of animated corpses I've heard of generally turns out badly for healthy, living humans in the nearby vicinity."

It was a good thing everyone on the streets was absorbed in their own lives. It was a convenient aspect of city living. Whether they were wearing headphones or not, humans tended to let the conversations around them blur into white noise when they were on the move.

Marie continued, "I'd like to observe him more closely, if possible. How much thought process does he have? Is he aware of his state of being?"

Joe nodded. "In summary, we follow him until he gets to wherever he's going, make sure he's alone where he can't eat anyone's brains but ours, and ask him, hey, do you know you're dead? Great. This plan doesn't have any holes in it at all."

FOUR

MARIE

Marie laughed. She'd been completely caught up in the practical considerations until Joe had delivered his irreverent summary. When he said it like that, it really did sound ill-advised.

"You don't have to come with me," she reminded him.

She didn't think he was going to leave at this point, but she preferred to always give the people around her an out. Call it a self-defense mechanism. Why that was, well, that was more complicated than she wanted to think about any time in the next decade.

"Oh, I'm not missing out on this," Joe assured her. His eyes glinted with mischief. "I love badly planned plans."

She wanted to protest, but really, this plan was impromptu and fraught with ways things could go wrong. It was a badly planned plan.

Kuro leaned in close at that moment, and every fiber of her being was aware of his proximity.

"Usually, Joe's the creator of said plans," he murmured, and Kuro's deeper voice sent delicious shivers down her back.

It was a good thing he hadn't said much, so far. Conversation with him did too many things to her that she'd rather not address in public.

Speaking of which, their person of interest had come to a stop. Apparently, the man remained in possession of enough of his mental faculties to remember that he commuted into downtown Seattle by bus. At this time of day, the bus stop wasn't super crowded, but there were a decent number of people around. She was starting to wonder if they were going to have to change their current tactic of just following and observing to something more proactive before someone else noticed just how abnormal this man was. A few people were already shooting sideways glances at the man and the way he stood rocking his weight from side to side, from one foot to the other, as if he was still walking even if he was standing still. Hopefully, they would conclude he was drunk.

Her companions slowed their pace. Joe brushed his knuckles over the back of her hand while Kuro gave a light tug just above her elbow of her other arm before letting his hand drop away. She came to a stop, choosing to take their wordless suggestion. They stood on either side of her, and she was reminded of the night she had met them and the way they had bracketed her up in the branches of a tree. It felt like they were keeping her safe, ready to catch her if she lost her balance, but equally ready to let her go if she made the choice to jump anyway. Maybe because of that, it felt even more okay to remain between them.

"What are the chances he's actually going to get on the right bus?" Kuro murmured, his voice only loud enough for the three of them to hear.

"It's not like we're going to know it's the right bus, no matter which one he gets on," Joe pointed out quietly.

"Maybe we shouldn't let him continue." Marie was all for reevaluating decisions when it made sense.

It felt like the risk of something going wrong was quickly escalating. A bus was an enclosed space, and their dead person wouldn't be on the move, but instead in a sort of holding pattern during the ride. She wondered if the lack of something to focus on, like walking somewhere, would mean the dead man would suddenly have the bandwidth to focus on something else. Like living, breathing humans who were passengers on the same bus. Any number of horror movies and television shows flashed through her mind with scenes of a bus crashed on the side of the road and everyone on it massacred. Their dead person wasn't acting like a zombie, one of the shuffling animated corpses driven by inexplicable hunger to feed on the living. Nor did it move like an undead servant, the way a zombie raised by a necromancer might have. This man had walked through the streets of downtown as if he was seeing another place, experiencing another environment. Something like the world they were all moving through, but not quite the same. The closest thing Marie could think of was when a human was given the Sight by Ashke's fairy dust. But her small fae friend wasn't anywhere nearby.

This was something different.

Maybe she should find a way to get this person back to the Darke Consortium, where there were other supernaturals available to mitigate the potential harm this dead person could do.

"I really don't think we should let him get on a bus," Joe said.

"Agreed." She could share at least that much of what she was thinking.

There were a lot more humans than supernaturals in the world. Even if both tended to gather in higher numbers in cities like Seattle, humans weren't aware of the supernatural community. There were a few trusted exceptions, but for the most part, people like her and her colleagues—and her new acquaintances—hid their paranormal natures.

If they could, they blended. If they couldn't, they existed in the shadows beneath the city streets or remained hidden by the blinding light reflecting off the city's high-rises. Either way, knowledge was a survival advantage, and humans didn't stand a chance of escaping unscathed when they didn't know what might try to eat them. Humans had a tendency to go about their daily lives confident in being the apex life-forms of this world, and it would shake the foundations of their existence to learn that not only was one type of predator hunting them, but several.

She bit her lower lip in thought. "It would be best to get him someplace away from the vulnerable populace."

"From humans, you mean." Amusement rippled in Kuro's voice.

"Doesn't your organization have colleagues that specialize in this?" Joe asked. "Fixers, I think you call them."

Marie let out a huff. "Yes, we have Fixers. But their purpose is damage control *after* any unfortunate incident results in the exposure of humans to paranormal occurrences. The teams are spread too thin to be expected to be proactive all the time. Part of the reason I get along with them well is because I do everything in my power to avoid needing them, rather than being sloppy and just expecting them to clean up after me."

Joe chuckled. "Ooh, that sounds like a story."

"The three of us are more than enough to discreetly isolate this person of interest without raising much alarm from the humans present at this time." Kuro stepped away from her side, exchanging a glance with Joe. "Why don't you get his attention and find out if you can coax him to move toward you? We'll bracket him from the sides, and the three of us can herd him into an alley. From there we can take him someplace more private."

Joe winked at her as he stepped away, mirroring Kuro's movement.

Marie opened her mouth to protest, then closed it, the words going unsaid. It was a simple enough strategy, and Kuro's reasoning wasn't incorrect. If anything, she would just be delaying them all to argue whether it was appropriate for them to work together in this moment. She shook her head. Her overthinking this was already making it harder than it needed to be.

"Excuse me," she called out. "Didn't I just meet you at Socrates Industries? Would you mind telling me if there's a more direct bus line to the building then taking the 50 and 120 lines from West Seattle?"

A few people turned their attention to her but glanced away again when they realized she wasn't talking to them. Her target, on the other hand, didn't acknowledge her at all. If he wasn't responding to her voice, she didn't have that many more options to get his attention. All of them required getting closer. And oh boy, she did *not* want to get within arm's reach. But she wasn't alone, and that helped her feel marginally better about what she was about to do.

She took a few steps forward, reaching a tentative hand out to tap the man on the shoulder.

An SUV came to an abrupt stop right there on the curb, directly where vehicles were not supposed to stop because they'd be in the way of the buses. Two more people in lab coats popped out of the back seat.

"There you are!" the older of the two newly arrived lab coats exclaimed. Gray hair and dark lipstick, with a feminine voice. Those were the brief impressions Marie got as the woman took their dead man walking by the arm.

"We thought we were all going to lunch together," said the other lab coat with a nervous chuckle. "But when we swung by your workspace to come get you, they said you'd left for the day. You said you definitely wanted to check out this restaurant, so we rushed to catch you before you left for home."

As the second lab coat, a middle-aged white man with brown

hair and medium build, continued to chatter, the two of them tugged the dead man toward the SUV. A Black woman opened the front passenger-side door of the SUV and stepped out with a slim backpack in her right hand. She slung the backpack over her right shoulder and kept her right hand behind her, cradling the bottom of the backpack as she moved to hold the rear passenger door open for the trio.

Marie had to make a conscious effort not to narrow her eyes as she noted the very precise way the Black woman had moved. She had an air of fitness about her that seemed at odds with the trio of researchers wearing lab coats. One of Marie's colleagues and close friends, Thomas, had that vibe about him. It had nothing to do with being a supernatural, and everything to do with having some sort of military training. The woman's sharp gaze was sweeping the area and landed on Marie.

Marie gave her best vague and harmless smile, then glanced up at the bus map. Nothing to see here. Totally harmless. In moments, car doors closed, and the SUV smoothly merged into traffic.

Well, that was unexpected.

She had no idea what to do next. It wasn't like she could go after the dead man on foot. And she didn't have the means to instigate a car chase, either. She glanced around trying to come up with something clever in the moment, but there weren't even scooters or electric bikes available for rent via app. As if she wouldn't have been incredibly obvious following the vehicle if one had been available.

Couldn't you just conjure up some kind of solution?

The words popped into her head in her ex-friend's voice, and Marie mentally squashed the sentiment. It had been a mistake all those years ago to confide in the person she'd thought of as her best friend. Marie still immediately thought of what she would say in any moment of doubt or uncertainty, letting her live rent free in Marie's head even though they weren't friends anymore.

She was one of a few past acquaintances whose unrealistic expectations of Marie's witchcraft had no foundation in what she could actually do. That was before Marie learned not to lean into friendships so quickly, not to trust so much.

This current situation was not something Marie's particular magic could solve. Maybe if Bennett or Thomas or even Punch had been here, there would have been a better solution for following the vehicle. Hell, Ashke would have been able to follow the vehicle unseen without any problem at all. But Marie just wasn't that kind of supernatural.

Speaking of other kinds of supernaturals, she realized both Joe and Kuro were nowhere in her line of sight. It didn't mean they had gone, but it didn't mean they had stayed either. She decided to walk back to the Socrates Industries building to find out whatever she could. It was better than remaining there, confused. At least if she was on the move, she had a chance of gaining more information.

She made it about two city blocks before Joe and Kuro fell into step on either side of her. She felt short walking between them, and that didn't happen to her often, since she was a couple of inches taller than the average female-presenting person in the United States.

"The SUV already made it back to the building," Kuro said in a matter-of-fact tone. His hands were in his pants pockets as he walked casually beside her.

"It pulled up to a docking bay at the back of the building where they take large deliveries," Joe added, tipping his head toward her so a few of his tousled locks fell across his forehead.

Kuro's shoulder brushed hers as he leaned close. "We went up and followed along the rooftops to keep line of sight. Once there was no way to continue observing them, we came back for you."

She didn't know what to say. Confusion and gratitude and a little bit of frustration jumbled up inside her, mixed with a good dose of the fluttery sensation tickling the inside of her chest as she reacted to the warm tone in the last few words Kuro had said.

We came back for you.

Joe bumped her shoulder with his. "No one was screaming, and there didn't seem to be any kind of struggle inside the car. There's that, at least."

"Those other people seemed to know their colleague wasn't quite right." Marie decided to give in and join the conversation even if this whole thing was a little on the chaotic side. She should really be contacting her colleagues at the Darke Consortium to fill them in on what she'd witnessed.

"Shady," Joe said.

She fought the urge to smile and lost. "You're not wrong."

"What are you going to do next?" Kuro asked.

There were a lot of things she should do. She should call Bennett or Thomas or Duncan. She should head straight back to the Consortium manor. She absolutely should brain dump every detail she could remember about the entire incident and her meeting prior to it in case she had picked up on something that she didn't immediately understand the import of when it happened. She should plan what she'd be alert for the next time she returned to the company, because obviously her mundane contract had escalated into a matter for the Darke Consortium.

Magic was involved, of that there was no doubt. Considering the amulet she'd seen the dead man wearing earlier, she thought a magical object was involved. One of the primary missions of the Darke Consortium was to take objects of myth and magic—particularly dangerous ones—out of the hands of humans who could do themselves or others harm. There was already one dead body here, even if she had lost it. A body count definitely fell into the harm category.

"Wow," Joe said.

Coming up out of her deep thoughts, Marie looked at him with wide eyes. "What?"

He gave her a smirk, and there was a teasing glint to his eyes. "I can almost hear the gears turning in your head."

"Join us for lunch," Kuro said abruptly. There was a coaxing note to his words.

The fluttering was back, like a thousand butterflies inside her chest, each of them excitedly whispering random thoughts. Was she being asked out on a date? That was good, right? Was it even time for lunch? Well, didn't she like brunch anyway? Did it matter? Date! With just the one? Or both? Did she want to date just one of them? Which one? Did she have to choose? Why not both?

She took a deep breath and mentally stuffed every single butterfly as deep down inside herself as she possibly could. These two worked for an organization in direct opposition to the Darke Consortium. One of their colleagues had kidnapped and sold Peeraphan to a collector. In fact, Marie shouldn't forget these two had been a part of it.

The only reason she was giving them the time of day at all was because they had immediately regretted their part in the whole situation and helped Marie make it right. But as far as she knew, they were still working for an opposing interest. It would be too strong to say they were the enemy, per se, but the phrase "fraternizing with the enemy" was still coming to mind.

She gave Kuro and Joe what she hoped was a sufficiently serious look. "I think it's obvious that this is about to become a conflict of interest."

The corner of Kuro's mouth twitched upward slightly. "I disagree."

"Same," Joe added. "And if you join us for lunch, we'll give you our reasons why we should work together."

MARIE

That's everything I can think of at the moment," Marie said, wrapping up her debrief.

Punch, Bennett, Thomas, Asamoah, Ashke, and Duncan all looked back at her from the screen of her phone with various expressions of thoughtfulness.

It was Punch who spoke first. "Okay, since it seems like everyone's going to need to digest the information Marie just gave us, I suggest the rest of you drop off the call and get back to whatever it was you were doing. This situation can percolate in the back of your minds in the meantime, and you can bring any questions you have to Marie—either as a group text or the next time we call in for another videoconference. I'm going to stay on the call with Marie because I have some follow-up questions."

"I have—" Bennett cut himself off as Punch glared through the video call, theoretically at him and anyone else who intended to keep talking. Punch and Bennett were in the same physical location, so she might have given him a nudge off-screen, too. "...no urgent questions at this time. Just be careful, Marie."

A giggle bubbled up from Marie's belly and tickled her throat. Bennett was changing, his general mood less broody when Punch was involved. It was really nice to witness her friends enjoying some well-deserved happiness.

Thomas's eyes were narrowed but he just grunted what sounded like an agreement with Bennett and dropped off the video call. Asamoah grinned broadly and nodded to everyone in general before dropping off the call.

Ashke laughed outright. "I sense an interrogation coming, and I want in."

Marie shook her head. "Maybe another time, Ashke."

Ashke shrugged, the tiny winged fae doing a little flip in front of the camera. "Hey! I'll remember that. I want all the juicy info and I'm not above heading downtown to find out for myself."

She didn't tell him not to. That'd just guarantee he'd be there even faster.

Duncan interjected before Ashke could press her further, wearing his perfectly professional blank expression. "If you need support from another Consortium member, remember you only need to call and I can be there in a matter of hours."

Marie nodded, biting back the urge to thank him. Duncan was sidhe, a powerful type of fae. When working with the fae, even if you were friends, it was best not to thank them. The reasons were complicated, but the simplest was that any gratitude could be interpreted as owing far more than whatever the original favor cost the other party.

Duncan might never intend to take advantage of Marie, but he had lived a long, long time, and being fae was more a part of his nature than blending in with the much younger human species. It was a lot easier to trust the people around you if you avoided leaving yourself too open to unfortunate circumstances.

Once only Punch and Marie were left in the video call, Punch leaned forward eagerly toward her camera so her eyes filled the screen. "Give it up, Marie. It's just you and me now. You were invited for a boba tea by two exceedingly attractive men, then lunch, and you have nothing to say about what happened?"

Punch knew about Marie's encounter with Kuro and Joe months ago. The entire team working for the Darke Consortium did. But it had been Punch who had picked up on how flustered the encounter had left Marie.

"Well, it got complicated so fast," Marie protested.

"Yes, yes. Dead person walking." Punch waved that away. "These aren't just any two hotties, my friend. These two literally pulled you out of a tight situation not too long ago and cuddled with you until the danger passed."

Marie laughed. It had been years since she'd indulged in the light chatter that a friend could provide. That was what happened when you decided to purge your life of all the toxic influences that only ever caused you misery and focus instead on setting up personal boundaries. Maybe she'd been a little aggressive about maintaining those personal boundaries, but hey, she was a work in progress.

Meeting Punch had broken her out of the sort of stasis she'd been in when it came to her life. Now Marie was exploring what it took to have this kind of friendship again.

"I wouldn't call it *cuddling*," Marie said finally. "We were in close proximity by necessity. The three of us were perched up in the branches of a tree. And I'd have figured out a way to handle those security guards if I had to. I do have a few talents of my own."

"Mmm." Punch nodded in acknowledgment. "But they saved you the trouble, and they redeemed themselves in the process."

Marie lifted her eyebrows and pressed her lips together. "Their involvement in your kidnapping still ought to count against them."

"It would, if they knew what they were involving themselves in," Punch countered. "You said they didn't."

"*They* said they didn't."

"You believe them."

Marie sighed. "I do."

Punch clapped her hands together. "And there was chemistry. Serious chemistry. Which one gets your heart rate going, hmm? I have my theory, but I want to hear it from you."

Joe's bright grin was sexier than any cheerful expression had a right to be, and Marie could fall forever into Kuro's stare.

Marie scowled at her friend. "You know it's not one or the other."

Punch bit her lip, but it didn't hide her delighted smile. "Both! Excellent. And they found you together."

"I didn't have lunch with them," Marie admitted. "I came straight back to my place to connect with all of you. That was a clear priority."

Punch drew back from the camera, so Marie could see her entire face, and rolled her eyes hard. "Please tell me you established some way to contact these two guys. Phone numbers? Do they use KakaoTalk? Line? WhatsApp? I'd ask about social media, but you avoid that like the plague."

It had been Marie and Punch establishing an ongoing chat in their messaging app of choice that had prompted the rest of the Darke Consortium members to create their own profiles in the same app. It was one used fairly widely in Japan and Southeast Asia. Apparently, most of Punch's family living in Thailand and the United States were already on it.

Thomas and Ashke had worked together to establish some kind of magical influence on the profiles of the members of the Darke Consortium. Their chats had an added layer of magical security so they could all speak freely about Consortium matters. It was a convenient way to keep in touch, especially with Punch and Bennett currently on a trip to Thailand to deliver a recently acquired magical object, the Noose of the Phayanak, into the safekeeping of the regional consortium.

"Same as ours, so I friended them," admitted Marie. "Actually, it was Joe who asked me if I had a profile."

Punch made a high-pitched sound that might have been a squeal but was muted because she clapped a hand over her mouth. A moment later she dropped her hand and asked, "So have they messaged you yet?"

Marie's face warmed, both because this line of questioning was a little embarrassing and because she was pleased to see notifications saying that there were messages waiting for her in a different chat. "Yes, and before you ask, no, I haven't had a chance to read them yet because I've been talking to you."

"But you intend to talk to them again, yes?" Punch asked pointedly.

Marie pressed her lips together. "It makes sense to talk to them again given the situation we encountered today, and to work out what their intentions are regarding Socrates Industries and the magical artifact there. But other than that, it seems like conflict of interest."

"Marie." Punch must have been looking straight into the camera lens of her phone rather than Marie's image on the screen in order to really project the impression of eye contact. "You don't interact with colleagues from other consortiums in anything approaching a dating scenario. You also never accept dates from any of your day job clients. Good practices. I support this. These two are neither colleagues nor clients. Why not them?"

Marie sighed. "It's a bad idea to mix the professional and personal. It's asking for trouble. And when it comes to my day job clients, they're almost always human with not a clue about the supernatural, paranormal, or even the peculiar that exists in the world. Kind of hard to develop a meaningful relationship when I'm holding back that much about my life."

Punch nodded. "These guys are also very clearly supernatural."

"Still a conflict of interest," Marie pointed out. "They're literally competitors for the same artifacts our consortium is trying to take out of human hands. Also, they have questionable ethics, even if you seem to have forgiven them for the part they played in your kidnapping just a couple of months ago."

Punch held one hand up as if she were weighing something in it. "Let's say they're flexible. They still seem to go by their own moral code and that led them to helping you, which goes a long way toward me making my peace with their involvement in the situation. The glowing look you have on your face talking to me about them helps me warm up to them, too."

Marie looked from Punch's image to the image of herself in the chat screen. "What? No."

"Yes. I told you talking about them makes you blush. I mean seriously blush. I can tell you like thinking about them."

"I'm pretty sure they're significantly younger than me." As soon as she said it, Marie realized the futility of that particular comment.

Punch laughed. "Centuries. Bennett is older than me by *centuries*."

"Fair." Marie nodded. "The two of you have been working to connect on various viewpoints."

Punch and Bennett had met under stressful circumstances, what with Punch being cursed and Bennett bringing Punch to the Darke Consortium to break the curse before it killed her. They'd fallen hard and fast for each other but there'd been a fair amount of denial, especially on Bennett's part. It meant they'd spent a large portion of the time since unpacking what it all meant to them.

"One thing I've really enjoyed is figuring out how to communicate with each other," Punch admitted. "I mean, we each have our ways of trying to get our points across. It's been an adventure learning to understand what each of us has to say, whether we're using words or not."

"You're figuring it out, though, both of you," Marie said quietly. She was so happy for them.

"Yeah." Punch's expression had a soft glow to it. "It helps that he's so supportive about me exploring my abilities as a kinnaree. It's a lot less scary when you have someone around to spot you as you literally step off a ledge to see if you can summon wings in midair."

"I get it." Marie smiled.

She and Punch had both done their share of figuring out their identities as supernaturals. Neither of them had generational knowledge, having been born to human families and disconnected from any magical mentors. Everything Marie had learned about her nature as a witch had come from trial and error, pulling together snippets of research and experimenting to figure out the rest. Punch was doing the same to learn more about what it was to be a kinnaree.

"Anyway," Punch said, bringing their conversation back on topic. "Age gap is not the biggest challenge to overcome for people like us. Besides, you make a hot cougar."

Nope. Done now. "I'm ending the call, 'kay? Thanks. Bye."

Her face might be burning up.

"Wait, wait, wait," Punch called. "Before you hang up, I need to know. Were you wearing pants or a skirt today?"

Marie was absolutely certain she was going to regret giving Punch the answer to this. "I was wearing a dress suit. It was the first time meeting a client. You know I like to make a sharp impression."

Punch looked incredibly pleased. She might have been smirking, even. "Excellent. I'm sure you absolutely did make a stunning impression."

Marie glared at Punch's image on her phone. "Goodbye, my friend. Go do mischievous things that would scandalize your ancestors."

"Only if you do the same!"

Marie ended the video call and tossed the phone on her bed, deliberately not checking her other chat to find out what Joe or Kuro had sent her. She wasn't ready to let the fluttering feeling loose from where she'd shoved it deep inside herself.

She was half tempted to let herself flop down next to her phone. Curling up and making a nest out of her down comforter and pillows felt like a wonderful idea, but her stomach growled, and she stayed on her feet, if only because the thought of filling herself with tasty food first was an even better idea.

Her apartment in downtown Seattle was in a brand-new high-rise and was a sort of hybrid between a one-bedroom apartment and a studio, in that it was mostly an open-plan layout, but there was a sliding door separating the sleeping area from the rest of the living space. She had filled the main living area with potted plants arranged on various stands at multiple heights to take the best advantage of the light from the floor-to-ceiling windows comprising most of one wall. There was a single long counter that provided her with her cooking area next to a sink, a very compact dishwasher, and a space-saving refrigerator and freezer.

Still, it was more than enough space for her to cook for herself. If she was ever in the mood to cook for a bigger group, she could always take over the kitchen at the consortium manor and cook for the members of the Darke Consortium. They gathered and had a big meal at the long dining room table at the manor fairly frequently.

Her rice cooker was already keeping rice warm for her, so she only had to make something to go with it. Opening the refrigerator, she took stock of what she had and started pulling out ingredients to make her take on soondubu jjigae. It was autumn, and despite it being warm enough to have worn a dress today, the hot Korean stew was still appealing now that the sun had gone down. Twenty minutes later, her soondubu jjigae was simmering and she was just finishing pan-frying a fillet of sablefish to go with it.

She decided to plate it all separately with her rice in one small bowl and her soondubu jjigae in another bowl, with her fried fish on a plate beside it. She carried it over on a tray to rest on the small side table next to her chaise longue, so she could eat her dinner looking out over the city.

She ate most of her meals alone, but she still liked to plate her meals in ways that appealed to her. Her father had been a chef, and she remembered being allowed to watch from the counter right next to the kitchen as he checked the finishing touches on plates before they were whisked away to be served to his customers. There was a reason why people said you eat with your eyes first. Her father always made sure a meal was tantalizing to both sight and smell before a customer ever got a mouthful to taste.

Using her long-handled spoon, she took up a bit of rice and dipped it into the gorgeous red tinted broth of her soondubu jjigae, getting a little bit of the silken tofu and a piece of kimchi as well as one of the tiny clams she had added to make the dish a seafood stew. When she took that carefully assembled bite, flavor exploded across her senses.

She liked her soondubu jjigae to have an umami flavor layered throughout her dish, starting with the fermented sharp tang of kimchi and the salty umami of fish sauce, rounded out by the savory spice of the gochujang and sharper spiciness of the gochugaro red pepper flakes. The tofu was almost custardy-soft and carried the flavors of the broth. She had added the clams just to spoil herself. She'd finished it with a drizzle of rich sesame oil and the freshness of thinly sliced scallions to give added dimension to the meal.

This dinner was one of her favorites, but it would have been interesting to find out where Kuro and Joe would have suggested they go for a meal. Seattle was a good foodie town, and you could learn a lot about a person by the kind of food they liked to eat. All she knew about their tastes so far was that both of them were reasonably interested in boba tea. That didn't tell her much of anything, considering how popular the drink was. There was a boba shop within a few minutes' walk of just about anywhere in Seattle.

Her next bite was rice and the crispy pan-fried sablefish to calm the spice in her mouth. The meal was pretty much the epitome of comfort food for her. The only thing she didn't do this time, because she didn't have any, was crack a raw egg into her piping hot soondubu jjigae and let the heat of the stew lightly poach it. Well, there was always next time.

Would there be a next time with Kuro and Joe? She shouldn't care, should she? Really, she should be more focused on heading back to Socrates Industries to investigate their walking dead person. Her walking dead person. Well, the walking dead person. There was that amulet he had been wearing and also those plants that really shouldn't have been among the cuttings intended for use in the gardens she'd been hired to create for the building.

She turned away from her dinner and pulled her tablet from her shoulder bag. Pulling up a web browser, she started a general search on various amulets and chest plates from Egypt. She was relatively certain she had seen something like it before, but Egyptian art and history were not her forte.

It took another half hour or so of internet research in between bites of her dinner to find the amulet. Once she found it, there were very few articles available that told her anything but the same few repeated facts. It was a curiosity for most of human academia, with more import assigned to where it had been found than anything else.

The amulet wasn't at the center of some folktale or legend. Who had made it, why it had been made, and what its purpose was weren't easily discoverable. But what she found was a good starting point.

When it came to one of the plants she had seen in the storeroom, there was actually a whole documentary available online. The veracity of the content within said documentary remained unknown until she had a chance to watch it and take notes so she could follow up on any facts presented, but watching it sounded like a good way to close out her evening.

Super exciting night. That was just the way she did things. So wild, much zing.

Six

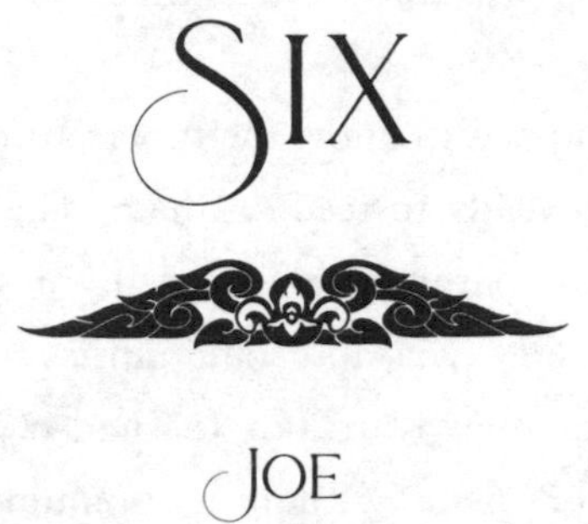

Joe

"Found a hot spot," Joe said. There was a growl to his voice, despite the anticipation growing inside him. "I wonder if she likes this kind of night out?"

"It's for the best that she isn't here," Kuro murmured. "You need to hunt tonight."

Joe scoffed. "Best time to feed is under cover of darkness, for either of us. It was broad daylight and barely even midday. She would have been safe with us in a public place, and we could've gotten to know her better."

He and Kuro would've kept her safe in a place like this. Between the two of them, they were more than enough for any solo danger that might hunt the streets of Seattle.

Kuro growled through the earbud, way up on his rooftop perch, watching Joe head to a popular nightclub. Joe decided to ignore it.

This was one of the bigger places in downtown Seattle, multilevel with both lounge and nightclub spaces that attracted a broad range of night-goers even during the workweek. He generally enjoyed the atmosphere, which helped him blend easily into the crowd who'd come to party. It was best for either him or Kuro to do their hunting among a population where their victim wouldn't be missed, regardless of whichever one of them was actively hunting on a particular night.

Humans didn't need to know the supernatural and the paranormal were real, and ready to feed on them. The human population far outnumbered the paranormal, especially in metropolitan areas. Sure, there were small towns and communities that were exclusively supernatural. But neither Kuro nor Joe had ever come across one that had a place for them. Without a community to rely on, they avoided altercations with human law enforcement as a matter of survival. Fear and larger numbers were what made humans dangerous, even to each other.

In any case, Kuro and Joe weren't hunting the innocents chasing joy under the strobing lights and thumping music. No. Such places attracted all sorts of predators, both supernatural and human. He and Kuro liked to choose humans who would prey on their own kind as targets. The two of them were just higher up on the food chain.

"She's a perceptive witch," Kuro pointed out. "She would have started to pick up on the sharp edge of your mood if we'd spent any real time with her."

"And that's a bad thing?" Damn it. A note of hurt slipped out, and Kuro was bound to have heard it.

"Of course not," Kuro responded quickly. Of the two of them, Kuro was not the best at expressing his feelings, so Joe gave him a chance to clarify what he'd intended.

"I'm saying that approaching anyone with the intent to get to know them requires care," Kuro explained. "And if we cut her with either of our tempers, she doesn't have a reason to forgive us. Maybe the best way to start is to present her with the best of each of us first."

"Fair," Joe responded. He wasn't going to argue when Kuro was right. Joe would've come to the same conclusion on his own if he'd been thinking more clearly. "And neither of us wants to be tempted by her life energy."

They both fell silent for a long moment. Marie had been full of life, bursting with energy and sweetness and warmth. As starved as Joe had allowed himself to become, he could've been a danger to her.

Kuro was right. If they'd found a moment to get close, to kiss...

Joe shook himself all over. The situation hadn't happened, and he had the motivation to keep himself properly fed now. He spoke again with an upbeat tone. "On that note, I'm going in to find myself a juicy hothead to deflate."

"I'll be here if you need me," Kuro assured him.

A pang of regret hit Joe in the chest. There were times when the two of them were in good enough condition that they could each go hunting and just meet up at the end of the night, sated and ready to greet the dawn. Lately, though, Joe hadn't been in the right headspace to go out. He'd been letting himself go longer and longer between hunts, which made it harder to control the bloodlust building inside him. Something Kuro didn't experience.

No matter how well Kuro complemented Joe as a partner, the two of them didn't have the same needs. Kuro was a kitsune and Joe was a gumiho—two different types of fox spirits and supernatural beings. If Joe went too long without sating his appetite, only sipping at his prey's life force and letting them stumble away alive wouldn't suffice. He craved the fresh taste of heart or liver.

A person didn't walk away from that kind of feeding.

As Joe approached the entrance to the club, he managed to charm a few ladies as they approached the line. It didn't take more than a bright smile and a witty joke or two. Not a drop of magical influence required.

Not for the first time, Joe thanked the increased popularity of K-pop in the States. He had the visuals to pull off the look, with a face longer than it was wide, gently curved along the jawline. His forehead was wider than his tapered chin and his complexion was smooth, so long as he shaved daily. He kept his hair medium long on top and cut somewhat close around the sides, allowing him to play with any number of trendy hairstyles.

Tonight, he'd worn his hair in tousled waves, allowing a lock or two to fall across his eyes when he tilted his head just so. He'd worn a no-makeup sort of makeup look, subtle enough that someone unfamiliar with makeup wouldn't realize he was wearing any at all, but what he was wearing gave him a flawless complexion and accentuated his best features. He wasn't particularly tall, but was tall and fit enough to be attractive to most people.

When the bouncer surveyed the group Joe had formed around himself in line, Joe was able to project just enough magical energy to encourage the bouncer to let them all in. Staff at the door liked to control the flow of people in and out, favoring good looks and a decent ratio of gender representation. If the bouncer was asked later to remember any single person, Joe wouldn't stand out in the other man's memory. Joe and Kuro had learned to take such precautions to prevent discovery if either of them ever slipped up on a hunt.

The interior of the club had a futuristic spaceship sort of feel to it, with rounded walls and a wavy collection of pillars in a space designed to feel cavernous. A mix of strobe lights and projections lit the darkness with huge video displays on the upper walls. At one end, a DJ was spinning popular dance music, and the floor was filled with people happy to burn off the nervous energy of a workday.

It was a fun vibe. Mixed in with people who'd obviously come directly from office high-rises were drag queens and goths, a couple of furries, and maybe a cosplayer or two. Joe smiled and let his canines lengthen a bit. If there were a few more furries present tonight, he'd let his fox ears manifest. As it was, he'd stand out a little more than he'd prefer if he risked it. Instead, he let the ladies he'd entered with melt into the crowd on the dance floor so he could continue deeper into the club solo.

Music pulsed through him and the lights flashed, lifting his mood as he made his way to the upper level. He didn't stand directly at the edge, but hung back a layer or two from the people whose faces were lit by the sweeping spotlights. He could still see down into the main dance floor as he danced with a sexy lady, a hot guy, a gloriously androgynous person with the cutest freckles rocking pink-and-yellow-streaked hair, then got sandwiched between two other people. Really, he enjoyed them all as he kept watch.

It didn't take long to find what he was looking for.

No matter how great a venue was—welcoming and inclusive, with a positive regular crowd—there were always the worst elements of the human race present too, being terrible to the people around them. Joe watched a man go from person to person on the dance floor, grabbing their hips roughly from behind and grinding into them with no warning or request for consent. Just pawing and scowling when the other person turned and rebuffed them. A few times, the man even shoved the person for rejecting his advances. One woman let him dance with her, and he immediately groped her, going for a breast and reaching between her legs with his other hand. Obnoxiously lewd and just gross. She yelped loud enough to be heard over the music and struggled out of his grasp.

Yeah, the man was exactly what Joe was looking for.

It took a few minutes for Joe to work his way down to the dance floor. A bouncer was already on his way to grab the man and escort him out of the club. Perfect. Joe slipped to the back of a small group of people heading out, making sure to get his hand stamped so he could reenter the club later if he chose.

He trailed along behind the group, wrapping his magic around himself in a very subtle notice-me-not sort of way. As a gumiho, his magic had a broad range of applications, mostly having to do with his appearance or the way he was perceived by others. Through experimentation over the years, he'd found that it was most effective when used with subtlety.

Even his influence over other things was most effective when he was just giving it a nudge, like changing traffic signals. Trying to make something do what it wasn't designed to do in the first place or trying to change something's state to something it wouldn't naturally take on was outside of his range. At the current moment, no one was paying attention to him anyway, so it was very easy for his magic to ensure he remained unnoticed.

The door of the club opened and music blared out into the night along with the sound of shouting and a scuffle as one of the bouncers forcibly ejected the man Joe had been observing earlier. Yeah, Joe hadn't thought it would take long. This particular club was pretty good about booting out anyone obviously problematic. The man was brushing off his pants and straightening the fabric of his shirt across his shoulders, muttering about his right to be in the club anytime he wanted and suing them for assault.

"I don't even understand what her problem was." The man's grumbling was getting louder as he started to walk down the street. "She liked it, she just wanted it behind closed doors in the dark so nobody would realize how dirty she was."

This guy had an ugly soul, the kind that ruined everything for everyone around him.

Joe followed on quiet feet, keeping his posture relaxed and casual as if he was just headed in the same direction. There were a couple of smaller lounges and bars a few blocks away, but they were just a little frustrating to get to on foot. Unless, of course, an impatient person decided to cut through one or two dimly lit alleys.

The alleys in question were reasonably clean and clear of vagrants. But the people who took those kind of shortcuts tended to be people who thought of themselves as impervious to disaster. When bad things happened, they never saw it coming and were absolutely sure they hadn't done anything to deserve that kind of karma.

It was like going through life convinced you were the center of the story, gifted with protagonist armor. But the reality was that this man had already exhibited deplorable behavior, and was now making the choice to cut through a questionable alley, with a predator like Joe already on his trail.

"Why can't women just be honest about what they want?" the man asked out loud, smirking as the words bounced off the buildings framing the alleyway. The guy liked the sound of his own voice. "Why do they gotta pretend they want the nice guy, when they don't want the nice guy because he can't give them what they actually want? What's a guy gotta do?"

"Do you really want to know?" Joe asked, stepping up right next to him.

The man flinched hard. "Oh shit!"

"Did I scare you?" Joe widened his eyes and raised his eyebrows in mock surprise.

Of course the man was scared. His heart was pounding so hard Joe could hear it. Joe's heightened senses weren't as acute as a vampire or a werewolf's, but they were better than a human's and the earbuds he wore were set to allow ambient noise to filter through. He'd had them on sound-canceling while he'd been in the club to protect his sensitive hearing.

The man looked Joe over and must have decided Joe wasn't a threat. Tugging at his sweater, the man fussed over his appearance again before throwing back his shoulders and puffing out his chest with false bravado. "'Course not. I just don't appreciate people listening in on what I'm thinking."

As if the man hadn't been saying every thought out loud just to smirk at the sound of his own voice.

"Ah." Joe nodded slowly. "Sure. But you seemed to be having an interesting conversation with yourself, and I was just wondering, do you really want to know?"

Because Joe could give him the answer. It was a part of the exchange his magic as a gumiho could provide. Knowledge in return for sustenance. Joe didn't think it was a fair trade, to be honest, but there were people in the world who felt it was worth it.

This guy scoffed as his eyebrows pulled together and his mouth twisted with what was probably confusion. "What would I need to know? You're going to tell me why women are bitches?"

Joe made a clicking noise with his tongue. "Such language. That's part of it."

The guy shrugged. "Like I give a fuck. I don't trust anyone who refuses to curse."

"Nothing wrong with cursing when it's called for." Joe shrugged and leaned in a little closer, letting his voice drop deeper. "Sometimes there isn't a better word to express exactly what I mean when the word *fuck* comes out of my mouth."

There it was. The man's gaze dropped just the slightest bit, looking at Joe's mouth as he formed the word *fuck*. Excellent.

"Some people need a little warm-up before they get that raw, that real." Joe had his attention now, and the man didn't even notice he was being backed up against the wall of a building. "They want to know their wants, their needs, are being taken into consideration. They appreciate going at their own speed, unless it was their decision to let someone else set the pace. Does that make sense?"

"Huh?" The man was still staring at Joe's mouth, and his own was hanging open slightly. "No. That's a bunch of bullshit. It's like there's this complicated playbook, and guys like me didn't get the info. There's gotta be insider intel, or a cheat code to the game. Something."

Obviously not listening, even when Joe was giving him insight for free.

"Let me give you the knowledge you seek." Joe was practically whispering now and the man's eyelids were half closed as his gaze remained fixed on Joe's mouth. If the choice of phrasing was odd to the man, it wasn't enough to break his focus.

Joe struck, sealing his mouth over his prey's and reaching deep with his tongue. His magic flowed, diving into his victim, and began drawing on the human's life essence. The man stiffened in surprise and even started to melt into Joe for a second before starting to struggle. But Joe had him pinned against the wall and even if the man was stockier, Joe was stronger.

He drank in his victim's vitality, savoring the high level of bitterness that came with it, like a really strong pale ale. The accompanying sour flavor of the man's soul was an acquired taste, but Joe had learned to like it. It was confirmation Joe had judged his target correctly and this wasn't just an off night for the man.

He was a long-term, full-time, terrible representative of humankind. And the flavor of him was getting weaker and weaker on Joe's tongue. Joe pressed his mouth harder against his victim's, reaching deeper down his prey's throat, chuckling as the metallic taste of blood seeped across his tongue. Oops. Joe's teeth were a little sharp. The man was going to have a bloody lip.

"Enough." Kuro's voice was sharp through Joe's earbuds.

Joe growled deep in his throat, not easing off his prey.

"Stop." There was a harder push behind Kuro's voice now, a command in his tone. "Let this one go and you can hunt another."

Joe lifted his lips in a snarl, breaking the seal he had over the other man's mouth, and drew back his magic. In the space between the man's mouth and Joe's, a tiny bead floated, pulsing with swirling red light. Joe inhaled quickly, drawing his yeowoo guseul, his fox bead, back into himself.

"Shit," Joe muttered. If he'd been in a proper state, he would never have allowed his bead to be exposed that way, instead extending it into his victim and drawing it back while he still had a physical connection with him.

His victim slumped down the wall, staring up at Joe with a horrified look in his gaze. Tears welled up in the man's eyes.

Joe stared down at him. "Now you know."

When a human had his yeowoo guseul, they gained knowledge. Time flowed differently, and the human would experience visions. As they looked out over the land in their vision, they would gain the history of whatever place they found in their mind's eye. Then there were the people. As the experience continued—and more life energy was drained away—the human would gain insight into more and more people in their life, extending in ever expanding association until they might have an understanding of the existence of humankind in its entirety. If they had the stamina and the gumiho allowed them to keep the fox bead for long enough, a human might look skyward and gain otherworldly wisdom from the heavens.

Theoretically.

Joe crouched down so he was at eye level with his victim. The man tried to scramble back in fear, but only managed to slide to one side. There was knowledge in the man's eyes, but not wisdom. He hadn't looked up to the heavens during his experience. Joe always checked, curious about what a person would experience if they had the presence of mind to have done so.

Ah well. Joe sighed. "I'm a little curious as to what you'll do with your newfound knowledge, but not enough to find out. Be glad you have a rest of your life to live. Maybe try to be better to your fellow human beings."

Joe stood and walked on through to the other side of the alley. If anyone had been watching, they'd only have witnessed two people engaged in an intense kiss in the alleyway. The experience was probably already fading from his victim's memory. Too much information flooding a mortal mind tended to wash away like water over a sandy beach. The mind could only absorb so much before it was gone again. That was the way Joe's "gift" of knowledge worked.

Joe swiped at his lower lip with his thumb. There was a bit of blood. He sucked it clean, wishing it would take the edge off his craving for a more satisfying, bloodier feed. The man's heart or liver would've tasted even better, richer.

"You good?" Kuro's voice asked through the earbuds.

Yes. Joe was a good person. By choice. He could resist the urge to rip and tear and feed.

Joe turned onto the main street and nodded to nothing in particular, knowing Kuro could see him. "Yeah. Thanks."

"I've got you."

It was reassuring, knowing Kuro was there to hold Joe back from taking his hunt too far. As much as Joe craved the blood and organs of his victims, he didn't want to be a serial killer. He'd prefer to give his victims the kind of harsh experience and epiphany that just might nudge them into changing themselves for the better. A change in perspective and worldview, really. Even if his victims forgot the paranormal element of their life-changing moment, they'd still learn more than they'd ever bargained for. If they'd really bargained at all.

Joe smiled into the night, already scanning the street and the bars for his next target.

People always thought they wanted the answers to life, the universe, to everything. He could give those, but only for a price no person should want to pay.

Seven

Kuro

Looks like we'll make it home before dawn," Kuro said.

"Yeah, let me just walk this guy to someplace safe," Joe responded through their earbuds.

"Haven House is just a couple blocks away," Kuro offered.

It was a halfway house that took in humans who were struggling to build a foundation for themselves, stone by stone, upon which they could build a new life. The key was that Haven House chose humans who were still persevering. They didn't take in those who had given up and were just grabbing opportunities, only to slide back into despair.

Kuro and Joe made sure to know where the shelters and halfway houses were in the city. They'd had no choice but to stay in those places in harder times, when even their pooled resources weren't enough to give them shelter and food.

And as a bonus, some of the worst examples of humankind lurked around the homeless, preying on their own kind. When Kuro or Joe needed sustenance and didn't have time to be subtle, those were targets they could take that no one would miss if one of them lost control.

Haven House seemed fairly new, established in the last couple of years. They also were open at the oddest hours. It would be a good place to drop this man, as safe as they could manage, at least.

"Hopefully, they take newcomers this late," Joe grunted.

"I've got a hunch they do," Kuro responded.

"I'll take your hunches over another person's facts anytime."

Kuro watched Joe leave his prey slumped against a dumpster in the alleyway just below. The mugger had been Joe's third, after a night of club and bar hopping. On the other side of the dumpster was the man's victim, a young man barely old enough to buy his own alcohol. The guy—boy, really—had been slurring his words and unsteady on his feet when the mugger had jerked him into the alleyway and started to divest him of his wallet and valuables. The attacker hadn't been gentle about it, pausing to get in an extra nasty kick here and there.

Joe had intervened and fed off the attacker. At that point, Kuro only had to remind Joe to stop because of temper rather than hunger. It was a good thing Kuro had been up on the rooftop, where distance had helped him keep a leash on his own temper.

"The two of you really do work well together."

Kuro spun around to face the speaker. The stranger stood in the shelter of the rooftop structure that gave access from the stairwell up to the top of the building. The night seemed to deepen around the figure, swallowing light from the surrounding buildings and streets in an unnatural way. The man had the presence of mind to be standing downwind too, so Kuro couldn't even catch his scent.

Whoever it was, they weren't an average human or Kuro would have noticed his presence earlier. Magic was in play, wrapping the user in shadows to avoid detection, at least until Kuro knew they were there. Now that he was aware of them, he could see through the magic to the person hiding behind the illusion.

Vampires had a similar ability, but this man was breathing and had a healthy flush to his complexion. Besides, most of the vampires

Kuro encountered seemed to have taken on an otherworldly attractiveness, while this man was, honestly, overwhelmingly average.

Werewolves didn't tend to bother wrapping themselves in magic to hide. Their pack magic helped a hunt go unnoticed too close to populated areas, but as a fox spirit, Kuro had enough wildness to sense when pack magic flowed through an area.

The man could be fae. There were so many kinds out there, there were most likely some that used shadows this way. But Kuro was pretty sure that any fae with the attitude this man was projecting would've glamoured their outward appearance to be somewhat more remarkable than this, and not so…basic.

Kuro tipped his head and considered. No crow feathers or raccoon tail. This man wasn't likely to be a tengu or tanuki. He was regrettably not as familiar with South or Southeast Asian supernaturals. He and Joe hadn't run into many in their travels around the United States. If this man was from another continent, Kuro had no idea what kind of supernatural he was.

And he was taking too long thinking about all of this. He shook his head, trying to focus his thoughts. There had to be something wrong. He normally removed himself from a potentially dangerous situation, then considered the possibilities. Was there a spell in progress?

Kuro let a growl roll up from his chest, his upper lip lifting to show a hint of teeth.

"Don't shoot the messenger." The man held his hands out to the sides. "I'm just here to give you a message from Babel."

Kuro guessed the man was speaking metaphorically. It wasn't likely he knew that Kuro was carrying a firearm loaded with silver bullets. It was equally unlikely the man knew Kuro was also armed with a steel knife and a pair of wooden chopsticks that would do in an emergency. It was always wise to be prepared for the usual supernatural suspects. Or maybe the man did know exactly who and what Kuro was, and it still didn't matter.

"What's the message?" Kuro asked.

"Our mutual employer simply wanted me to remind you and your partner that you need to make amends for the contract that was broken earlier this year," the man said lightly, as if the message he was passing on was of no particular consequence.

"We have every intention of making up for our perceived breach of contract." Kuro wasn't going to actually confirm that either he or Joe were in breach of contract.

There was a little wiggle room for interpretation. Better that it was referred to as claimed by Babel and the people who had drawn up the contract. The moment he and Joe stated they were in breach of contract was the moment Babel could own their lives.

"You are a smart one, Yamamoto Kuro." The man chuckled. "Nine-tailed. Kitsune."

Alarm shot through Kuro. None of those was his true name, but they had been ways to call him for long enough that the three of them used together had a measure of power. The other man began muttering too low for Kuro to hear, and adrenaline kicked in, clearing the remains of whatever spell had messed with his thoughts earlier.

Witch.

Kuro threw himself to one side, desperately hoping to dodge whatever new spell was coming his way. He was too far from the edge of the building to jump off the roof, and having been named three times, attempting to evade the spell was probably futile. But he had to try.

He felt the spell wrap around him, even if he couldn't quite see it. It smelled of sour sweat and carried the tang of spilled blood. It was a spell wrought with power gained through fear and pain. It coiled and twisted around him, slipping over his form as he struggled against it, drawing tighter and tighter around him.

Kuro rolled on the rooftop surface, struggling to regain his feet. Fighting to breathe.

The naming hadn't been completely accurate, that was why it wasn't taking hold immediately. The witch would've had to invoke Kuro's true name three times for that. Kuro struggled, releasing a measure of his own power in a burst, trying to break free.

It might've worked—the magic loosened briefly—but the witch pointed a finger at Kuro and a fresh onslaught of magic wrapped around him, reinforcing the spell. It tightened around him again as he stumbled toward the edge of the roof, his senses jangling with the beginnings of panic.

He was kitsune, a kind of yōkai, a supernatural of Japanese descent. One of his forms was a fox, and his power was such that he had not one, not three, but nine tails. At some point in his life, Kuro had gone by those three names for long enough to give the naming enough of a hold on him to be dangerous if it was backed by sufficient power. And there was a terrible amount of power behind this spell casting.

Kuro opened his mouth to cry out at the pain of the spell contracting around him, his skin burning and his joints grinding. No sound made it out as the spell stole the air from his lungs.

Apparently, Babel had felt it was worth supplying this witch with the number of victims needed to cast a spell on a nine-tailed kitsune and make it stick. That would have been a lot of torturous murders. Kuro crouched low, struggling to take action. Even if he managed to throw himself over the side of the building, the spell would follow him.

The man laughed again. This time the sound rolled across the rooftop, a grating laugh full of malicious intent. The spell constricted

Kuro from every direction until he felt compressed, forced to lie on his side and curl up into a ball. It went further than that, applying searing pressure to every square centimeter of his skin, like he was being forced into a mold too small for him.

It was more than physically painful. The spell hooked into his spirit with a hundred thousand tiny piercing pinpoints and burned the edges of his being until he couldn't even pant anymore, barely able to hold onto consciousness. Footsteps approached. Kuro didn't have the energy to lift his head and watch his attacker come near. He could only open his eyes and look up, way up, at the man standing over him.

"It took a lot of sacrifices to gather the power for this spell, fox demon," the pain witch said. There wasn't a hint of regret in his statement, only that pleasant, matter-of-fact tone. "Babel was willing to pay a bundle to send this message to you and your partner. I'm interested in how this will change your dynamic. That oh-so-efficient coordination between the two of you. Remember that mistakes made have unpredictable consequences."

The man walked away as Kuro stared up at the night sky. The cold breeze ruffled his fur. He'd returned to his fox form, been forced back into it, like he'd been stuffed inside his own body. His magic wasn't responding to his demands to change shape back to his human form. Hell, his body wasn't responding to his order to stand on his own four paws. He was lying there, vulnerable. Too exhausted to move. And the pain witch was getting away.

A metal door was pulled open with a creak, the door to the stairwell.

"You know," the witch called, "I honestly thought a nine-tailed fox would be a bigger adversary."

Rage flared in Kuro's chest, searing through him as his own magic shoved against the bindings of the spell the pain witch had cast on him. If Kuro hadn't already been bound, his power would have been enough to destroy his attacker and the entire rooftop with him. But he'd been overconfident, stupid.

It burned. The admission, his power confined within the witch's spell—everything burned until the backlash of it seared through every fiber of his physical body. Even the individual hairs of his fur coat hurt.

He was helpless, and he hated it.

Marie

Marie jerked awake, bringing her hand to her forehead and rubbing to soothe the sharp throb. Then she scowled at her mini tablet lying next to her face. It hadn't been smart to transfer to her smaller device so she could watch the documentary lying down. It wasn't the first time she'd dropped her tablet on her face as she dozed off, but it usually happened when she was reading.

The documentary had been a little slow, with people speaking in low, awed voices about the rituals the ancient Egyptians might have practiced using blue lotus. There'd been soft background music for a mystical ambience, too. She wasn't even sorry she dozed off. She could always backtrack and pick it up in the last place she remembered. The real question was whether she was actually absorbing the information she was trying to research.

The memories of Joe's ready grin and Kuro's intense gaze bubbled up in her thoughts. Nothing in the documentary mentioned anything that would bring those two to mind. The closest imagery related to Egyptian mythology had been Anubis. Whether Anubis was depicted in animal form or his anthropomorphic representation, the Egyptian god was shown in the form of a jackal or another canine, but he never had multiple tails. Not like her fox spirits.

Not *hers*. Them. The fox spirits. Joe and Kuro. Which were definitely not her fox spirits even if she did seem to keep encountering them.

Maybe she should call it a night and get ready for bed.

She shook her head and swung her legs off the chaise, planting her feet on the floor. Time to get her head out of the clouds and back to reality—like walking dead guys, ancient Egyptian amulets, and mystical blue lotuses that helped people travel into the afterlife.

Marie resolutely headed for her bathroom to wash her face. Maybe she'd feel refreshed enough to take another pass at that documentary. She was midstep when something set off her wards, threads of her magic vibrating through her. Whatever it was, it wasn't an immediate danger, it wasn't one of the wards set directly on her apartment or even on the building. But it was within the near vicinity.

Turning off the lights in her apartment, she stepped to the windows, staying to one side so she could dodge out of sight if need be. Seattle downtown was always brightly lit, even late into the night. The trees along Pine Street were wrapped in strings of LEDs, adding to the streetlamps and illumination from inside the nearby buildings. Still, there were nooks and crannies, alleyways and corners where the light didn't reach.

She peered out in the direction of the ward that had been disturbed. The building next to hers caught her attention immediately. It was a parking deck, the rooftop several floors below her own. It usually had ample lighting because people snuck out there all the time to conduct photo shoots with the city as a backdrop or to shoot videos. Right now, it was dark. It wasn't as if someone had knocked out all the lights. She could still see the glow of the outdoor lamps. It was more like shadows were pooling on the roof, swirling in thick currents.

That magic had been what had set off her wards and it had the feel of another witch, but not the kind of witchcraft Marie practiced.

Her magic was drawn from and fed back to growing things, like her house plants and the urban greenery all around Seattle. Her power amplified when she spent time in gardens or in the forests around the manor of the Darke Consortium. This witch's magic was gained from living things too, but it was stolen through blood and tears, fear and grief.

She shrank back from the window, brushing her fingers over the rosemary she had in a planter there. Careful not to disturb her own wards, she added a few layers of magic inside her existing protections. Unless the other witch knew exactly which window to look into, Marie's magic would cause a casual glance to slide right past. The added magic would ensure no movement inside her apartment would catch attention.

If she had to defend herself against another supernatural, she could, for the most part. But it took time to gather power the way Marie did, allowing it to trickle into her slowly from the life around her. If she tried to draw it forcibly, it would harm the source. So she carried different talismans as reservoirs when she left her safe spaces, and generally did her best to avoid confrontation in the first place. She was very good at spells to allow herself and her home to blend with the surroundings.

Feeling reassured about the added precaution, she studied the rooftop next door more carefully. She couldn't make out anyone on the roof. Maybe the door to the stairwell had just opened, because it was swinging slowly closed now. She bit her lip. Just because she hadn't seen someone didn't mean someone hadn't been there. At this distance, sound and smell weren't an option. She murmured softly, letting her fingertips slide over the starburst blossoms of dong quai growing tall in the pot next to her plant stands. Its sweet scent washed over her as she reached out with her boosted magic, hoping to sense what she couldn't detect with her eyes, ears, or nose.

There weren't any humans on the roof, but there was a living being. Curled up on its side, it was small and its pain was a bright psychic flare in the shadows. Whatever it was, it was vulnerable. She wasn't immune to the temptation presented by the power she could draw from that. No witch was, as far as she knew. She'd wondered, early on, if that was a sign that she was bad or wrong somehow. With experience and time, she'd figured out that in many ways, the practice of witchcraft was a choice.

She didn't draw her power from another's pain. Wouldn't.

The other witch obviously did, so the question Marie had now was not as simple. Why did they leave such a juicy power source alone and exposed on that roof? It could be bait to capture an even more tempting victim. A solitary green witch, for example, like Marie.

It was a possibility, but not a high one. There was a strong coven of witches in Seattle whose magic had been built over generations and was shared through familial bonds. They made it their business to ensure witches who practiced pain magic were driven out of the city as soon as possible. Solitary witches like Marie were left to themselves, the coven wouldn't bother them, but it wouldn't go out of its way to help them either. So it wasn't likely that a witch practicing pain magic would even know a witch like Marie was in the vicinity. And they certainly wouldn't risk drawing the attention of the coven just to lure a hapless green witch out into the open.

The small form down on the rooftop moved slightly, and she could finally make out several fluffy tails spread across the pavement, each of them a deep burnished red fading to charcoal at the tips. She knew those tails.

Darting for the door, she wrapped as many protections as she could around herself, so many that even the concierge at the entryway of her building didn't notice her run past. Similar to the spells she had around her apartment, they provided a you-can't-see-me sort of effect that dampened any sounds she made and even her scent. It wasn't perfect, but she'd been working on strengthening it for moments like this, when there were other supernaturals active in the vicinity.

Seattle was a dense city with supernaturals scattered sparsely throughout. She rarely came into contact with them outside the Darke Consortium unless she was specifically seeking them out, and of those, she really only encountered the ones who allowed themselves to be found. Tonight, there were at least two on the same city block as her. And there wasn't even a cosmic convergence she was aware of to explain any of it.

She approached the street corner and peered around the edge of the building. A figure wrapped in shadows—dramatically unnatural, that effect—left the stairwell of the parking garage and crossed the street, slipping down an alley with haste. Her heart pounded hard, providing her with a convenient way to count off ten before she walked as quickly and quietly as she could down the street and ducked into the stairwell. The elevator would attract too much attention.

She climbed the stairs, staying alert to any sound or sign of someone else lying in wait. At every landing, she paused to catch her breath and cast another spell. Some were simple warning spells, to let her know if anyone followed her up. Others were detection spells to check for any nasty surprises left by the pain witch or give her an idea of who else might still be in the parking garage. And still others were protections wrapped around herself, more misdirection to make it hard to land any kind of hit on her.

Take a set of stairs. Breathe. Cast. Repeat. Exhaustion was tugging at the edges of her awareness as she stretched her energy reserves, but she had practiced to handle situations like this. She could manage.

Finally, she reached the rooftop, thankful it was only twelve floors and not as tall as her own apartment building. She checked her surroundings carefully as she emerged from the stairwell, but the fox with nine tails was still lying exposed across the roof from her. There was nothing for it but to walk out into the open and retrieve him as fast as she could.

KURO

The door to the stairwell creaked open again, and Kuro struggled to move, get to some kind of cover, lift his head to look his attacker in the eye even. *Something*.

"Kuro?"

That voice. Feminine. Gentle and low, slightly husky. He knew that voice. Marie. Footsteps approached, light and more delicate than the ones that had just walked away from him. Or maybe the man had left a while ago. Had Kuro blacked out? She needed to get away from here. It was dangerous. He tried to get to his feet, but he only managed to flop awkwardly on his side, his paws scrabbling against the concrete.

"I'm just"—a pause—"I'm just going to get you away from here. Okay? Don't bite me or anything."

He panted, unable to do much else. When she coasted her palm over the fur on his side, he let his eyes close. Her touch soothed the searing pain. Maybe she could disperse the spell. She was a witch, too. Her hands smelled of fresh rosemary and another woody, floral scent.

When she gathered him into her arms and lifted him, he managed to rest his chin on her shoulder and pry his eyes back open. The least he could do was keep watch behind her as she carried him across the roof and toward the stairwell. He couldn't sense the other witch anymore, and he figured she wouldn't have come out if there was immediate danger. Which meant he was safe with her, at least for the moment.

Inside the stairwell, she began her descent. It was a long ways down. While he didn't have a problem running up or down that many levels in any of his forms, she was limited to her human form with the same strength and stamina as a normal human. At least as far as he knew. She was definitely not moving faster than a normal human could, but maybe that was out of care for him. He wasn't sure.

Her body tensed as she froze on the stairs and her arms tightened around him. The sound of someone running up the stairwell finally pierced his clouded thoughts, and Kuro realized he'd been almost completely absorbed in his mental stream of consciousness and barely aware of his surroundings aside from the feeling of being held by her.

"Joe?" Marie called softly.

"Marie?" Joe answered in turn. "What happened? Why is Kuro with you in that form?"

"I'm not sure, but we need to talk somewhere else." Marie's words were terse, assertive.

"Okay." Thank all things running on two legs or four that Joe had fed fully tonight. He didn't seem ready to argue with her. "I can carry him. Do you know where we can go?"

Right. Going back to their apartment was potentially a bad idea.

"My place is warded," Marie answered.

She didn't sound happy as Joe took Kuro out of her arms. Kuro gathered a burst of energy and turned his head quickly enough to give her a lick on the cheek. Joe chuckled and Kuro didn't have enough in him to give his partner the glare he deserved.

"Safety first," she said. Her tone had softened slightly. "Then we'll figure out what happened."

Nine

Marie

I can't believe you got to kiss her first."

Marie shook her head and decided to ignore Joe's comment as she let the both of them into her apartment. She removed her shoes and placed them on the shoe rack inside the hallway closet, pulled off her face mask to hang on the hook by the door, and hung up her jacket in the closet as well. She hesitated, figuring shoes inside her living space was a fairly low priority consideration given the current circumstance. But Joe gently nudged her to the side with his shoulder as he toed off his shoes and kicked them under her shoe rack. Kuro wasn't wearing shoes in this form, so that wasn't a problem at the moment.

"Come in," she said to Joe and Kuro. "My wards go up as soon as I shut the door. There are additional safety measures around the outside of the building to give me an early warning if something or someone is approaching."

Joe was still carrying Kuro cradled in his arms. "Can I put him on your couch?"

"Yes, absolutely." She paused, glancing down at her shirt. "I didn't see any blood anywhere. Do you think he's hurt? I could go get a towel for him to lie on in case we have to give him any kind of first aid."

As Joe gently placed Kuro on her chaise longue, Kuro struggled up into a sitting position with obvious difficulty. But he looked straight at her and shook his head in a clear negative.

"I think that's a no." There was amusement in Joe's voice despite the worry on his face as he gazed down as his partner.

"Can I get you something to drink?" she asked. "I'm definitely making tea for myself."

"That would be great," Joe responded. "Can I trouble you for a really tall glass of water, too? It's been a long night for me and I'm in serious need of hydration."

Marie nodded, glad to have something simple and constructive to focus on for a moment as she gathered her thoughts. She decided to make a whole pot rather than separate mugs, measuring out her own blend of tea including kudzu, ginseng, and citrus peel in the steeping chamber of her glass teapot.

"Ginseng to reduce inflammation. Orange peel for flavor and improved digestion," she muttered, reinforcing the intent with which she was using the ingredients for a magical boost. "And a little bit of kudzu, to prevent hangovers and any aftereffects."

Joe was definitely dressed for clubbing, and she thought she smelled a touch of alcohol and smoke around him. The herbal tea would help his metabolism deal with whatever toxins he'd been exposed to at the clubs, and it was especially effective infused with her magic.

She filled the teapot from the hot water dispenser she kept on her countertop. She had it set to keep the water at a constant 195 degrees Fahrenheit so she could have up to four liters of hot water ready to dispense whenever she needed it. No waiting for a kettle to boil. Three minutes later she was placing a tall glass of tepid water on the side table next to Joe as well as a bowl of water for Kuro. Ice water would've been too upsetting for the stomach considering how overheated both of them seemed to be. Then she poured out two cups of steaming herbal tea.

"My water glasses are a little too slender for you to drink comfortably from," she said to Kuro. "So I figured a bowl would work out better. Let me know if you want a glass instead."

Kuro lapped neatly at the water, then lifted his head to gaze at her. She wasn't sure what she expected. She'd never really spent any time with a real fox, much less a nine-tailed fox spirit. But there were two of them in her apartment right now, and one of them was the size of a true fox, currently waving nine tails around himself. The memory of his fur under her palm tickled at her mind and she quashed the desire to ask to pet him again. She was suddenly intensely curious as to whether the fur around his ears was silky soft.

Joe was looking around her apartment, and his gaze took in her large windows. As he peered out into the night, he asked, "You've got a great view of the roof of that building. Did you see what happened?"

"No." Marie took a sip of her tea, letting the spicy warmth of the ginger soothe her. "Whatever happened, a powerful enough spell was cast to brush against the wards of this building. I was alerted that something big was happening, but by the time I looked out, all I saw were magic-generated shadows. It took a few minutes for the magic to dissipate enough for me to make out Kuro lying down there."

Joe turned to look at her. "And you recognized Kuro right away?"

"I thought so," she admitted. "I remembered the coloration of his tails. Besides, it was a fox in the middle of downtown Seattle, and I could see there were more tails than any normal fox would have. I've only met two of you in my entire life. I figured chances were high it was him."

"So you came running." Joe's words were tinged with wonder. "You could have stayed hidden. You barely know us."

"A witch was involved," Marie insisted. "And the spell that brushed my wards was definitely powered by pain magic."

A low growl filled the room, and Marie looked at Kuro to find the fur all around his neck and shoulders raised.

"All the more reason for you to have steered clear," Joe said, as if he was in agreement with Kuro's wordless sentiment. "You don't have the scent of pain magic around you. You draw your power from a different source."

That last statement was left dangling, like a question. Or maybe it was an invitation to share. Maybe she would clarify the type of witchcraft she practiced, eventually. Right now, she had questions.

"Let's focus on Kuro for the moment, okay? What happened to him is more urgent." She shifted her gaze from one to the other until they nodded in agreement.

"He's not going to be able to tell us anything in this form." Joe tilted his head to the side as he regarded his partner. "We had a call going, but our earbuds don't really pick up other people speaking near us. It's part of the background noise filtering technology. I could hear someone talking to him, but not what they said."

"And nothing happened to you?" Marie felt something out of place about the both of them, different from when she'd met them earlier in the day. It wasn't just Kuro.

"I was coming back from dropping someone off at a nearby halfway house." Joe's forehead creased as he drew his eyebrows together in thought. "Someone brushed past me, but I was straining to hear what was going on with Kuro. I didn't think twice about it."

Kuro had come to stand on his four paws and was sniffing Joe all over.

"I think something happened to you, too," Marie said quietly. "There's something that's changed about both of you. I can tell."

Auras weren't her forte. She could see them if she tried, but she had no real basis for comparison since she'd never taken a look at their auras previously. But now that she was looking, there was something wrong about each of them. It was the same as a person walking through a cloud of cigarette smoke and having tendrils of the smoke cling to them as they continued on their way.

"But Kuro is the only one who's like this." Joe motioned to the kitsune next to him. "If he could change back, he would've by now. He hates not being able to interject when he's got something to say."

Kuro nipped at Joe's ear.

"Hey!" Joe clapped a hand over the side of his head to guard against Kuro's teeth. "It's true."

Marie huffed out a laugh. "This is serious."

Joe's expression sobered as he lifted his gaze to meet hers. "This *is* serious," he confirmed. "But it isn't going to be any easier to face if we're dire about it all. Keeping it light helps me get through."

"Okay." Marie gave him a faint smile. He had a point, and she wasn't going to question how he dealt with difficult scenarios. Everyone had their own methods for handling stress or processing things. "Other than not changing back into a human, is there anything else off about what Kuro can and can't do right now?"

She wasn't certain what kitsune could do, really. She was only familiar with folktales and mythology, and most of that she'd read months ago after her first encounter with them. If there was one thing she'd learned over and over again from working with the Darke Consortium, what the legends indicated was often only a hint of what the reality was.

Joe seemed about to say something, but a ball of blue flame flared to life in the space between the three of them. The warmth of the flames caressed her skin as if she sat close to a campfire. Only this ball of flames rose and fell in the air. As it moved from one side to another, Marie looked past the light to find Kuro's gaze on her, the reflection of the blue flames showing in his eyes.

Joe cleared his throat. "Seems he can create fox fire just fine."

Marie nodded. The ball of blue flames kept pulling at her attention, and she imagined she could lose herself staring into the fire. The flames winked out and the room seemed darker suddenly, the air definitely cooler.

"Try not to stare into fox fire for too long," Joe warned. "It's not the kind of calm people get from looking into a fireplace or a campfire."

Marie swallowed and nodded. She'd try to remember. Curiosity bubbled up, and she wanted to ask about the consequences. But this wasn't the time or place for any deep dives into supernatural abilities.

Instead, she addressed Kuro. "So you have your usual abilities for this form, you're just not able to turn back to human form?"

The kitsune nodded.

She sighed, looking out her window again. Most of the night was gone. It'd been well past midnight when her wards had warned her of the pain magic outside her home. Bringing the guys here and this conversation had taken a decent amount of time, too. Her tea had gone cold.

"Dawn can't be too far away." She sighed. "I've got limited space, but you're both welcome to use my chaise longue and crash for what's left of the night. Maybe after a few hours' sleep, we'll have enough brainpower to figure out how to handle this."

This was probably not the best idea she'd ever had. Thomas and Ashke would have opinions about her bringing two people she hardly knew into her home. She could picture Thomas's expression once he found out she'd also allowed them to stay over while she slept, with just a sliding door separating them from her.

Thomas was a colleague and a friend, nothing beyond that. But he was fiercely protective and he had a formidable temper, even among werewolves—supernaturals already known for extreme moods. She wasn't particularly looking forward to dealing with Thomas's temper, but she would be letting Thomas and Ashke know about this anyway.

The two of them shared different aspects of security for the Darke Consortium, and that included the safety of each member, not just on the small island where the consortium was physically located. As a member and a friend, she would be keeping them in the loop. But she was also incredibly tired, and the immediate danger had passed. She would contact them in the morning.

She gathered up the teacups and took them to the sink. "Let me get you some extra blankets."

The tiny hairs on the back of her neck lifted, and magic filled the apartment the way steam would, billowing gently outward from a single source. She turned back to Joe and Kuro just in time to see Kuro's fox form blur and lengthen until he was standing in front of her chaise.

His dark hair hung loose and wild around his face, with locks falling across his eyes, almost long enough to brush his jawline. His expression was brooding, and the corners of his mouth were turned downward in a frown. She was struck by how attractive she found him, standing there in the middle of her apartment as the night sky lightened outside her windows.

"Hey!" Joe exclaimed and wrapped his arms around Kuro.

Kuro blinked, his dark expression relaxing slightly. Then his arms looped around Joe's waist, returning the embrace. Joe must have been a lot more worried than he let on, because he buried his face in Kuro's neck and Marie thought he might be shaking slightly.

It hit her then that she was an outsider intruding on this moment between them. She turned away, moving as quietly as she could to get blankets for the two of them. It'd be a much tighter fit for them on the chaise now. It'd make a lot more sense for one of them to take the floor. Maybe she could give them some extra towels to create a makeshift pad under the blankets. She empathized with them having just gone through a scary experience, but she wasn't giving up her bed.

"Marie." Kuro's deep voice resonated in her chest. She felt it right in her sternum, and her nipples tightened.

Okay, she needed to get ahold of her reactions. She was too damned tired to be arguing with her own libido.

She put on a smile and headed back to them with an armload of blankets and towels. "Glad to have you back in human form. I was a little worried you might need a fresh set of clothes, the way werewolves sometimes do, but it seems your magic preserves whatever it was you were wearing?"

Okay, that might've been perilously close to babbling. She could've stopped at the welcome back to walking on two legs part.

Kuro only smiled faintly, his gaze holding her in place while she clutched the blankets to her chest harder. "Thank you."

The words hit her like a warm splash of water, washing through her unexpectedly until she found herself blinking back tears.

"Hey, hey, hey." Joe's tone was much gentler than it had been when he'd greeted Kuro.

Suddenly, Joe was taking the blankets from her, and Kuro was leading her over to the chaise. The concern and care coming from both of them only overwhelmed her more.

She didn't want them to worry, so she tried to put her feelings into words. "It's just been a while since someone thanked me. It's silly, honestly. It's just really nice to be appreciated."

There were several fae in the Darke Consortium, so no one thanked anyone out of an abundance of caution. Her friends and colleagues respected her and placed their trust in her. They did little favors for one another as a show of their appreciation, but they never said the words.

Beyond that, though, several of the toxic relationships she'd ended not too long ago had been ones where she'd been taken for granted. A lot. She honestly couldn't remember being thanked so sincerely by anyone. Even with her own family, thanks and love were expressed with indirect actions, not in words. Kuro's quiet, intense thanks had hit different.

"Not silly," Kuro said and pressed a kiss against her temple. Then he drew back, concern furrowing his brow again. "Is this all right? Or am I overstepping?"

He was close, sitting next to her on the chaise with his thigh pressed against hers. Joe was just as close on her other side, his palm lightly rubbing a soothing circle between her shoulder blades. She suddenly wanted those blankets back, so she could have something to do with her hands. Because with the two of them right there, on either side of her...

"No," she breathed out the answer to Kuro's question. "You're not...overstepping."

That slight smile played across Kuro's lips as he leaned even closer, his gaze holding hers until he was so close she couldn't maintain eye contact anymore as he brushed his lips over her cheek in the same spot he'd licked in his fox form earlier in the evening. "Thank you for coming to help me."

His breath was warm against her cheek as he spoke, every word causing his lips to brush over her skin.

"Thank you for giving us sanctuary in your home," Joe whispered in her ear. His teeth grazed the upper shell of her ear and she gasped at the sensation. He did it again, then asked, "Are you okay with me this close, too?"

She deliberately chose not to think, only to feel and answer. "Yes."

This was the sensation she'd craved since that day in the woods. The feeling of being held by them both. There'd been the promise of delight in this, a hint of what might be wonderful. She'd chased it in her fantasies. She probably would have dreamed about them tonight, after having encountered them on the street earlier in the day. Only she hadn't slept yet and dawn was coming and they were both right here.

"May I have a kiss, Marie?" Kuro's question was barely audible, but she heard it deep inside her head.

"Yes," she breathed.

His mouth closed over hers, taking over immediately as he tasted her. His tongue explored her until a whimper worked its way out of her throat. Her hand closed convulsively over his thigh, and she held on, desperately trying to keep her balance. One kiss and she was already melting into him.

When he let her up for air, Joe lifted her hand in his and pressed a kiss to her knuckles. "May I have a kiss, too?"

She looked at him with wide eyes and didn't resist as Kuro placed his hands on her shoulders to encourage her to twist her upper body toward Joe. Joe released her hand to press his forefinger under her chin and rub his thumb over her kiss-swollen lower lip. He lifted his gaze from her mouth to her eyes and raised an eyebrow.

"Oh." She hadn't answered him. He was waiting for her. "Yes."

Absolutely. *Yes*.

His grin was wide and bright and his eyes sparked with mischief as he dipped his head and captured her mouth. His kiss was light and playful. He sucked her lower lip and nipped at the corner of her mouth before settling his mouth over hers for a deeper taste. By the time he pulled back, her heart was pounding in her ears and her breath was ragged.

Sunlight peeked through the city high-rises and shone through her windows, bringing out the copper highlights in Joe's eyes.

Magic flared in the room again, and Joe's expression changed to panic as his face and body changed. A moment later, she was sitting with a nine-tailed fox in her lap where Joe had been.

She stared at Joe, and somehow the shock in his expression was just as clear in his fox face as it had been in his human face before he'd transformed. Behind her, Kuro's hands tightened convulsively around her waist.

Staring at Joe, she suddenly realized what the spell on each of them must have done. "Oh no."

Ten

Joe

"So you kissed him and he turned into a fox, not a frog?"

Joe glared at the tiny winged fae who was currently hovering at eye level with Marie. If he could talk—which he couldn't, in his current form—he would make sure the fae understood that he wasn't just any fox. He was a gumiho.

"Wrong folklore, Ashke." Marie crossed her arms over her chest and tipped her head to one side as she narrowed her eyes at the winged fae. "But you're perfectly aware of that, and I refuse to be baited. The only reason I mentioned the kiss at all is because we need to take into consideration all the possible triggers for the forced shape change. If a kiss turns a prince from a frog into a human, and true love's kiss can break any number of spells, it would have been remiss of me to leave out the fact that I shared a kiss with him right before he got stuck like that."

Hey now. Joe would have pouted if he'd been in human form. He was actually rather fond of his nine-tailed fox form. No need to refer to this adorable version of himself as *that*.

The winged fae, apparently named Ashke, held up his hands in a placating gesture. "I couldn't resist the opportunity to tease you just a little bit, Marie. You're usually the one getting us out of a mess.

Imagine my surprise when you called me at dawn to help you with a problem."

Standing next to Marie, Kuro frowned. His expression matched the way Joe currently felt. Joe didn't particularly like being referred to as a problem, and he also didn't want to cause Marie any more trouble than interactions with him already had.

Joe met Kuro's gaze and felt sure he could guess at what his partner's line of thought was. This was one of those times where an animal form would be best complemented by some sort of telepathic ability. In the years that he and Kuro had been together, they had never discovered that sort of ability among either of their supernatural talents. It would've been convenient in the past, and in this moment it would've been invaluable. But no such luck.

As much as he liked his current form, the prospect of being unable to shift, potentially being locked away from his other form, was more frightening than he wanted to think about. But the thought was there, at the fringes of his awareness.

"I'm guessing you tried this already," Ashke ventured with a hint of caution that had previously not been present in his tone. "But did you kiss him again?"

Marie opened her mouth with what looked like an angry retort, but she paused. Then she blinked.

She was so cute. Really cute. Joe let his lower jaw drop open in his foxy version of a grin.

She looked at him, glanced at Kuro, then made eye contact with him again. Then she said, "I didn't kiss either of them in fox form."

"Wait." Ashke darted over to hover in front of Kuro, then zoomed in to Joe's face. It was a good thing the fae immediately withdrew back to his position at eye level with Marie, because Joe snapped in irritation. Seemingly unfazed, Ashke continued his thought. "So each of them has been in fox form since last night. We'll come back to kisses in a minute. But let's actually talk about the fox form."

"Yes," Marie responded slowly.

Joe watched her carefully. He didn't know her well yet, but she wasn't showing signs of defensiveness or even tension. He'd have done something about it if anyone was making her uncomfortable.

"You said you were alerted by your wards that a powerful spell was being cast," Ashke continued. "So you left the safety of your wards—which we will discuss later, because I have opinions about that and I'm sure Thomas will too—and found one of them forced into fox form, but not the one who is in fox form now."

"Correct." Marie glanced at Kuro, probably to see if he wanted to add anything to this summary.

Kuro only watched the fae. Joe would have snickered if he could. His partner had trust issues. Joe might have volunteered more, just because he liked to be part of any conversation. Kuro was the brooding, silent type. Hot, but not so great for brainstorming sessions.

Ashke was still going. "Sometime right before dawn the original person forced into fox form returned to human form and there was kissing and then there was a fox form transformation again, but not the same victim."

There was another reason Joe wanted to regain his ability to shape-shift at will. He'd like to repeat the kissing, not just in discussion, but in action. Marie had been a delightful kisser. He was sure she had enjoyed it, too.

"Essentially yes." Marie nodded, definitely unaware of what Joe was currently thinking.

Joe sat back on his haunches. He had new respect for Marie and her ability to communicate, because the fae had delivered all of that at pretty high speed.

"It could have been the kissing." Ashke rubbed his jaw as he seemed to be considering. "One way to figure it out is to kiss each of them now and observe whether they switch."

Joe gave a sharp bark and let all nine of his tails wag. He'd wanted to suggest that in the first place, but Marie had been so upset by his shape change she had immediately called for reinforcements.

He hadn't been happy about that, and he imagined Kuro wasn't, either. First, the two of them had looked out for each other for so long, trusting anyone else to help solve their problems wasn't something that came easy for them. Second, the immediate response Marie had gotten to her call for help served to remind them that she had a support network and other people to rely on. She didn't particularly need them in her life.

Kuro's hand dropped down on Joe's head between his ears, then ran down his back and smoothly over a couple of his tails. Joe leaned into the comfort of his partner's touch and curled into Kuro's arms as Kuro gathered him up against his chest.

"I'm open to trying another kiss." Kuro's chest rumbled as he spoke, and Joe had no qualms about rubbing his face into his partner's chest.

Marie made a sound of protest deep in her throat, which made you wonder what other sorts of sounds could be coaxed from her. "It wasn't a kiss that turned you into fox form in the first place. And there wasn't a kiss before you turned back."

Oh! Joe wiggled in Kuro's arms. He looked from Marie to Kuro then back to Marie again and turned his muzzle up to lick Kuro's face in a long swipe from his jaw all the way up to his temple.

Marie gasped and Joe looked back at her excitedly.

Kuro turned his face into Joe's fur and muttered, "Was that really necessary?"

Marie's eyes were wide as she looked at them both. "Kuro did give me a quick lick on the cheek. But a lot of time passed before he turned human again."

Joe leaned toward Marie, trusting Kuro to keep him from falling. Instead of stepping forward to close the space between them and Marie, Kuro wrapped his hands more firmly around Joe. Joe growled in frustration, because he couldn't reach without either Kuro or Marie moving to eliminate the remaining distance.

"Would you be willing to allow him to give you a little kiss?" Kuro growled and added, "A much smaller lick than the one he just gave me."

Joe whined. He would have waited for her to tell him it was okay. He wasn't about to just indiscriminately lick her without permission. Besides, Kuro had totally licked her without permission in the first place. It was Kuro who owed her an apology.

Joe did his best to give Marie the most hopeful look he could manage. Marie giggled, and his heart leapt in his chest at the sound. He liked the sound of her joy, the pink flush in her cheeks, and the sparkle of amusement in her eyes. Sure, the fear of being trapped in just one form was still hovering at the edge of his thoughts, but he was glad he was able to be a part of bringing a smile to her face. It made him feel good.

Marie pulled out her phone and swiped it a couple of times. "Let me just set a timer on this so we know exactly how long it took if this works."

"Good idea," Ashke said, doing a little flip in the air.

Kuro remained where he was standing, holding Joe. Marie turned her attention back to them. Joe thought he detected a hint of nerves in her posture before she closed the space, so he waited. She met his eager gaze with a smile and gave him a little nod.

He did his best to keep his enthusiasm under control, but he had to admit he was wiggling a little in Kuro's arms as he leaned forward and gave her a little lick along the jawline.

He drew back, watching her for her reaction, his ears up as he listened carefully for any delightful noises she might have made. It wasn't that he expected her to be particularly responsive to him in this form, but it'd be nice to get confirmation that she wasn't repelled by him, either. He hadn't seen or smelled any sign of a dog, cat, or bird, or any kind of a familiar in her apartment or on her person. It was entirely possible she was only into plants and not particularly fond of animals at all.

She regarded him with wide eyes, her lips slightly parted. After a moment she huffed out a breath in a way he was starting to recognize as amusement from her. She looked him straight in the eyes and asked, "Is it okay if I pet you?"

Was it okay? He gave her his widest foxy grin and a nod.

She reached forward with one hand, her fingertips touching the fur on the side of his face uncertainly. He turned his head into her palm to encourage her, and when she curved her fingers to give him scratches around the base of his ears, he let his eyes roll back. Bliss. He rolled in Kuro's arms so his belly was up and he let his head loll back into her hand so she could continue scratching around his ears or reach for his belly, or hell, she could pet him anywhere and he'd be very, very happy.

All in all, experiments with Marie and Kuro were turning out to be pretty good. He personally was optimistic about the outcome.

Kuro chuckled. "So the timer is set. I wouldn't be averse to another kiss."

Marie was still petting Joe, her fingers buried in the fur around his neck. "Aren't you concerned that a kiss might change you back into fox form?"

"A kiss from you would be worth the risk," Kuro stated.

Joe lifted his head to look up at his lover. Damn, that was good.

The pink deepened across Marie's cheeks and spread up and back to the tips of her ears. "I don't want to force you into a form you didn't choose."

Also good. This witch. She might just be too good for this world. Okay, he was already sure she was too good for him, and he was absolutely, without a doubt, aware of the generous amount of narcissism he had going on. So if he was thinking Marie was too pure for him, then Kuro for sure was thinking she was out of his league. Which was totally ridiculous.

Therefore, it was absolutely reasonable to want her for the two of them. She was obviously responsive to each of them, so they needed to resolve this situation as quickly as possible and get back to wooing their witch.

"But it doesn't bother you?" Kuro asked in his serious and quiet way. "That we both have a nine-tailed fox form?"

Marie shook her head.

Laughter like mellow bells broke the tension between the three of them, and Ashke spoke. "She's worked with the Darke Consortium for years now. She spent plenty of time with Thomas in his human and his wolf form. Werewolves are *way* scarier than foxes."

Joe growled. Either he or Kuro could take on a werewolf one-on-one, any day. Werewolves tended toward packs, though, and that's where their greatest power was—both in strength of numbers and pack magic.

Marie shot a sharp look at the winged fae. "You're deliberately leaving that open to interpretation. There's mischief and then there's causing people unnecessary grief when they don't know each other very well. Cut it out, Ashke. I've had a little too much drama in my life recently and absolutely will kick you out of here for deliberately instigating miscommunication."

"Don't forget, witch. You called me." There was still laughter in Ashke's voice, but there was also a hard edge to his words now.

Marie nodded, her gaze steady. "And I'm regretting it."

Joe let out a soft whine. As much as he wanted her attention, he didn't want to be the reason she encountered friction with her colleagues and friends. The fae might be tiny, but his kind of magic was dangerous. Take away the mischief and he could make all of their lives a whole lot more miserable.

Kuro cleared his throat. "It never hurts to reinforce one's safety precautions with an added layer of protection, especially when the magic is of different kinds. It's good that you're here."

The tension held taut for another heartbeat, then Ashke zipped over to hover in front of Kuro.

"I like you, fox," Ashke said. There was a pause and then a sigh. "And I like Marie. If I test newcomers in her life, it is out of affection for a friend."

Joe perked up, ears forward. His encounters with the fae were fairly limited, and most fae he'd dealt with had been aloof and pretty damned arrogant. This was probably the closest he had ever heard one come to an apology. Marie's eyebrows had lifted. Joe thought it was a good bet this was the closest the winged fae had ever come to apologizing in her presence too, or at least to someone outside of their cool kids consortium club.

"While we've got an experiment going and we're not going to take the risk of testing it the other way..." Ashke zipped around in a circle and returned to hover in front of Marie at eye level. "I can investigate the area where fox number one encountered the other witch."

Joe gave a short bark. This time it was Marie who glanced at him and seemed to catch onto his prompt. "Someone brushed past Joe just as he was returning to Kuro last night. He was right on the street below us, a couple of blocks away. If there's any residual magic where Kuro was, I'd be interested to know if there is any from that encounter with Joe as well."

"And whether the magical signatures are similar. Gotcha." Ashke bobbed in the air and then darted out the window that was cracked open for him. The fae paused outside. "My barrier is layered outside your wards, Marie, so you can leave the window open if you want. But Thomas would insist you close it."

Joe suppressed a growl. Based on what Marie said earlier, there wasn't a thing between Thomas and Marie, but Joe would really appreciate some clarity on exactly who Thomas was in Marie's life. Werewolf or no.

Marie tugged the window closed, which irritated Joe more. He tucked his nose in between Kuro's arm and chest to hide his discomfiture. His reaction was petty, and while he owned it most of the time, he didn't want to be that way around Marie right now.

"Well, it's not gonna take him that much time to investigate the two spots, but he's not going to be back in the next few minutes, either." Marie stood, shifting her weight from one foot to the other, and Joe got the impression she was a little uncertain as to what to do next.

Then she was moving past him and Kuro to the counter area where she had a sink and a small stovetop. Her kitchen gave the feel of the setups he'd seen from vloggers who lived in Japan or Korea or China. Neat and tidy, making maximum use of the very limited available counter space. There were a few key items that seemed to have permanent places on the counters, like a multifunction rice cooker and an Asian-style hot water dispenser. The dispenser was super convenient. One touch for a steady stream of hot water, no waiting for water to heat up the way a kettle would require.

"How about some ramen?" she asked.

Hell yes. Joe barked once and hoped she'd understand.

Marie laughed again. Happiness bubbled out of her easily, like she gathered it from everything around her and shared it generously. "Just to be clear, I mean having noodles together. I watch enough Asian dramas to know that could be construed as a different kind of offer."

An answering chuckle rumbled up from Kuro's chest. Joe tilted his head. If he'd been able to talk, he would've wanted to ask which Asian dramas she watched. He enjoyed a few, and so did Kuro. The two of them had a tendency to binge Korean dramas together. Kuro liked to follow the epic long dramas out of mainland China a few episodes at a time. Then there were the BL dramas out of Thailand. *So good*. There were plenty more from other regions, too. It was a topic of conversation to explore later, when Joe was able to shape change at will again.

Because he would be able to. He was going to think it into truth.

"I've got beef, chicken, and pork tonkatsu flavors." Marie opened one of her cabinets. "What sounds good to you?"

Joe gave Kuro a significant look. Normally it was Joe who made conversation and took the lead for flirtation. Kuro was going to have to step up.

Kuro glanced at Joe then looked away quickly, clearing his throat. "No chicken for the gumiho."

Marie turned with a package in her hand. "No?"

Kuro held Joe out, balanced in his palm with his fingers crooked to keep hold of Joe. Joe wouldn't be hurt if he fell to the floor from this height, but he didn't appreciate being held out like a plush toy.

Kuro replied to Marie. "He is a gumiho, a Korean fox spirit. In the far past, the cries and blood of chickens were used to ward off gumiho. So for his kind, chickens are repulsive, and consuming chicken is not a pleasant experience."

Joe flicked all nine of his tails. It was true and he felt a little uncomfortable revealing a weakness, but this was Marie and he felt certain she wouldn't exploit it. He glanced at her and realized she was reading the food packaging.

"Hmm, this says it only has chicken flavoring but it would be better to err on the safe side. I'll make one of the other flavors." Marie looked at Joe. "Preference for beef or pork tonkatsu?"

She held up one for a moment, then lowered it and lifted the other. She paused and repeated the motion. Joe waited until she held the pork tonkatsu up and lifted a paw.

"Pork tonkatsu it is." Marie smiled at him. Joe liked the way she continued to talk to him, not over him, like he'd suddenly turned into a domesticated canine. She turned her attention to Kuro. "How about you? No chicken?"

Kuro's answering smile was slow and heart-stopping. "I enjoy the taste of a lot of things, chicken included."

Joe tipped his muzzle down and nipped Kuro's thumb. Obvious innuendos aside, there was also no need to rub it in. Joe was Korean American and wouldn't ever know what everyone was raving about when they talked about how good Korean fried chicken was. Usually, Kuro was good about not eating fried chicken in front of Joe.

It was Marie's turn to clear her throat. "Why don't I just make three pork tonkatsus?"

"You do that." Kuro's voice was still doing that sexy, deep thing, and Joe growled.

It was one thing to flirt with their witch, but it wasn't like Kuro to get this intense when they were just bantering about food.

Food.

Joe stared at Kuro. Kuro hadn't hunted last night, because he was looking out for Joe. Sure, Kuro hadn't let himself go for as long as Joe had, but it had been longer than was probably wise.

Joe turned and ran up Kuro's arm, nipping his partner on the side of his neck this time. Kuro growled, finally tearing his gaze from Marie. Joe planted his paws on Kuro's chest and stared into Kuro's eyes.

No feeding on our witch.

KURO

As distracted as he was, Kuro still closed his arms under Joe's rump to support him even while his partner got in his face. Irritated, Kuro stared into Joe's eyes as the gumiho stared into his.

In the moment of stillness between them, a red haze at the edges of Kuro's vision faded. Realization spread through his body like chills, originating from his chest and radiating outward. He'd been hunting and he hadn't been aware of it.

That was bad.

Like Joe, Kuro preferred to feed from the kind of people who did terrible things to their fellow human beings. In contrast to Joe, Kuro's mode of hunting was different. He didn't have a yeowoo guseul, a fox bead, to place inside his prey and absorb their life essence. Instead, he drew sustenance through touch, a specific type of touch.

It meant he had to be careful and in control when he was attracted to someone. And he was very attracted to Marie.

"I'm good," he murmured to Joe.

The gumiho sneezed in his face. Obviously, his partner had opinions about the truth of that statement. Regardless, Kuro was aware now and he wasn't going to inadvertently do something they'd all regret.

Marie was stealing quick glances at them as she bustled over the stove. She was aware something was going on, obviously, but she was willing to give them space to handle it. Or she was still wary of them.

Kuro didn't want her to feel unsafe. This was her den, her home. As he considered what he could say or do to ease the tension in the room, Joe hopped out of his arms. His partner trotted over to Marie and wound himself around her ankles the way a cat would.

"If I drop hot broth on you, it'll be your own fault," she warned. But her voice was steady and there was a touch of humor in it. "Do both of you like leafy greens and tofu? I've got some soy eggs already made, and some mushrooms, too."

Joe sat and tilted his head to meet her gaze, barking once to signal his affirmative. She gave him a small smile and looked to Kuro.

Kuro had remained in the living area. Keeping some distance between him and her was probably more prudent. At least, until he'd had a chance to go on a proper hunt. As it was, he could enjoy the look she had on her face as her gaze took him in from head to toe and back up again. It was dark in this part of the room, and he guessed she saw a lean shadow silhouetted against the plants lining her windows and the bright cityscape beyond.

If Joe was picture-perfect, Kuro knew he could come across with the kind of bad-boy vibes some people were drawn to. He and Joe had learned to play to their strengths over the years. But neither of them was trying to manipulate Marie.

"Yes, we'd both enjoy that," Kuro said after giving her a little more time to appreciate him.

Joe sneezed again and began grooming his tails.

Marie turned back to the counter, assembling their ramen in

separate bowls. "Great. Hopefully Ashke will be back by the time we're finished eating. You two weren't far from my place."

She carried two bowls over to Kuro, placing them both on the small table next to her couch. It smelled delicious, actually. Instant ramen was always a solid choice. He and Joe ate it all the time, in between real feedings. Human food was enjoyable, even if it wasn't real sustenance for either of them. But Marie had leveled up the ramen with an appetizing arrangement of all the add-ons she'd mentioned. The soy eggs were even the soft-boiled kind, split in half to reveal the jammy yolks.

"After we talk to Ashke," Marie was saying, placing a pair of chopsticks next to both bowls, even though Joe probably wouldn't use them. She was treating them both as guests, regardless of form. "I think we should do our best to get some sleep. Everything else is going to have to wait a few hours."

"You make it sound like 'everything' is a lot." Kuro took a seat, giving Joe enough room to hop up next to the nearest bowl.

Marie returned from the counter, having retrieved a third bowl for herself and was already neatly slurping noodles. "Mmm. Well, yes. First, there's both of you. We've no idea if or when this situation will resolve. Then there's the dead man we encountered yesterday. In addition to him, there are more things I need to investigate inside Socrates Industries, and I've got designs to complete for the job I'm contracted to do for the company."

"Well, when you put it that way." Kuro lifted his own bowl and started in on the ramen. It wouldn't make her any safer from him, but he still wanted to taste the food she'd prepared for them.

Joe was sitting next to him, eating straight from the bowl.

"Were you expected to go back today?" Kuro asked. She was a good cook, he decided. The added vegetables and egg served to enhance the salty goodness of the ramen, adding texture and contrast in flavor. The jammy soy eggs added a richness that was luxurious on the palate.

"No. Not right away," Marie answered. Then she tipped the edge of the bowl to her lips and sipped the broth.

Kuro smiled. She'd given them spoons, but he thought her choice was expedient since she was standing and holding her bowl in one hand, chopsticks in the other. Why juggle chopsticks and a spoon when she could sip from her bowl directly? It was a casual, comfortable sort of thing. It gave him, and probably Joe too, a feeling that she wasn't treating them with any kind of formality. This made the shared meal feel...close.

"I always take a couple of days to come up with proposed garden designs," Marie was saying. "But I want to get back there as soon as possible, to find out more about—"

"Our dead man," Kuro finished for her.

She narrowed her eyes at him. "Don't you think you've got more important things to be worrying about?"

Kuro considered her for a moment. She didn't need him or Joe. In fact, she was helping them. She was competent, intelligent, and had the resources to back her up if she encountered anything beyond what she could handle individually. Anyone proposing to be with her in any capacity would need to convince her they had value to add.

"I think it would benefit all of us to work together," Kuro replied. "You don't need us, but we bring skills to the table that will get you answers faster. Your consortium is spread thin, otherwise your other colleague would be here too, not just the fae. Besides, I hear werewolves are overbearing."

He needed to sell her on the benefits they could offer her.

"You need my help, don't you?" she asked softly.

Kuro frowned. Joe growled. When she put it that way, it really rankled.

"We don't accept pity," Kuro ground out. He kept his attention fixed on Joe, not wanting to see the emotion in her eyes.

She didn't deny it had occurred to her. At least she wasn't a liar. "You need a witch to counter a witch. If not me, you'd have to go find someone else."

The practicality in her tone eased his tight chest.

"The pain witch who confronted me said this was a warning, an added challenge while we're carrying out our task." Kuro couldn't keep his mouth from twisting into a sneer.

"A warning from who? Is there a witch coven involved with Socrates Industries?" Marie asked.

Kuro lifted one shoulder in a shrug. "We freelance, and our primary contracts come from Babel. Since the last contract we were involved in didn't go well..."

"Ahh." Marie gathered up the empty bowls, placing them in her sink. "So this is a punishment?"

"More like an added roadblock as we work on the current contract," Kuro clarified, struggling to express his theory. "Babel believes in chaos. I don't think whatever spell was cast is an attempt to permanently harm either of us."

"It's like making you play the game in hard mode." Marie sounded incredulous.

Kuro nodded. He wasn't sure how to put it, but that sounded about right.

Marie's head shot up and she looked out the window. A second later, the window opened on its own, and Ashke flew back inside. Kuro wondered whether it had been Marie's magic or the fae that had opened it. He didn't know enough about Marie's magic to know what she was capable of.

"Well, your boys are well and truly hexed," Ashke said, flying straight to Marie.

Joe flicked all nine tails, sitting up straight with his ears pinned back. The gumiho's posture indicated he was a mix of indignant and irritated. Kuro figured that was a match for what he was feeling. It's not like they couldn't have figured out they'd been hexed.

"I hope you've got more information to share than that," Kuro said. He kept his tone flat and deliberately refrained from any insults. A fae was still a fae, after all.

Ashke did a flip in the air, grinning at Kuro. "In fact, I do. Ask me if I'll share, fox boy."

Kuro swallowed multiple retorts, remembering the fae's earlier interactions with Marie. This one liked to bait people.

"Ashke." Marie sounded tired. Surely even the fae could hear it. "Please."

Ashke did seem to settle some. "There was residual magic on the rooftop for sure. And more on the street near Haven House, as you thought there might be. I can't tell you exactly what was cast but I can tell you blood sacrifice was a part of the casting. The sacrifice and spell were done someplace else and the hex was carried into downtown to be cast onto the targets."

"Designed specifically for them?" Marie asked.

"Probably," Ashke replied. "The magic did have a feel to it, not the same, but like different components of the same cologne. I can sense the full spell here with the two of them, but when I went out to investigate, only parts of the spell were present in each of the locations."

"So any reversal has to be for both of them, not one then the other." Marie said the words out loud, but her eyes had taken on an unfocused look, like she wasn't speaking to Ashke anymore.

Ashke flew closer to Kuro. "There she goes. Problem-solving mode."

Kuro shot a sideways glance at the fae, then looked back at Marie. She was looking pale, and there were shadows under her eyes.

"You mentioned wanting to sleep on the info this guy would have." Kuro jerked his head sideways to indicate Ashke.

"Do you have anything else you can share, Ashke?" Marie asked.

Ashke laughed again, the sound of it musical and mellow. "Now, if you had asked if I had anything else I could share or might share, I could have had more fun leaving some surprises for later. What I can share is slightly more specific. You're so good at that."

Kuro wouldn't have thought about carefully wording a question that way. But then, he and Joe mostly avoided dealing with fae whenever possible. It was tricky in the best of times. He got the impression the only reason the careful wording was being received so well was because the fae liked the witch, to whatever extent fae could like mortals.

Marie only politely waited, a pleasant and even sweet expression on her face.

"Careful, fox boys," Ashke whispered loudly. "This is one of her most dangerous expressions."

Kuro decided not to add to the commentary. He thought the fae was telling the truth, and he wanted Marie's potential ire to be directed at the winged man floating next to him.

Finally, Ashke flew in a circle above all their heads. "Night and day, day and night. We've already witnessed the effects of the hex. Makes it very hard to work together, if it's just the two of them, doesn't it?"

The fae zipped back out the window without another word, just the sound of his laughter echoing in the room.

Marie sighed. "He just had to be dramatic about it. I told him I didn't need drama."

MARIE

The thing about living alone was you got used to the sounds of your own space. An apartment in the middle of a high-rise, especially located in the center of a large city, was never completely quiet. The muffled city sounds became part of the white noise around her, and she took comfort in the familiarity of them.

She was usually alone when she stayed here, so she was careful to be alert for anything out of the norm. It didn't take much to wake her, even when she hadn't gotten enough sleep. Besides, the person moving around her kitchen wasn't trying to be sneaky about it. She had told Kuro and Joe both to help themselves to anything in her kitchen. From the sound of it, Kuro was making himself tea.

Marie reached for her phone on the nightstand. The display read almost 4 p.m. She'd slept the day away, almost six hours. That was a lot longer than the nap she'd been planning. She normally never napped longer than a few hours, so she hadn't thought to set an alarm. With strangers in her home, she'd honestly thought she would be lucky to get in thirty minutes.

She wasn't quite ready to face them yet. If they needed something, the sliding door separating her sleep area from the living space wouldn't have kept them out. She figured they could manage by themselves for another few minutes.

There were notifications on the main screen of her phone. She pulled up the messages from the Darke Consortium first. Thomas had sent a message via their private chat.

Ashke filled me in. He's staying nearby. Ping me when you wake.

Of course Ashke had. Equal parts irritation and warmth filled her chest. On one hand, she was a perfectly capable adult, with very solid security in place. Security Ashke himself had added to that morning. On the other hand, she was only one person, and she needed to sleep. It was comforting to know that one of her colleagues from the Darke Consortium—more of a teammate, really, and as close to a friend as she currently had if she was being honest about the current state of her life—was near enough to help if anything caught her by surprise.

She hadn't made the request of Ashke. The fae had his own duties and interests back at the Consortium manor, hours away. She smiled as she sent a response to Thomas.

Ping.

Pong, Thomas responded. Sleep well?

She briefly considered tapping the icon to initiate a video call, the way she normally would. It was faster than text chats, but her guests would hear the entire conversation. Better to keep it to text for now.

Yeah. Thanks. I've still got company.

I heard. Ashke felt they weren't an immediate danger to you. But that could change if they stay.

Not sure if they're staying.

She started to type a half dozen different follow-ups to that statement but decided to just wait for whatever Thomas was going to say next. She really didn't know what was going to happen with Joe and Kuro. Based on what Ashke had said about the hex on them, she had a strong suspicion about what was coming in about an hour, once the sun had set.

K. Whatever you decide, keep me updated pls.

Will do.

We're spread thin with Punch and Bennett away. I've got a situation in the San Juan Islands. Duncan is keeping watch at the manor with Asamoah and Ellery. That's not enough for the Consortium, so Ashke is going to need to head back.

She waited. She could see that Thomas was still typing.

A witch using pain magic that close to you is a problem. We're not close enough to provide sufficient backup. Would feel better if you came back to the manor. Make it easier to keep all our people protected.

I've got a contract, she responded.

Normally, she'd have found a way to work remotely. After all, Thomas was right to be concerned about a witch that used pain magic. Marie had a healthy amount of caution for that type of witchcraft. Although it didn't always equate to evil, pain magic was definitely the kind of heady power source that came with enough temptation to attract a lot of morally bereft souls. There was no way to know for sure what personal code of ethics those practitioners kept. Marie wasn't about to find out if the other witch would jump at the chance to use Marie as a sacrifice for more power.

So she described to Thomas what she'd seen the day before: the dead guy, the suspicious plants, and the amulet. Any one of those things might have been able to wait a while. Well, no, the dead guy couldn't wait. They really needed to investigate that.

She finished with a single line: It's obvious there's at least one other interested party.

Babel. We need to know more about them, but most of our intel is shallow. Our resources do better with old history. Any chance your boys might share?

They're not boys. Also not mine.

K…

Marie scowled at the phone screen. Thomas was teasing her. Best to leave that alone and focus on the question.

I don't know. I'll ask.

K. Kick them out if you feel threatened in any way. Ping Duncan or Ashke and they can be there in an hour or two. Wish we could do better. I don't like any of us in the city without immediate support.

Marie grimaced. His concerns were valid. She wished they weren't. It felt better that he had the same concerns about any of their team alone in the city, rather than her specifically.

A longer message came through.

Seattle is getting more competitive for objects of myth and magic. It's a major entry and exit point for black market items going in and out of the country. There've always been some independent agents carrying these items or seeking them. But Babel is bigger, with resources and means to coordinate freelancers like your boys. Hiring a pain witch to hex them, though? That's behaving like organized crime and I don't like it.

Also a good point. Seemed like a good time to get Thomas's opinion on Kuro and Joe's proposition.

They want us to work together to investigate Socrates Industries.

There was a long pause.

I'd feel better if I met them, but I trust your judgment.

Well, that was good. It would be even better if Marie had a better handle on what she was feeling about Kuro and Joe, aside from a whole lot of attraction.

They're still under contract to Babel. It was an important note to keep in mind.

Even after the bastards hexed them? Thomas didn't do emojis, but Marie could imagine his scowl.

They took action in direct conflict with their contract a few months ago. Based on what you told us they said, they have their own moral compass. Could be they intend to fulfill the contract to their standards, but maybe there's some flexibility when it comes to exactly how. Doesn't hurt to work together until conflicting interests can't be avoided.

Marie studied that chunk of text.

You switched to voice to text, didn't you?

Had a lot to say. Besides, I'm driving.

That was fair.

I'll get going then. Will check in.

Please do.

She let out a soft laugh. He didn't type it, but she knew him well enough to know that if she didn't check in somewhat regularly, he or

Ashke or both would come looking for her. It was comforting. There was something amazing about people who both trusted her and also didn't take her independence for granted.

"Hello?" Kuro's voice called low and soft from just outside her door.

"One second." She threw back her comforter and scrambled out of bed, reaching for the silk yukata she used as a robe. Pulling it on over her tank top and pajama pants, she pulled the sliding door open.

Kuro stood there with a mug of steaming tea. From the scent, he'd brewed some of her loose-leaf green tea with jasmine flowers. Behind him, on the chaise, Joe was still in his fox form, sitting up with a big yawn.

"Thought you might like some, since I heard you waking up." Kuro paused. "I wouldn't have bothered you, in case you decided to fall back to sleep, but I heard you laugh."

Ah. She nodded. "I was texting with someone."

Kuro nodded, holding the mug steady until she had it firmly in her own hands.

She lifted the mug to her lips, then lowered it. It was too hot to sip. The silence stretched out as neither she nor Kuro said anything, and even Joe just sat there looking at the both of them. It was so awkward. So awkward. Maybe it would be worth it to scald her tongue, just to give herself an escape from the tension.

"Did you sleep well?" she finally asked.

Kuro nodded. "The couch was comfortable, and you provided us with plenty of blankets."

"It's a chaise," she corrected, then winced. Who cared?

The corner of Kuro's mouth quirked. Her face warmed as embarrassment caught up with her. But she wasn't going to let it get the best of her. She forced herself to look up into his eyes.

His pupils were so dark a brown they might as well be black. The whites of his eyes showed on either side of his irises and even a tiny bit beneath. The effect was an intense gaze as he looked directly at her.

She realized, slowly, she'd been staring for too long. She should look away. Maybe say something clever.

"Hey! I'm back!" Joe exclaimed.

They both turned toward the chaise. Joe was standing in front of it, back in the same clothes he'd been wearing the night before. He was so incredibly hot. She glanced back at Kuro and swallowed hard. They both were. She'd managed to avoid thinking about it with Joe's shape change, but both men had invited her to share kisses and the potential in that was suddenly fresh in her memory.

Bad Marie. There were more important concerns to be thinking about. No cookie.

Kuro crossed the room and pulled Joe into a tight hug. Joe returned the embrace, laughing, then he fixed his gaze on Marie. "How long did it take for the kiss to kick in?"

Marie blinked. "What? Oh!"

She fumbled for her phone and swiped the screen to get to the timer, stopping it. She stared at the timer display, then back at the both of them.

"It was the whole day," rumbled Kuro.

"I don't think it was the kiss that did it." Marie looked past the two men and out her window at the sky.

Joe cocked his head to one side, then turned to follow her gaze.

Clouds were lit in colors of hot pinks and burnt oranges against a sky of blue and indigo. It was magic hour, the time right after the sun had set, when the light did indescribable things to everything it touched.

"Night and day, day and night," Marie whispered Ashke's earlier words. "I think the hex on both of you is still in effect."

"If you're right, I've only got an hour or less before I'm forced to change to my fox form." Kuro sounded grim.

She didn't blame him.

Joe let out a curse. "What do we do?"

"Babel is likely to lift the hex when we make good on the contract." Kuro's tone was flat, cold.

"Will they, though?" Marie asked. "A hex like this took a significant investment to fund. Will it be worth it to them to have it undone? Or will they just tell you how to undo it?"

Joe ran his fingers through his hair in a seemingly frustrated motion. Somehow, it only made him look even more like a K-pop idol straight out of a music video. "You probably have a better idea than we do."

"I don't get my power that way," she said quietly. She didn't think he meant to imply it, but she still had the urge to widen the distance between them. Not actually feasible since they were already about as far apart as one could get inside her apartment, with them standing by her chaise and her still standing in the doorway to her sleeping nook.

Joe muttered another curse. "I'm sorry. I meant to say you probably have a better idea of how spells work and what it would take to undo this hex. Not that you'd—"

"I'm a green witch." She decided it was better to push forward than wallow in emotional responses. "I draw power from the plant life around me and simple living things. It's a much more gradual thing. I have a longer-lasting reservoir of power, but it takes a lot more from me personally to do greater spells, and my recovery time is slow. I'm much more effective using my magic for subtler effects. I've never tried to break a hex, not like the one you two are experiencing."

"You don't have to," Kuro said quietly. His deep voice was warmer than it had been a minute ago.

A bit of the tension in her neck and shoulders eased. His words gave her the hope that he wasn't holding it against her that she couldn't just fix this.

Joe had tucked one side of his lower lip between his teeth, looking at Kuro. "We shouldn't bother you with this anymore. Pain witches like the one who did this to us get their sacrifices from somewhere. Don't some of them go after witches like you?"

She wasn't going to deny it. "Yes. But I'm also more exposed if I'm alone here in the city working on this thing at Socrates Industries by myself."

Both men stilled.

"You'd go back there? By yourself?" Joe asked.

A low growl rolled through the room and she thought it came from Kuro.

"It's what I do." She crossed her arms over her chest. "If it were just the contract to design the corporate gardens, I'd go back to the consortium and work remotely. But somebody from the Darke Consortium needs to investigate the dead man from yesterday and the item he was wearing. That person is me."

Besides, she also wanted to get a closer look at the plants she'd seen. It would take more than visual identification to be certain they were what she suspected.

She glared at them, daring them to try to argue with her. They barely knew each other, and she drew a hard line at people telling her what to do with her life. If they tried it so early in…whatever this was, it would tell her a lot about what level of respect they would have for her. Not enough.

It was Joe who let out a frustrated huff. "I don't want to compete with you. I don't think either of us does."

Some of the tension eased inside her. That was a better answer than what she'd been bracing for.

"Couldn't we work together?" Joe asked softly. His chin was tilted down so he could look at her through his thick lashes with those amazing eyes of his, all big and round.

Whatever defensiveness she had melted away. She let her arms drop and she picked her mug of tea up from the side table. Taking a sip, she let the fragrance of the jasmine fill her senses as the heat eased her throat.

"Let's explore investigating this thing together," she said finally. "Both of you mentioned teaming up, and I've been thinking about it. It seems like we all can benefit from it."

A happy grin spread across Joe's face, lighting up his expression. Kuro's features softened, and a small, lopsided smile pulled at his lips.

"Great!" Joe gripped Kuro's shoulder, leaning on his partner. Kuro stood there with his feet planted, solid as a tree, continuing to watch her.

Heat spread over her cheeks. Being around the two of them was a lot.

"I'm going to stay here this evening," she decided. "I've got to work on the designs for the gardens inside the building. They'll be my reason to go back."

Kuro finally stirred, sitting down on the chaise and pulling Joe with him to sit far enough to one side that there was room for her to sit on the end. "Whether I change or not, we should head back to our place to find out if it has been tampered with."

"It's just a temporary unit," Joe added. "We rent month to month."

"And I need to hunt," Kuro said curtly.

Marie didn't cross the room to join them, despite the unspoken invitation. It didn't feel quite right with the current discussion. "Ramen doesn't quite sustain you, huh?"

Both of them shook their heads.

"We both feed on life essence," Kuro offered.

"But we don't kill if we can help it," Joe added. "And we only prey on bad people."

"Define bad." She pitched her voice so it sounded like a suggestion. It wasn't like she could judge them. Supernaturals had to live their lives in accordance with their natures. What mattered was the choices they made while they survived. She'd worked alongside Bennett, the vampire steward of the Darke Consortium, long enough to understand that.

"People who do harm to others, mostly," Joe answered readily. "Physical stuff is the easiest to notice. Sometimes we encounter somebody that has been harming others emotionally or mentally. In places like this, cities mostly, it's not hard to find that kind of thing."

"And you don't kill them?" Marie felt it was important to be clear, and they weren't exactly giving details. "How do you feed? Not like vampires?"

Joe shook his head. "It's different. It would take a long time to explain, actually. I would offer to show you, but I don't know if that would upset you or not."

"By feeding on me?" Red flag.

Joe shot to his feet. "No, no, no. We wouldn't. I meant that we could arrange it so you could watch from someplace safe. Usually when one of us is hunting, the other is on lookout, just making sure nothing gets out of control."

Joe's face flushed. Marie wondered what he wasn't saying. Maybe it was too complicated for a quick explanation.

"But aside from the feeding part of it, watching might make you uncomfortable." Joe bit his lip again. "To an observer, it looks really sexual. I'm not going to say it's not, depending on which of us it is, but it's complicated."

Marie considered what Joe was saying, unwilling to press him more because he was so obviously struggling with discussing this with her.

"It wouldn't be as difficult if this were just a working arrangement," Kuro stated, drawing her attention back to him.

He stood slowly and approached her, giving her plenty of time to move back or tell him to stop. She didn't. Joe hesitated, then joined them until all three of them were standing within each other's personal space.

It was Marie's turn to bite her lip. She wanted to know, so she asked. "You want this to be more than a professional collaboration? Both of you?"

They both nodded.

"Is that something you'd consider?" Joe asked. His voice had dropped low and quiet, almost intimate.

"I have been thinking about it," she answered honestly. She wanted to know more about their feeding, because it felt like it could be a hard line for her. She'd been in open relationships before, knew the importance of discussing hopes and boundaries, but this was a whole different level of complicated.

"With the two of us?" Kuro asked. "We've been open about our interest, but want to be clear."

"Yes." She met each of their gazes. Complicated might be worth it, for them. She wasn't sure, but she also wanted to know and didn't want to regret not taking the chance. "I've been in polyamorous relationships in the past. Not many, but enough to know what I'm hoping for and where my hard lines are. I'd like to get to know each of you better, and hear more about what you want from me."

Both of them gave her smug smiles. Under the intensity of their regard, her body was responding. Her nipples tightened, and she resisted the urge to look down to find out if they could tell through the thin fabrics of her camisole and yukata.

"First"—Kuro paused, waiting for her to meet his gaze again—"we're not looking for a one-time thing."

"We're interested in getting to know you, too," Joe confirmed. "You can stop anytime, and we'll back off, but we're not just looking for a hookup. We'd like to spend time with you."

Marie started to answer, but then Kuro's eyes widened, and he quickly shoved his tea mug into her hands. Then he was shrinking. And there was a fox sitting at her feet.

"This is definitely going to impact the way we all get to know each other," Marie muttered.

THIRTEEN

KURO

That could have gone better," Joe said.

Kuro glared at him, ears pinned back, still in his fox form.

The two of them were on another rooftop, on a building somewhere in between where they had been staying and Marie's high-rise apartment. This rooftop wasn't intended for public access. It had no lighting, which was perfect for them. No one would wonder what Joe was doing out here in the hours just before dawn. And no one was going to wonder what the heck a fox was doing in the middle of the bustling city—especially one with nine tails.

"Do you want to head back to our witch?" Joe looked out over the streets below. "Seems like this would be the best time to slip back into her building. I don't sense anyone following us."

Kuro growled. Keeping eye contact with Joe, Kuro sat. The movement seemed very deliberate.

"Or we could hang out here for a little while." Joe ran his fingers through his hair and sighed as frustration churned in his belly. "Not being able to talk freely is really getting to me."

Kuro made a sound deep in his chest. It might have been about as close to one of his normal grunts as Joe had ever heard his partner make in fox form.

Joe turned and sat with his back against the low wall bordering the roof, knees up. Kuro moved to sit right between Joe's feet and leaned forward until he bumped Joe's nose with his own.

Joe laughed. "That's cold and you know it."

Kuro settled back on his haunches, looking smug.

"Okay, yeah. It'll be good for the two of us to talk privately." Joe realized the timing worked out.

They had remained at Marie's apartment well into the night. She'd pulled out her tablet to get some work done and set up her laptop for Joe and Kuro to watch streaming videos. It'd been awkward for the first few minutes, but she'd been adamant about continuing to work on her research. She'd wanted to look for whatever information she could find regarding their hexes and research the situation at Socrates Industries.

Apparently, a dead person walking around was a major cause for concern to her. Maybe he should've been more worried himself, but the body hadn't appeared to be interested in eating anyone. It hadn't seemed like the beginning of a zombie apocalypse, so Joe was a little more focused on his and Kuro's immediate circumstances.

For him, it wasn't about how the scientist was walking around after death, or even how he ended up dead. It was purely about getting ahold of that amulet the scientist was wearing. That was what Babel wanted.

Joe chuckled. "Marie's really something, isn't she? She made her list of things to do and got started on it, right away."

He'd wanted to talk to her more, but the way the conversation had been interrupted by Kuro's change, it'd been like getting splashed with cold water. The sooner they had more information regarding the situation at Socrates Industries, the sooner they could put together a plan to get inside.

Babel had arranged this situation to ensure Joe and Kuro had a vested interest in completing the contract, after all.

Joe tipped his head back to rest on the stone wall behind him. The cold was seeping through his clothes. The weather might be fairly temperate in Seattle, but the late fall was still cold. He looked up into the night sky. There was cloud cover tonight, and the city lights reflected back eerily. But the sky was lightening, even if it wasn't easy to tell. Dawn wasn't too far away.

"If we've figured out the cycle of the spell correctly, you should change back to human soon," Joe said to Kuro. And Joe would be forced into his fox form.

He didn't even try to suppress the shudder that ran through him. He'd had his shape-shifting ability since puberty. It had been one of the first aspects of his nature as a gumiho to manifest. More and more of his abilities developed as he continued to mature. By the time he grew to his full height and filled out his frame around the age of twenty-five or so, he was comfortable in his human form, his nine-tailed fox form, and a range of partial shifts in between. He'd never been trapped in a single form, never been unable to choose the form he wanted to take.

A paw pressed firmly into his chest, bringing Joe's attention back to the here and now. He looked into Kuro's face.

"You remember when we were first getting to know each other in college?" he asked Kuro, chuckling. "You were so serious. It was so damned hot, and you caught me stroking myself in the showers, thinking about you. I was so close, I lost control of my shift and my fox ears came out."

The sky lightened further to the east and Kuro's form grew, changed, until he was kneeling between Joe's legs with his hands resting warm on Joe's knees.

"Fox ears and nine tails on a stark-naked human body dripping wet under the shower spray," Kuro's voice came out husky and low. "With your hand wrapped around your cock. You were gorgeous."

The memory of it and hearing the sound of Kuro's voice, especially with that note to it... Joe's cock was straining at the fabric of his pants. He reached up and fisted a hand in the fabric of Kuro's shirt. His partner leaned in, kissing him hard. Kuro's big hand wrapped around the nape of his neck, and Joe let Kuro take the lead between them.

When they broke off the kiss, it was because they were in dire need of air. Kuro rested his forehead against Joe's, and they stayed that way, without any sound passing between them but their ragged breathing.

"It's hard, not getting to hold your hand," Joe said softly. "I guess after this many years, I took it for granted. I mean, I thought we touched all the time, no matter what form we were in. And there's nothing stopping us from touching, really..."

"But it's not the same," Kuro said just as quietly.

Joe shook his head. "It's not."

Neither of them were attracted to the other when they were in fox form. They weren't actual foxes, after all. It wasn't quite the same as maybe werewolves felt. He'd never known one well enough to ask. He and Kuro both had been born human, grown up human, and sure, mythology said gumiho were supposed to be actual foxes who lived a century or more before gaining the power to become human, but in actuality, he was thirty and Kuro was thirty-one, and no matter what form they were in, they thought and felt like humans.

He didn't want Kuro in fox form the way he craved Kuro's touch in human form.

"As much as I want to follow up on that kiss," Kuro rumbled, "we have less than an hour to talk freely."

"Usually, an hour would feel like forever." Joe laughed, his sense of humor kicking back in with a bitter edge. Patience was never a virtue he had any interest in pursuing. "But for the first time, it's not enough."

Not nearly enough.

As quickly as the laughter had come, Joe felt hollow inside, and that space was starting to fill with cold fear.

"We should start timing it," he said impulsively. "For Marie. She'd want the information. Did you see how she takes notes? Dates and times and measurements."

One corner of Kuro's mouth tipped up. He reached into his pants pocket and pulled out a phone. "All right, then."

That was another difference they had from werewolves. They didn't lose their clothes when they changed shape, and that included what might be in their pockets or on their person at the time. Beyond that, Kuro had ways of storing stuff as a kitsune that Joe didn't as a gumiho.

"Staying with Marie is a good idea, if she'll have us," Kuro began, shifting his weight back so he was crouching on his heels. He returned his hands to rest lightly on Joe's knees for balance. "Safety in numbers."

"And it doesn't seem like the pain witches knew she lived nearby. I don't think they would have hexed us so close to a witch who might have been able to help us if she'd known." Joe chewed on the inside of his cheek briefly. "But what if we bring trouble to her?"

They'd gone back to their place. There hadn't been signs of disturbance. Neither of them had sensed anyone following them on the way there, or on the way back, either. But obviously the pain witch—and their accomplice—had found him and Kuro somehow. They weren't always as careful as they should be discarding things like used straws or tissues. A witch could trace a being's location with something like that, an item carrying a part of the person who had used it.

As good as cities were for supernaturals, there weren't so many among the populace that they encountered each other all that often. Not unless they deliberately went to a place that catered to them. Joe and Kuro really didn't interact with many others, unless they sought them out, like Marie.

"We can use my power to make space for ourselves in her apartment that no one else will be able to detect," Kuro said. "We won't impinge too much on her, then."

Joe nodded. They'd have to explain that to Marie. "Okay. And what do we do next?"

She was going to ask for ideas. Joe had been thinking about it. He figured Kuro had been, too. He wanted to be sure they were in alignment. Because at this rate, it was Kuro who would be doing the talking when next they were in Marie's company.

"I'll go with her," Kuro said without hesitation. "During the day. We shouldn't leave her without someone to watch her back with pain witches paying attention to this contract."

"Yeah." Joe met Kuro's gaze. "If we were contracted to confirm items of interest were in that building and retrieve them, then Babel will be aware of potential competition."

"At night, you help her research," Kuro said.

A thought occurred to Joe and he started laughing.

Kuro tapped his knee. "What?"

"It's just..." Joe couldn't stop laughing. "This isn't the first time we've had to give a lady a chance to get some rest. But we're not even thinking about sex."

Kuro's quiet laugh joined his. "Yet."

Heat bloomed in Joe's chest.

"Yet," he agreed. Then he reached up to grasp Kuro's forearms. "That reminds me, we're each spending time with her. Just not together. You okay if I get close to her?"

Kuro smiled fully, then, and the expression changed his face in a way that made Joe's heartbeat stutter. "Yeah. If you're okay with me doing the same."

Joe had been thinking about that, too. "It's good for her to have a chance to get to know us each individually. I'm not sure we ever did that when we were dating anyone else. It was always us inviting them to join us both on dates and stuff."

Kuro turned his head and dropped a kiss onto Joe's knuckles. "It could be a stronger foundation for a relationship."

"You want this, with her?" Joe asked quietly.

He hadn't been able to stop thinking about Marie since they'd sat with her in the trees, months ago. She was more than a passing interest. Interacting with her yesterday and the day before only attracted him more.

"I feel the potential," Kuro answered. "But I'm not leaving you if it doesn't work out with her. She's the one who'll decide if she wants to build something with us."

Joe searched Kuro's face, not for any hints of uncertainty or duplicity. That wasn't Kuro. Joe was soaking in the conviction with which Kuro made his statement. If Kuro said it, he meant it. Joe took a lot of comfort from that. It anchored him.

"I'm not leaving you, either, if she decides being with the both of us isn't what she wants." Joe grinned. "But how can she resist the two of us? I think our chances of wooing our chosen witch are solid."

Kuro snorted. "We'll see."

"For now, we each get to know her in the time we've got with her." Joe gave Kuro's arm a squeeze. "And make the most of the time we get after sunset and before dawn."

Kuro nodded. Then he leaned forward again, until he was on his knees. Joe straightened from his seated position, turning his face up to Kuro's. As they met in a kiss, Kuro's hands came up to frame his face and Joe clutched at his waist.

This kiss was more carnal than their earlier one. It was more of a hungry clash of tongues and teeth. There was more strength in the way they held each other. A hint of desperation.

Kuro was the one to pull back. He unzipped the duffel Joe had brought from the place they were staying and pulled the stone out. It was hollowed out, with a sliding cover on the bottom, the kind of thing people used to hide their house keys in.

But when Kuro used it, as a kitsune, it was magic. "Let's take this someplace private."

He tucked the stone against the doorjamb of the stairwell access so it would be concealed behind the door if anyone were to open it. Then he went still. There was no flash of light or thunderclap, nothing to draw attention. Between one breath and the next, Kuro created a pocket universe inside the hollowed-out stone and turned with his hand outstretched toward Joe.

Joe grinned and took hold, letting Kuro tug him inside.

It was an odd feeling, stepping from the outside world into the space Kuro's magic created within the stone. As far as Joe knew, Kuro could make a pocket universe out of any stationary crevice. It was just easiest if it was a contained space to begin with.

There was no sensation of being shrunken down to fit inside a stone that could sit in the palm of Kuro's hand. It was more like stepping through a doorway. One moment, Joe was out on the rooftop. The next, he was following Kuro into the room that had been created by Kuro's kitsune magic in response to their combined desires.

It was a simple room with a connected bath. The room itself was decorated in a modern minimalist style, but the fabrics were luxurious, especially the sheets and blankets on the king-size bed. The bed also had a ridiculous number of pillows.

The heavy drapes were drawn, but if Joe decided to look out, he'd see city lights shining in an indigo night. There were no doors. The way out of Kuro's pocket universe always resembled a portal to Joe, never to be mistaken for a door.

Kuro hooked his hand around the nape of Joe's neck, capturing his attention and his lips at the same time. Their kiss was rough, burning off the stress both of them were carrying. It turned carnal as they opened to each other in a clash of teeth, desperately tasting and drinking each other in.

Joe let his hands wander over the flat planes of Kuro's chest and over his ribs. Kuro reached around and grabbed Joe's ass with both hands, pulling him close as Kuro ground their hips together.

"Fuck, Kuro," Joe groaned as Kuro scraped his teeth down Joe's neck.

"I know you want me," Kuro breathed against his neck. "But I want to know how much you want *her*."

"What?" Joe stilled.

Kuro hadn't ever talked about a woman when it was just the two of them. They'd been with women before, individually and together. But Kuro had always kept that unspoken boundary around the two of them that couldn't be crossed.

Kuro walked them toward the bed, pressing Joe down onto the mattress. "Marie. We both want her."

Joe lifted his hips, grinding up into Kuro in return. "Yes."

Kuro's hand palmed his erection through his pants. He leaned forward, his voice gravelly in Joe's ear. "Now that we've talked about exploring with her, I want to know. How much do you want her?"

Joe decided to go with this without overthinking it.

"I want to taste her," Joe muttered. He grappled with Kuro's pants and got them undone, wrapping one hand around Kuro's hard length.

"Yeah?" Kuro's hand pressed harder against Joe's erection, dragging a whimper from him.

"On *you.*" Joe sat up enough to kiss Kuro again. "On your tongue. On your cock. I want to taste the two of you at the same time and know you're both mine."

Kuro growled and thrust into Joe's hand. Then he lifted off Joe enough to get Joe's pants open and pull his cock free of his boxer briefs. They writhed together, each holding the other.

"I want to be balls-deep inside you," Kuro ground out, "while you're buried inside her."

Joe swept his thumb over the head of Kuro's penis, smearing the precum down his shaft.

Kuro let out the air in his lungs in a huff, his hand moving quicker over Joe's length. "I want to know how she feels coming around my cock while you're filling her up from behind."

"Nnngh." Joe couldn't form any more words. All he could do was imagine Marie between them, the scent of her, the sound of her voice crying out with the pleasure they'd give her.

They came at the same time, thinking about what it would be like if she was with them.

FOURTEEN

KURO

Kuro knocked on the door to Marie's apartment. There was nothing in the hallway or on the door to indicate it was different from any of the other units, but he was almost sure his steps would have brought him here, to this door, regardless.

She opened the door and immediately stepped back to let him in. "Did the code work okay for you?"

Something eased inside him. Kuro nodded. "Door code let us into the lobby, and we caught the first elevator up. Just like you said."

The moment he was inside the entryway of her apartment, she let the door close behind him and turned the bolt. He felt her wards go back up. He toed off his shoes and placed them on her shoe rack. He paused, realizing there were now two pairs of house slippers that hadn't been there when they'd first arrived. She must have put them out for him and Joe. Warmth bloomed in his chest to match the warmth of his partner against his back. Sure, they were the disposable kind one put out for guests, but they were an indication of their welcome in her home and the consideration she had for them.

"Is that..." Marie asked from behind him. "Is that one of those dog backpacks?"

Joe squirmed in the pack on his back. Kuro glanced back at her. "Yes."

Her eyes were wide and she lifted a hand to cover her mouth, but he caught the sparkle of amusement in her gaze. "That's a good solution. All his tails are stuffed in there?"

Joe whined.

Kuro tipped his head toward him. "It's not comfortable, but it works. The concierge said he was cute and asked if he was a Shiba Inu."

A muffled giggle came out of Marie. "The building is dog friendly. That works."

She looked down at his shoes on the rack. Hers were tiny compared to his. Hah. He could probably slide one of her flats right inside his shoe. He slid his feet into a pair of the slippers she'd left out.

He turned back to her. "Thanks for these."

"Oh." She blinked. "No problem."

She had plant stands with natural light lamps set up along the hallway and they shone softly on her face. She was dressed in loose, comfortable lounge wear that looked soft to the touch. Or maybe he just wanted a reason to reach out and touch her.

Joe whined again and managed to stretch his neck enough to nip Kuro's ear.

Marie jumped. "We should get him out of there. Would it be easier for you to set him down, or do you want to turn around and I'll open the backpack?"

Kuro lifted one side of his mouth in what he hoped was enough of a smile for her to know he was amused. Then he turned so she could let Joe out.

Moments later, Joe was in her arms, panting happily. He even gave her a lick on the cheek.

"Hey."

They both froze and looked at him. Joe, at least, appeared completely unrepentant. But Marie's eyes were wide and her shoulders had hunched a little, whether she was aware of it or not. Kuro regretted how abruptly that had come out.

For her, Kuro would try to be clearer about expressing himself, at least until she got to know him better. "That was for Joe. He shouldn't just go around licking you without permission. I apologize for doing it myself the other night."

Joe immediately tucked his nose under a paw. Good. Just because he was in a form she found cute, neither of them was going to sneak a familiarity she hadn't agreed to moving forward.

Marie smiled at him. "Thank you. I appreciate that."

She bent and let Joe down to stand on his own. Joe's ears drooped and he kept his head low, looking up at her.

She held her hand out to him, palm up. "I'd have appreciated you asking. You both asked when you were in human form and that made me feel really good."

Joe rolled onto his back, showing his belly.

"You don't have to do that," Marie protested. "I'm not that mad. We're just still…still…"

She seemed flustered. Kuro stepped forward slightly.

"Getting to know each other?" he offered.

She straightened abruptly. He swallowed against the sinking feeling in his gut. She was nervous around him. He didn't think she was this jumpy when she was with Joe in human form.

"Yes, exactly." She sounded slightly breathless. Still, she met his gaze and that wasn't nothing.

They continued to stand there. He wasn't sure what to say next and he didn't want to make her even more uncomfortable. Maybe he and Joe should have tried to find somewhere else to stay, near enough to be of help to her but not right in her space.

"I cooked, if you're hungry," she offered quietly. "I'm not sure if it's the kind of thing you like, or if you even eat breakfast so early. It's the sort of thing that keeps, though, so you can feel free to wait until you feel like eating."

He hesitated, but best to get it out there. "I am hungry, but the food won't help."

Great. That could be taken any number of ways and did nothing to reassure her or encourage her to get comfortable with him.

She was staring again, and her face was flushing. "I'm sorry. You both were starting to explain earlier. I don't know why I… I wasn't thinking…"

Normally, he'd have given up and retreated. The less said, the less damage he could do with miscommunication. But Joe wasn't going to be able to smooth anything over while Kuro found a way to express with actions what he'd failed to get across in words. Kuro figured he should try again.

"I can eat human food," he said quietly. "So can Joe. We enjoy the experience. But we could eat and eat and still be hungry. It won't sustain us. Human style meals are something we like taking part in for other reasons."

She pressed her lips together. "What can we do to help sustain you, then? I remember you said you wouldn't feed on me."

"No." He confirmed that as quickly as possible. He didn't want her to worry about that with either of them. "Even if we weren't worried about harming you, a single person couldn't sustain even one of us for long, much less both of us. We won't ask that of you."

Joe pressed a paw into the top of Marie's foot, expressing his agreement in his own way. Still, it was an issue to address, before Kuro became a danger to them both.

"I'll go out later today," Kuro said. It came out quick, the words clipped. "Joe will stay here with you, and I'll be back before sunset."

Her stare cut through him. She had a way of looking at a person, as if she could see through all the layers, all the walls a person might erect to protect themselves from the world. It wasn't judgment, not in the negative way people used the word. It was more of an assessment, made in less time than it took to blink. All at once, her posture changed in some infinitesimal way. She'd come to a conclusion and he had no idea what it was.

"Won't you need someone to keep watch?" she asked quietly. "You and Joe do that for each other, that's what you explained earlier."

Kuro hesitated.

"Joe can't go out in broad daylight and be your wingman or whatever. The dog backpack is only going to help so much." She stood taller and lifted her chin. "Joe can stay here inside my wards and I'll go with you."

"What?" Kuro blurted the question at the same time Joe yelped. The offer had taken them both by surprise.

"You—or was it Joe? One of you, anyway, offered to show me. It's something I'll need to know about you, as friends at least, and I think we're headed for more. There's no reason to delay it when there's an equally practical reason for it to happen now. I just..." She hesitated for a moment, then gave herself a little shake. "I'm not going to march out there with you and demand you go do whatever it is you do while I watch. I'll need instructions to be there for you in a way that's helpful. Is it too soon for us to share that kind of thing?"

It was faster than Kuro had ever considered with any other partner. Even he and Joe hadn't compared the ways each of them needed to hunt until they'd been spending real time together for a few months. They'd only had days with Marie, most of them in unusual circumstances.

Kuro glanced at Joe. His partner was watching him, waiting. Kuro swallowed hard. It would've been better if this conversation had happened with Joe. Joe was better at communicating with others, putting his thoughts into clever words.

Kuro could speak with random people just fine, when he didn't care what they thought or felt. When he didn't care if they took his brevity for rudeness. This was different. It mattered that Marie understand him and he didn't want to cause her distress if he flubbed it along the way.

There was also the actual way he fed.

"I'm not embarrassed of how I feed," he said.

"I didn't mean to imply—"

She sounded like she was about to apologize and he held up a hand to stop her. He continued, "I was talking out loud. Finishing a thought. Sorry. I started in the wrong place."

"Okay." She didn't sound upset. Maybe a little confused. That was justified.

He could do better if she wasn't standing there in the hallway of her apartment, with a hundred percent of her attention focused on him.

"You said you had breakfast ready. Let's go in, and you can sit and eat while I tell you about it." He blew out a breath. "That would be easier. You wouldn't have to stand."

That was what was distracting him, really. It wasn't her attention. He liked her attention on him. Her mind was sharp, and even if he didn't know what she thought of him, he liked the way she gave her attention so fully to him when he talked.

He wasn't the talkative person in the room, ever. Joe was more often the center of attention. Kuro didn't mind. He preferred it, actually. It made it easier to observe the people around him. But when it came to a lover, someone he was in a relationship with, he wanted someone who paid attention to him every bit as much as Joe did.

Marie didn't say anything, only nodded her head with a hesitant smile and motioned for him to join her. She stepped farther into her apartment, motioning to the counter. "I made congee and there's a bunch of side dishes to go with it."

Her rice cooker had been pulled to the center of the counter, and next to it was an array of glass containers. Kuro recognized a few of the things. At least one of the containers contained napa cabbage kimchi, and another had radish kimchi. There was also some kind of grilled fish, probably mackerel, and what looked like flaked, salted salmon. There was a container of eggs, still in their grayish-looking shells and another of soy eggs too. She also had a plastic tub of what looked like pork floss.

"You didn't cook all this while we were gonc." Wait. No. He wanted to smack his own head with his palm. That hadn't come out right at all. Joe was sitting there, glaring at him.

But Marie was bustling at the counter, getting a bowl for herself. "No. I live alone, and I travel back and forth from my cabin on the consortium grounds. So I make these side dishes and carry them back and forth in an insulated tote. All these containers have lids with tight seals. Makes it easy for me to have a few fresh veggies for a meal or two and just keep dry staples here like rice and noodles. Then I have these to add to my carbs to make them not-boring."

"Not-boring," he repeated, chuckling. He liked the way she put it.

She shrugged and smiled. "Seattle has a lot of good food choices, so I sometimes eat out. Some of my favorite restaurants are within walking distance of my place. With this system, I don't feel guilty about not finishing what I have in the fridge when the mood strikes me to eat out. All of these will hold for more than just a day or two. It doesn't matter if I skip eating them for a meal out. At the same time, these are go-to favorites for me. So I don't have to think hard when I know I should eat but don't have the energy to figure something out."

As she spoke, she spooned herself a generous helping of congee.

Steam wafted through the apartment, the comforting smell of cooked rice. He thought it carried a savory element too, maybe some kind of umami.

"That's not just plain rice."

Joe walked over and sat on Kuro's foot. Okay, that hadn't sounded like the polite inquiry or conversational prompt he'd intended, either. He wasn't sure how to fix it. Really, he was much more eloquent when he was with Joe. Hadn't he been smoother when they'd first invited Marie out for boba tea? Maybe they needed to go for boba.

She glanced at Kuro and raised an eyebrow. "You can smell it from over there? I usually add chicken broth, but since I wasn't sure if Joe would have some, I used vegetable stock instead and a mushroom powder seasoning. I love it for the umami it can add."

Kuro lifted his foot, not quite scooping Joe into the air, but giving his boyfriend's ass an impromptu lift. Their lady seemed to be understanding Kuro just fine. He could and would try to do better with communication, but there was a certain distance she'd need to come to meet him or this wasn't going to work. So far, she seemed perfectly willing, and even had a knack for adjusting to the way he conversed.

She didn't add everything onto her congee, he noticed. This morning, she added a generous bunch of the pork floss, then she shelled one of the grayish eggs, revealing the distinct dark brown translucent jelly look of a century egg. She cut it into thin wedges and arranged half of them in her bowl of congee next to the pork floss. She set the other half aside, maybe for later. Joe had wandered over, his nose lifted and twitching as he considered the scent.

"I'll have a bowl with the other half of that century egg," Kuro said hesitantly. "If you don't mind."

He didn't want to take it if she was saving it for later. She had another, so it wasn't like she couldn't have another if she wanted one. It was just that a little went a long way with century eggs, so she might not have wanted to eat a whole other one. He'd help her eat it if that seemed to be the case later.

"Sure." Marie seemed completely unbothered. She turned and gave him a smile. "No questions about what any of this is? I know we're all Asian American, it's hard to miss. But that doesn't tell me much about what foods you might enjoy, especially when you don't need this for sustenance."

She handed him a bowl. She had spooned a helping of congee into the bowl, steaming and silky looking, and arranged half the century egg pieces on top. The steam from the congee lifted the sharp scent from the creamy yolk into the air.

"I didn't like century eggs as a kid," she admitted. "There was too much bitter in the flavor, and I didn't like the color."

She moved to one side with her bowl and motioned for him to help himself to the rest. He gave himself a small helping of the mackerel and the salmon, just a bite each really. Smiling, he also took some of the pork floss. It'd been years since he'd had any over congee.

"I grew up calling them thousand-year-old eggs," Marie said as she stood next to him. "Did you want any?"

Kuro glanced at her and realized she had directed her inquiry to Joe. His partner shook his head and wandered over to her chaise, hopping up and making himself comfortable. She followed, so Kuro followed as well. He hung back a little so she would take the other side of the couch, rather than leaving it for him and Joe like she had previously.

"The first time I had one, it was a terrible experience." Contrary to her statement, she scooped a segment of the preserved egg with some congee and popped it into her mouth, chewing slowly and thoughtfully. "My father was a chef before he retired, and we were in one of his friends' restaurants. We were in the kitchen, and they gave me a whole one and told me to try it."

Kuro stopped and blinked. The process of preservation gave the egg white a firm jelly texture in addition to the dark, clear tea appearance. The yolk became extremely soft and creamy, but also developed extremely strong flavors. "That would have been..."

"Kindest way to describe it would be an umami bomb in my mouth," Marie finished for him with a wry grin. "As a kid, I thought it tasted like I imagined sulfur would. I didn't try it again for years, even though I intellectually knew it was meant to be enjoyed a little at a time with a lot of rice. My dad used to cut it up into teeny tiny pieces and mix it into his congee. Now, I think my adult palate is better at recognizing the complexity of the flavors, and I know to enjoy it a bit at a time. But it's funny what a rough introduction to a food can do, because first impressions stick with us for so long."

And that was what concerned Kuro about introducing Marie to the way he and Joe fed. Even though Joe grappled with a more voracious, bloodthirsty nature, Kuro's way of feeding was its own kind of harsh. He was nervous about upsetting Marie, or worse, scaring her.

Kuro nodded. "I was born here. Both my parents are Japanese, but my mother was born in Japan, and my father was born here. They met in college, married, had me. I grew up bilingual, and we mostly ate a mix of Japanese and American foods in the house. I didn't try century eggs until college, when a bunch of friends stopped in Philadelphia's Chinatown for something to eat after we went clubbing."

"You grew up on the East Coast? Me too. Though I went to college in Colorado." Marie hummed as she continued to enjoy her breakfast. "We always had rice in the rice cooker. Sometimes we'd take a scoop of the regular steamed rice and just add hot water from the electric hot water dispenser."

"One of my favorite appliances to have in a kitchen," Kuro murmured. "Convenient to have liters of water kept ready at a constant temperature for instant noodles, tea, whatever. Better than having a kettle taking up space on the stove or waiting for an electric kettle to heat the water every time."

Marie smiled. "They really are convenient. Other times, my dad would have an actual pot of congee on the stove in the kitchen. We always had side dishes and leftovers in the refrigerator, so breakfasts were easy. We didn't really do eggs and toast or bowls of cereal or oatmeal, the way a lot of my school friends did. But my dad and I would make scrambled eggs and scrapple with toast on Saturday mornings."

Joe sneezed. Hard to say whether it had been a coincidence or in protest to the mention of scrapple. Kuro wasn't going to call him out on it.

"I never understood the appeal of scrapple." Kuro shrugged, spooning another mouthful of congee so he couldn't say something worse.

Marie scrunched up her face and stuck out her tongue briefly, then smiled. "You're missing out. Cooked with skill, scrapple is amazing."

"I'll take your word for it." He wasn't aware of any place that even sold scrapple in Seattle, and while he was sure it could be acquired, he wasn't particularly eager to find some.

"My dad did a lot of mixing up of food, though, using a lot of recipes that were Chinese mainland in inspiration with a global interpretation." Marie glanced up at her array of sides on the counter. "He was always ready to try combining elements of foods we encountered outside our home with the foods my parents made. My mom didn't love cooking as much or as often as my dad did, but she had her absolute favorite Korean foods from when she was a kid.

They grew up in the United States too, so a lot of what we ate and what I eat now is a couple of generations removed from anything anyone might call authentic, I guess."

Kuro considered that. "I'm interested in whether flavors are traditional versus fusion just for the story of why the choice was made, but I'm not too worried about the definition of authentic."

She looked at him, seemingly startled, then she bit her lip and nodded. "Agreed."

Joe was sitting next to her, his tongue lolling out as he grinned wide. Kuro ate more congee to hide his embarrassment. He guessed he must've gotten comfortable enough to have said something right. Best to leave it at that and not ruin the moment.

KURO

“Wait here.” Kuro figured the coffee shop next door to where he was going was the safest place he could leave Marie. It was public and there were plenty of other people around. No one was going to approach her here. She had a table where she could see anyone approaching her, as well as the front door of his destination. It wasn’t the kind of vantage point he and Joe would normally choose, but that needed to change anyway.

“Just wait?” Marie asked.

“Wait and listen, but not closely.” Kuro tapped his earbud. “You just need to be alert for an emergency or if I ask you to come to me as an excuse for me to leave.”

She reached up, lightly touching her own with a fingertip. Hers were a different brand, but served the same purpose. They allowed her to be on call with him. The only difference was that Marie tended not to use the sound-canceling feature in the city, preferring to allow ambient noise through for awareness of her surroundings.

“Okay, I can do that.” She nodded.

Her brows were drawn together slightly in a look of concentration. She was really cute when she was thinking hard, and he knew he shouldn't say that out loud because he didn't want her to take that as him belittling her. He just liked to watch her think.

She was so quick, obviously intelligent, and it was an experience trying to follow her line of thought as she flashed from one to the next to the next. He had always been the type to stand back and assess a situation, wait for the right moment, be certain of what he wanted to do next. She was so decisive and fast, blink and you'd miss the thought process that led to her conclusion. So he was enjoying watching her carefully. He didn't want to miss a thing.

He hesitated, then pushed on, because it was better to prepare her than have her hear or see without context. "You're going to hear some things."

The lines between her brows creased a little deeper. "Are you going to be hurting someone?"

"No," he replied quickly. Then he cleared his throat. "Not unless they ask for it."

"Oh." All the lines disappeared from her face, and her eyes widened. "*Oh*."

He sighed and ran his fingers through his hair. It was a gesture he'd picked up from Joe. "I draw life energy from intimate contact."

Her lips parted. "So you need to be intimate with someone."

"It doesn't have to be sex," he clarified. "But that's what works most efficiently. Especially if it's been too long between hunts."

"In an ideal situation, how would you…feed?" Her voice was soft. No signs of disgust yet.

That had to be a positive sign, or he hoped it was. So he answered her. "I'd go to a nightclub, like Joe does. I'd dance with a number of people, maybe spend some time in a dark booth with them. I'd draw from multiple people from multiple clubs in a night. None of them would feel more than a hangover in the morning."

"But this isn't an ideal hunt." There was a harder edge to her tone now.

The best thing he could do was keep giving her the context she needed to understand. It wouldn't do any good to hide any part of this from her. If he was going to give her insight into this part of his life this early in their relationship, he was going to be transparent. She'd have to decide if she could accept it, accept him, or not.

"No. It's been too long." He glanced at the apartment building, then back at her. "I can't take the time to observe and find multiple appropriate individuals. This way, I know who my target is and I know exactly how to get what I need in a single encounter. We don't have time for me to feed another way."

"Are you going in there to have sex with someone and leave them dead?" Marie's voice was steady, neutral.

It sounded strange coming from her, because she was normally so expressive. It reminded him that she was more than just a woman he and Joe had met and both been attracted to. She was a successful, competent individual across two distinctly different vocations that were complementary but each extraordinary in their own way. One of those was an expression of what she *was*, not just what she did. She was a witch, a powerful one, through both talent and practice. And that was the aspect of her he was answering now.

"Not dead. They'll definitely feel like they've come down with the flu or something similar for more than a week. If they don't take time to recover, they could come down with a serious illness." Kuro figured that was the most important part. But she was still gazing at him steadily. "I don't intend to have intercourse, but it depends on what you personally define as sex. I need them to orgasm to release enough energy to feed me."

There it was. All laid out. Marie tucked her chin downward, her hair falling forward around her face.

It wasn't just the understanding of what he needed to do to feed. She was going to be listening to him do it. It would be difficult for even the most understanding person to accept. He took a step back. He should go, give her space. Let her think on it. Be prepared to do this and return to find Marie gone.

"Kuro."

He stopped, looked at her. She was standing there, with her shoulders slightly hunched and her hands stuffed into the pockets of her overcoat. She wasn't smiling, but her gaze was earnest. She was still looking at him and seeing him.

"I'll be listening," she said quietly. "Call me if you need me and after this, I'd appreciate it if you could help me understand why you chose this person."

That was fair. More than fair. He nodded. "Okay."

He turned then, and headed into the apartment building. He texted his target and she signaled the main door to open. He proceeded directly to the elevator, letting his hair fall forward over his face enough for it to obscure his features while still looking fashionable. His magic would do the rest.

If anyone ever checked security footage, they'd see an average height, average build, male-presenting person with longish brown hair and pale skin. There wouldn't be enough to further determine his age, ethnicity, or much of anything else. No tattoos or other markings to help with identifying him. Just your average person who looked like any number of other people coming and going throughout the day. Maybe he lived in this building, maybe he didn't. The concierge didn't even look up as Kuro walked past. They wouldn't have enough of an impression of him to definitively say whether they'd seen him before.

It was an extension of his shape-shifting magic, the ability to give the impression of the nondescript and unremarkable person.

Pleasant enough to be immediately dismissed from people's minds as he passed them by. It was honestly an ability he should be exercising all the time. Not just when he was coming and going from a hunt. He'd become complacent, and that was why a pain witch had managed to hex him in the first place. He didn't intend to allow himself to be caught that way again.

His destination was one of the highest floors in the rather tall building, but he didn't go directly to that floor. Instead, he got off the elevator a couple of floors below and took the stairs the rest of the way.

A young white guy opened the door. Kuro stared at him. The other man stared back.

"Come in!" a familiar voice called. "Frank, don't just stand there in the doorway. Be polite and invite Eric in. Or actually, just let him in. He knows he's invited."

Kuro didn't wait for Frank, who was flustered and blushing so hard his ears were red. Frank might be old enough to order his own drinks at a bar. Maybe. Hopefully. Kuro was younger than their host by a few years, but this other guy was just out of college. It wasn't about the years. It was about maturity, and this guy was young.

"Eric," Julie purred. "I was so glad to get your text. It's been so long, I thought I might not hear from you ever again."

Kuro didn't smile. "I wasn't expecting a party."

"Oh, don't be mad." Julie sat on her luxe white sectional, with one of those ottomans big enough to be a bed on its own, and picked up a glass of wine. "We came here to do some project work since the new open office floor plan is just so noisy. I was developing a migraine. When you texted, I thought it'd be perfect timing for a break from work."

Kuro nodded. He glanced at Frank. The younger man's face was still very red. Maybe that wasn't just embarrassment. There was a second glass of wine on the glass coffee table.

"My husband is out of town, and work has been so busy." Julie pouted. She fluffed her hair. "Frank, here, has been a lot of help in the project, but he's still got a lot to learn."

Frank was starting to sweat and shift his weight from side to side. The guy was obviously uncomfortable with the situation. "Maybe I should go pick up lunch and meet you back at the office, M—Julie."

Yeah. If Kuro needed a reminder of why this particular person was his target today, poor Frank was definitely a good reminder. It was obvious the other man didn't want to be here. Julie was married and too smart to have an ongoing affair. She did find herself plenty of company, though, and part of the reason she was eager to have Kuro was because she hadn't been the one to discard him.

"Oh no, Frank. You should stay." There was some emphasis on the last word that made it an order, not a suggestion.

Frank flinched.

The power dynamics in the room were not to Kuro's taste.

He stepped toward Julie. "I don't play well with strangers."

Julie smiled up at him, running her tongue over her lips before she smacked them together loudly. Her eyes were glazed and her cheeks were flushed. The glass of wine in her hand was probably not her first. "I believe I mentioned already that he's got a lot to learn. You'll be an excellent example for him."

She set down her wineglass and laid back across the ottoman suggestively. Kuro glanced back at Frank. The young man's eyes were open so wide, they might fall out of his head. Well, this was probably the first time Frank had been maneuvered into this situation. It didn't seem like he had the wherewithal to walk out, so Kuro was going to need to make some choices.

Kuro crossed over to Julie and knelt on one knee. She watched him, propped on her elbows, her expression full of anticipation. Her knees fell apart slightly and she might not have even been aware of it.

She was an older woman, successful, and she was hungry for Kuro's touch. It was a side effect of who and what he was. Because he didn't kill his victims, they remembered the pleasure they got when they were with him, even if they didn't remember the details of their encounters and weren't aware of what he'd taken from them.

Some of them developed a hunger for his touch. It kept them coming back for more, if he allowed it. She was someone who had wanted him back, on her terms. He hadn't given that to her, which only made her want him more.

He touched the outsides of her knees, featherlight, ran his hands up her thighs and under her skirt. It was a pleated skirt, somewhat reminiscent of a school uniform, but the fabric and color made it part of a dress suit. It didn't complement her shape, but her image of herself wasn't the same as what he saw when he looked at her. It didn't matter. What mattered was that he could already feel her life energy, sizzling under his fingertips.

She moaned. "You barely touch me and it feels so good."

Kuro didn't reply.

"I should go," Frank muttered to one side.

Kuro had positioned himself so he could keep an eye on Frank and the door. As a result, Frank could see everything that was happening.

"You should join us, Frank," Julie purred.

Kuro gripped her thighs, digging his fingers in just where her thigh started to curve into her ass. She gasped. "I don't play well with others," he repeated.

"Watch, then. Can he watch?" Julie's eyes were starting to glaze over with pleasure. She liked a lot of different pressures. Liked to play rough. That was fine. Kuro could do that for her. He wasn't going to allow her to pressure someone else into this when they obviously didn't want to. But a hard look crossed Julie's face. "He can't leave. I don't want him to leave."

This was taking longer than Kuro wanted. He wasn't interested in power plays. It would take too long to convince her that letting the other man go was her idea.

Kuro growled.

Julie smiled. She was taking it as agreement. Because that's what she wanted to hear. "Excellent."

Kuro hooked his thumbs into her panties and pulled them down. A thong. Of course. He left it hanging around one of her ankles and hooked his hands behind her knees, lifting her legs up and wide so she was completely exposed.

"Do it," she urged. "Eat me."

Kuro looked up at her. "You're going to come for me and I'm going to walk out of here."

She squirmed, trying to lift her hips toward him. "I want more."

"You get to come." He let his breath ghost across her skin. "I could make you feel good and leave you before you come."

"No!" He saw the belief that he would do it in her panicked gaze. Good. Because on any other day, if he wasn't so hungry and if he didn't care about sparing Marie another hunt, he would have.

"I really should—" Frank was starting to walk away.

Good. The guy should take his chance and get out of here. Actually, he'd had multiple chances and hadn't walked out. At this point, there was only so much Kuro could do to give the man opportunities to extricate himself. If he didn't in the end, that was on him.

"Frank." Her voice snapped, hard. Then her tone turned syrupy sweet. "If you want to keep your job, you stay and learn."

Some people stayed with the devil they knew rather than taking a chance at the unknown. It was a choice. Granted, Kuro didn't know the other man's situation. It might be an awful decision to have to make.

Kuro nipped the inside of her thigh, taking more energy from her. The hunger inside him unfurled, expanded outward. He was drawing from her at every place where their skin touched, every point of contact, like an electric current. If he touched her too long anywhere, there could be physical damage.

No commentary out of Frank, only obedience. Kuro decided not to give the guy any more chances. He was going to need to learn to free himself from these kinds of circumstances on his own. Otherwise, the corporate world would chew him up and spit him out. There were too many people who took advantage of power dynamics, regardless of gender or age, not always sexual, but always taking advantage.

Kuro let one of her legs rest on his shoulder and brought his palm down on her butt in a light slap. It was enough to make her squeal, not enough to even redden her skin.

"You have my attention," she gasped. "I'm so wet for you. Do you see? Do you like it?"

He didn't answer. He didn't need to. She didn't actually care what he thought. He only bent over her and showed Frank how fast he could get this woman off.

Kuro stood when he was done, leaving her panting and limp. Her body still shuddered slightly from the intensity of the orgasm he'd pulled from her. He could have brought her to the edge once or twice, increased the intensity for when she finally came. It would have fed him more, but what he'd gotten from her was enough. He didn't like making Marie listen to more than the absolute minimum necessary.

He walked into the bathroom and washed his hands, rinsed his mouth. As he emerged, Frank was still standing there, staring. Julie had literally dozed off, sated and drained. There was nothing stopping the other man from slipping out, but here he was with an erection and the fabric of his suit pants wasn't up to the task of hiding it.

Maybe he didn't want to leave that badly after all. Kuro didn't have a way to know for certain. Frank looked up as Kuro headed toward the door.

"There are other jobs, you know," Kuro said, holding the other man's gaze.

"Hmm?" Julie stirred, her skirt still gathered around her waist. "Eric? You'll text, right? Text me later."

Kuro left. He didn't bother to respond. Maybe he would choose her to feed from again. Maybe he wouldn't. It definitely wouldn't be any time in the next several weeks. Her husband was never away for longer than a week or so on business. Besides, Kuro didn't dislike her enough to kill her.

Marie fell into step with him as he walked by the coffee shop. She removed her earbuds, slipping them into their case before stowing them away in her pocket.

He wasn't looking at her, but from the edge of his peripheral vision he noted how carefully precise each of her movements was. She was being careful around him, and he didn't want that, but he wasn't sure how to ease the brittle tension around them. He wasn't sure how she felt about what she'd overheard.

"Are you very different, with the people you hunt?" she asked finally.

It wasn't a question he'd been prepared for. Then again, he really hadn't known what she would say. Relief rushed through him like a cold splash of water, because honestly, he'd been tensing, ready for her to say she didn't want to have anything to do with him.

"I think I'm honest, no matter who I'm touching," he said finally. "It's different from person to person. It depends on what they want and who they want me to be in their heads. It's easier to be that for someone I don't care about."

She nodded. "Would it be easier to find your…to find sustenance if you were working through some sort of escort service that vets clients for your safety?"

He sucked in a breath, started to say something, then stopped. He hadn't thought his safety would be the first concern she'd raise. Honestly, he was trying to wrap his head around her suggesting strategies for him to find prey.

"It just seemed like it was a surprise to you that there was more than one person there, and the first thing I thought about was how dangerous that could be," Marie explained. "Obviously, it sounded like the third party didn't know what was happening and really didn't want to be there, so that worked out okay this time. But what if someone does that to you in the future? Has it ever happened before?"

The words were speeding up as she spoke, giving him a hint of the worry she must have felt for him. *She'd worried for him.*

He ought to go to hell for the happiness warming his belly at the realization. He didn't want to make her experience any kind of anxiety.

"That's why you were on the line with me," he said. "If I felt I couldn't handle the situation, I'd have said something out loud to indicate you should come up and get me. Maybe barging in like a jealous girlfriend or something."

She huffed out a laugh. "You seem really confident I would have realized that's what you wanted. No signal phrase or code word or anything."

"I have faith in your intelligence." He was being completely sincere. Though she had a good point about the signal phrase or code word. He should have thought of that. He and Joe had been comfortable with their buddy system for so long now. After a moment, he offered her another truth, because she was being so understanding and silence felt awkward. "I did try an escort service for a short while, before Joe and I started to coordinate our hunts."

"Oh?" Marie almost bumped into someone. The streets weren't crowded, but they also weren't empty. It happened more because she was looking at him instead of watching for what was ahead of her.

Kuro extended his elbow without removing his hand from his jacket pocket. She took it without hesitation, slipping her hand in the crook of his arm. The warmth he'd felt earlier expanded through his core. She really wasn't afraid or disgusted by him. She was touching him.

What had they been talking about? Oh. It was his turn to talk.

"It felt wrong, to use an escort service as my means to find victims," he admitted. "It was human owned, and the owner was a good person. It's a transactional business. Honest, in its own way. Expectations are clearly discussed and protected by contract. Clients are vetted. I didn't want to use a respectable business like that for predatory reasons, even if someone else might, and even if some of the clients probably fit my preferences for feeding. I was pretty sure most of the clients were relatively good people. Just lonely or curious or whatever."

Marie nodded. "It does seem like people who are looking to hurt others, or who feel entitled to treat others badly, wouldn't subject themselves to a vetting process. I'm sure there are some. But for the most part, I can understand why you and Joe frequent clubs and bars. There's a constant flow of people of all sorts coming and going."

"Yes."

"I..." Marie hesitated and her hand squeezed his arm gently. "I feel uncomfortable and it's not even about the sex, because we haven't discussed any kind of exclusivity, and you're being completely transparent about it, but I also get that it's part of what you have to do to feed. I don't pretend to understand. Not yet. But I'm trying to keep an open mind and just learn for now. I want to consider what you're sharing with me and I appreciate that you're being so open. It can't be easy."

He smiled. "It's not."

"Thank you." Her voice was soft, like a caress.

He wanted to lean into that feeling, hold her and soak up the warmth she was offering him. For the moment, he just said, "No, thank *you*."

SIXTEEN

MARIE

"Miss Xiao! I was notified you'd checked in at the front desk. I thought I'd swing by to say hello."

Marie turned to see Tobias Mancini—Toby—emerging from the security turnstile. She wasn't surprised someone had come to inquire as to what she needed, but she hadn't expected him to come personally. She schooled her face into a pleasant expression, with a sweet smile. "Hello, Mr. Mancini, I'm just here to take notes on the lighting in several locations. It wasn't my intention to interrupt your day."

"I asked you to call me Toby," he reminded her.

Actually, he hadn't asked her. He'd told her. And she hadn't offered the use of her own first name in return. Apparently, that was something he'd noticed but wasn't going to address directly yet. He wasn't even looking at her at the moment. Instead, his attention was on something over her shoulder.

"Oh, I'm rude. I'm so sorry." She angled her body to include Kuro in the conversation. "This is Kuro. Kuro is learning about the type of consulting I do, so he's shadowing me for parts of this project."

"I see." Toby smiled, but it seemed a touch forced. "Well, it's good to have a strong back to lift some of those heavier pots and buckets in there."

Charming insinuation. If Kuro had truly been a team member on a project she was leading, she'd have countered Toby's words. But she and Kuro had discussed their approach on the walk over to Socrates Industries, and they'd decided it would be to their advantage for him to be underestimated. Allowing Toby to assume Kuro was manual labor was in alignment with their strategy, so, as much as it irritated the hell out of her, Marie let it slide.

"I'm likely to be back here over the next few days, at different times," Marie said. She tipped her head to one side, successfully drawing Toby's attention back to herself. "I'll need to confirm the lighting in each of the areas to be sure I have good placement for each of the plants in my designs. I'll probably need to take photos, too."

Toby nodded. "Sure, sure. I'm glad you're being so thorough. The previous designers didn't even ask. They just sent us proposed drawings based on the blueprints we provided."

"Ah well, everyone has their own approach." Marie wasn't going to put down other professionals when she didn't have context for why they'd done what they'd done. "We'll be down here a while, then we'll walk to each of the locations in the building. I'm sure you're quite busy with meetings. I appreciate you scraping together the time to check in on me personally."

Toby cleared his throat, looking from Kuro to her and back again. "Of course. You let the front desk know if you run into any problems. If you're still in the building by the time I wrap up for the day, I'd be happy to walk you out."

Marie just nodded. She wasn't going to give him any kind of response that could be interpreted as a confirmation. It was possible he wasn't extending an oblique invitation, but she didn't want to deal with it if he had those kinds of intentions.

"Mr. Mancini." A voice called out in the hallway. It didn't sound happy. "I thought we had reached an understanding."

A woman in a lab coat came striding toward them. She was an older Black woman, with springy salt-and-pepper coils that danced around her collarbone with every movement. Her facial features were elegant, with sculpted cheekbones and an angled jaw. She wore an ornate chain to hold her glasses.

"Now, Leslie, I'm just here to see to the needs of one of my subcontractors." Toby held out his hands, fingers splayed, as if he was trying to tone down a mood that wasn't all that heightened at the moment.

Judging from the sparks in the woman's dark eyes, it wouldn't be surprising if she could escalate it if the situation called for it.

"Uh huh." The woman crossed her arms over her chest. "Yet somehow you managed to encounter one of my direct reports the other day, took umbrage with the way he was traversing a public corridor, and decided an accident was grounds for firing him."

Ah. Well, that shed a little light on how the dead man went from safely inside the research and development department to roaming the streets of downtown Seattle.

Toby seemed to puff up, his face turning red and his rather significant eyebrows drawing together until they met across his forehead. "It is well within my purview to terminate employees who are in violation of the company—"

"You literally asked, 'Do you know who I am?' and fired him. Within an hour, representatives from human resources were down here to escort him out of the building," Leslie stated. Her voice was still at conversational volume, her words clearly enunciated, and her tone sharp. "Rather than risk my key researchers in encounters with you, it was my understanding that you would steer clear of the research and development areas unless there are official meetings for executive management."

Marie was doing her best to keep a neutral expression. Kuro had managed to fade entirely into the background somehow, and no one was even registering his presence. She, on the other hand, noticed Leslie glancing her way. So Marie was careful to project as much distance as possible between herself and Tobias Mancini. She was going to need access to this floor and department, for more than just the plants provided for her project.

Leslie was continuing to set boundaries for Toby, and Toby was not getting in a word edgewise. The other woman had built up a decent amount of momentum and still hadn't raised her voice. "... because you took over a storage room down here in our area without consulting my team or staff. We have sensitive research going on in this department. Any contractors need to adhere strictly to the no-photographs policy in this area."

Marie said nothing, only nodded her understanding.

Leslie finally turned her attention to Marie. Marie didn't change her posture, still standing upright with her head held high. She might have looked to one side or the other to indicate she didn't wish to engage directly in the conversation between Leslie and Toby, but now Marie wasn't flinching from Leslie's regard.

Fine lines smoothed away from Leslie's forehead and at the corners of her eyes. Her mouth relaxed from the frown she'd been wearing. She took in a breath, starting to speak, but someone else came around the end of the corridor.

"Leslie? We're ready to start the next test run."

Leslie turned to face the speaker, and it was lucky for Marie that she did. Marie was absolutely positive she hadn't managed to control the shock on her features as she recognized the man speaking to Leslie now. It was the researcher who had bumped into Toby the other day, and later crashed through the conversation she'd been having with Kuro and Joe. It was their dead man.

Only his skin was flushed a healthy color, and his movements were normal. He was talking, and the look in his eyes was alert. Obviously not dead. Now.

And he wasn't wearing the amulet anymore.

"I have to go," Leslie said. She glanced back at Marie. "We'll introduce ourselves formally another time. Or not. If you need anything on this level, you come find me first. Ask for Leslie. I'm the only one in charge on this floor."

"I'll remember to do that," Marie responded.

Leslie looked her up and down for another moment, then headed away to follow her very much alive researcher.

"I've got a meeting," Toby said, his face still flushed. "I'll leave you to it. Like I said, go ahead and let the front desk know if you need anything."

Abruptly, Marie and Kuro were alone, standing in front of the storage room. She looked at him, and his face was resting in a decidedly bored expression. He was, she thought, really good-looking in a bad boy kind of way, even when he was just standing there not doing anything.

She let out a slow breath, releasing tension she hadn't realized she'd been carrying in her neck and shoulders and abdomen. It was like she had progressively braced herself for some kind of impact. "That was a lot."

He nodded.

"Let's finish taking pictures of every plant here. We've got special permission within my contract to do so. Then we'll go up to each of the garden locations in the building and take notes on lighting, just like I said." She took out her phone and tapped the camera app. She stepped closer to him, lowering her voice. "Once we've done that, we'll come back down and go looking for the restroom. Figure out what we can gather from an innocent walk around that corner."

He nodded.

She smiled and started taking pictures of plants. It might be paranoia, but she didn't want to risk speaking freely about any of their intentions while inside this building. She didn't have the skills to spot listening devices, and she was sure she'd miss some if she tried to look for them. She could probably come up with a spell to reveal them, but that might damage them, and then they'd be replaced. Plus, all of them becoming inoperable at once would be suspicious and draw unwanted attention. So it was better to just act like they were there and not actually worry about finding them. It was easier to be discreet.

They had finished their tasks, both in the storage room and at the various locations for the gardens elsewhere in the building, when she felt it. A surge of magic. It was witchcraft, of a sort. It wasn't blood sacrifice, but the feeling of death tinged the energy flowing throughout the building.

She hurried back to the elevator. Being caught in the rotating entryway while security confirmed her was especially uncomfortable. All of her senses were jangling, on edge. Kuro was there with her, standing close enough that she could feel his solid warmth at her back. She stopped at the storage room and looked in, just for appearance's sake, then headed right down the corridor.

Kuro followed her without a word. Which was good, because she was following her intuition at the moment and wouldn't have been able to explain anything even if she'd tried.

Turning the corner let them into an open-plan cubicle area. She could see over the cubicle walls, down the length of the long room. There seemed to be more hallways along the inner wall. There weren't any heads visible to indicate anyone was sitting in the cubicles at the moment, so she walked down the aisle hugging the inner wall to peek down the hallways.

There wasn't a lot to hint at what was there. Each hallway had two doors on either side, marked with door numbers. They could be conference rooms or they could be labs. No way to know unless she opened a door. She thought they would be conference rooms, though. Some of her other clients had laboratories, and those all had windows to see into the laboratory space.

One of the cubicles, at least, had notes on the dry-erase board. She did her best to pause and unobtrusively memorize the sketch of the blue lotus on it. If she lifted her phone or appeared to be taking a photo in any way, she was certain a security camera somewhere would have caught it. Instead, she reached out and pointed at the cute corgi calendar pinned next to the dry-erase board, then walked away. She had a strong enough visual memory to re-create what she'd seen: notes on extracting blue lotus essential oil and formulating a standard dosage.

She didn't breathe freely until they finally left the building. "Well, that left me with a whole bunch of new questions."

"Is that good or bad?" Kuro rumbled.

"I honestly don't know."

Kuro was silent for a moment, then he asked, "What's the worst outcome you can think of?"

She considered that as they walked. "They could be intentionally resurrecting dead people. And that's just one accident away from starting a zombie apocalypse."

SEVENTEEN

JOE

There was a welcoming committee waiting for them on the tiny boat dock as they approached. Joe craned his neck to see around Kuro's head. The backpack was a decent solution to get around while they were in downtown Seattle, but now that they'd taken the cutter to this little spot in the San Juan Islands, he was hoping he could get out and move freely.

There were two, no, three people waiting for them. Joe hadn't immediately noticed Ashke hovering over the shoulder of the fierce-looking Asian guy.

Now that was a striking man. He was long limbed and rangy, probably somewhere between Joe and Kuro when it came to height. That was pretty tall for someone of Asian descent, honestly. Both Joe and Kuro were taller than average in their human forms. This guy's skin was golden tan accented by his thick, dark brown hair. His face was long and oval, with a slightly squared chin and his eyes were cut long, slightly double lidded. He was, in short, an incredibly sexy Southeast Asian man. He had a fierceness to him, though, that made Joe consider approaching with caution. Actually, if he had any natural fox instincts at all, Joe knew he shouldn't go anywhere near the other man. He wasn't human, that was for sure. There was too much energy radiating off him, too much potential for violence.

Next to him stood an even bigger man. This man was Black, his skin a mellow brown, his hair trimmed close to his scalp in a neat fade. He wasn't just broad across the shoulders. He was a literal wall of a person. Fortunately, he wore a pleasant expression. His full lips were curved in a smile, and his dark eyes sparkled with amusement as he regarded them all.

Joe wondered whether Kuro had ever come home to anyone waiting for him like this. Joe hadn't. He'd had a relatively happy childhood, but he'd been an only child. While his parents had always made certain one of them was home when he returned, the other was almost always busy working. Kuro was also an only child. It was one of the things they'd had in common, in addition to having a furry form and nine tails. So Joe imagined Kuro might not have had something like this either, unless one counted the frat experience in college. It would have depended on the fraternity, really, and Kuro didn't talk much about his.

This, though. If one counted their silent boat man—and Joe would have to be a fool to dismiss one of the sidhe—this was a group of people very interested in Marie's return to the island that fell under the protection of the Darke Consortium. It didn't feel like a gathering of academics or scholars or even quirky librarians. It felt like a family where every one of them starred in a series of their own action movies, chronicling their adventures and quests in search of objects of myth and magic.

He'd bet at least one of them hated snakes.

It was the lean and sexy guy who caught the rope the sidhe tossed and helped tie up the boat. It was the big man who offered Marie a hand to step off the boat. Kuro—good man—was there to steady her at the elbow. Joe gave his partner's ear a quick lick in solidarity.

Once Kuro had both feet on the tiny pier, Joe started to wiggle. He wanted out. There were a whole lot of people intent on taking care of the witch they were trying to woo. Joe would feel better about it if he at least didn't have to ride in a backpack. A quick glance at the sky confirmed the sun would be setting soon. He wanted to be on the ground when he changed back to human form.

"You all didn't have to come down to meet me," Marie said. Her tone was grumpier than Joe had ever heard from her. "I was coming up to the manor anyway."

The big man chuckled. "Duncan texted us as you were boarding the boat. Said you had company. Thomas and Ashke bolted down here right away. I decided I didn't want to miss this, just in case there was any excitement."

Marie shot a glare at each of them, including Duncan, their sidhe boat captain. "Why would there be anything other than a nice, calm introduction?"

Yes, why? Joe couldn't bring himself to resent it, though. Marie had people who cared for her. It was good to witness. He'd have been angry if she'd been alone in the world, unappreciated. This, though, this was somewhat intimidating. He and Kuro had a lot of work to do in order to coax her into making room in her life for them.

Ashke zipped over to her, doing a little flip before hovering at eye level. "No reason. You just haven't dated in the ten years or so that you've been a part of the consortium. At least not that any of us have known about. I read that family gets to roast potential suitors. I've tasted fox, so I figured we count in the absence of your relatives, since they mostly live on the East Coast or out of country. What kind of fire does one use to roast a suitor? Does that even work on fox spirits?"

The big man laughed out loud.

Kuro had been leaning over, letting Joe out of the backpack. Hearing Ashke's commentary, Joe hopped free of the backpack and shook out all of his nine tails, drawing himself up to appear as large as possible. He was not going to go down easily.

"No one is roasting anyone," Marie stated. "Also, Ashke, the term roast was most definitely used in a figurative sense, not literal. No fire for you."

"Fine." Ashke's wings dipped for a fraction of a second, before he recovered. "It's not like anyone here has fire at their beck and call anyway."

Well…

Kuro lifted his left hand, palm up. A ball of fire flared into being, the flames blazing yellow and orange in the shaded light beneath the tall evergreens around them.

A low growl cut across the quiet of the island. Joe tensed, turning toward the sound. The lean man was standing there, arms loose at his side, hands in fists. But his eyes were narrowed as he glared, and his pupils were starting to change from brown to gold.

"Thomas," Marie called gently. "Please."

Thomas was most definitely a paranormal. All of them were. Joe hadn't figured out what the big man was yet, but it was becoming very obvious that Thomas was a werewolf. That explained the radiating energy and Joe's nerves.

For his part, Kuro banished his fox fire as easily as he had summoned it.

Ashke flew around his head. "I gotta admit, that was nice timing. Well played, fox boy."

Joe suppressed a growl of his own. Fae tended to be long-lived. Joe understood that both fae were likely decades, centuries, possibly millennia older than either him or Kuro, but he disliked being called a boy. Especially in front of Marie. Unless, of course, they also considered her a youngling. After all, for them, the age difference had to be negligible. She couldn't be more than a dozen years older than he or Kuro. And witches could live a long time.

"We've prepared dinner out on the back patio," the big man said, his tone calm. He still looked relaxed and amused. Joe wondered if all of this was normal for them.

"Thanks, Asamoah." Marie sounded relieved. Joe was, too. At least someone seemed at least marginally friendly.

"No more magic, not anything that can be interpreted as dangerous," Thomas said. His voice was rough and his eyes were still yellow-brown.

Back to thinly veiled aggression.

"You say that like some of us don't trail magic behind us like we live and breathe it." Ashke flew on ahead, his tone still lilting.

Joe resisted the urge to roll his eyes. Someone was likely to notice even if it wasn't immediately obvious that they were studying him. Generally, Joe and Kuro didn't interact with that many supernaturals at the same time. Their interactions with Babel had been small meetings to review contracts and receive necessary briefings. Often, it had been a single vampire or human presenting the details. Otherwise, Joe and Kuro worked on their own. They'd been called in to aid Francesco a few months ago, and the experience had confirmed their preference for only accepting contracts on their own. Outside of working with each other, they didn't really like to be added to a team on demand.

As a result, Joe and Kuro were used to being the only supernaturals in a given situation, and thus the most dangerous beings present. This was a completely different playing field. It said a lot about Marie's capabilities that she moved as an equal among them, while they obviously cared about her well-being. Every one of the people around them was a heavy hitter, with both strengths and limitations.

Joe wasn't immediately sure who was the most formidable person in present company.

Ashke was right, though. Refraining from surprise magic wasn't exactly an option. Sunset was coming quickly. Joe hoped they all made it up to wherever they were going before he changed and set off the werewolf. Of all the situations Joe had imagined, he really hadn't thought he'd be hoping *not* to change back into human form. Actually no, it wasn't that. He just wanted control over his shape change. Wanted it back bad.

He trotted alongside Marie with Kuro on her other side, same as he would have if he'd been in human form. He was the same person, after all, regardless of shape. The werewolf was behind them, but he responded to a few of Marie's questions. It kept Joe on edge, but it could've been worse. The werewolf could have been stalking behind them in silent mode. That would've been unbearable.

The path was uphill and a little winding, not hard to navigate but intentionally not a straight line to the manor. Joe was pretty damned sure of it. There was security here. He'd done enough jobs for Babel to recognize at least the most obvious measures. That didn't stop him from appreciating the surroundings, though. All of it was set up in a way that didn't take away from the general atmosphere of the island.

Coming from the Northeast, Joe was no stranger to evergreens, but the woods in the Pacific Northwest had a unique feel to them. The forests smelled different from the ones in the Northeast, too. The trees on this island in particular smelled of Douglas fir, cedar, and spruce. There were other trees as well, but Joe didn't know them well enough to name them. Here and there, a maple tree was easy to identify for its broad leaves in bright autumn display.

They emerged into a clear area, and Joe would have let out a low whistle if he'd had a mouth that could whistle. The grounds all around the manor were clear, and the building had the feel of a small castle. What the big man, Asamoah, had referred to as a back patio was more like an expansive stone terrace. There was a table large enough to seat twenty people, set with plates and silverware. Covered platters were placed at one end. Marie approached the table, running a hand lightly over the tablecloth.

"Did Ellery set this? They outdid themselves. It's lovely." Marie's voice was pitched a little loud considering present company were all supernaturals. Joe was fairly certain they all had some kind of enhanced hearing as compared to humans.

Joe cocked his head to one side, considering her. She only had eyes for the table, lifting the covers to peek at the contents of the platters. She wasn't making eye contact with any of their welcoming committee. It was like she was projecting her thanks to the castle, or someone else. Probably whoever Ellery was.

How many people were a part of the Darke Consortium?

The others were seating themselves. Kuro pulled out a seat for Marie at the same time the sidhe did, the man who'd driven the boat to get them all here. Joe froze, waiting. Long, silver gray hair was tied back with a simple cord. Everything about the sidhe was ethereal, elegant. It all screamed High Court. Joe didn't know much about the courts of the sidhe, but he understood that the High Courts held the most power. Marie was choosing between Kuro and potentially insulting one of the most powerful fae anyone could encounter.

"You're very kind, Duncan. Will you be joining us?" Marie murmured, as she sat in the chair Kuro had pulled out for her.

Joe twitched his ears forward, tensed and ready to leap forward if she needed him.

The sidhe only sighed. "You have been spending too much time with Punch. She is always asking me to join the meal."

"Maybe so," Marie agreed cheerfully. "I'm not sorry."

Joe suddenly found himself the focus of the sidhe's attention. Cold stabbed him right in the chest as he waited for whatever the sidhe was about to do.

Duncan only turned his hand to indicate the chair he had pulled out for Marie. "Perhaps our nine-tailed guest would like to sit on this side of you. It seems the fox in human form has the other seat."

This was not anything like what Joe had expected when it came to sidhe.

"Greeting guests is a part of my duties here at the Darke Consortium," Duncan said. "I am also the household manager, overseeing the maintenance and upkeep of the manor and any guest structures on the surrounding property."

The most powerful butler Joe had ever encountered. Of course, Joe respected Duncan's choices. There really wasn't any other way to go if one wanted to associate with such a fae and live. And he was going to have to associate with the sidhe—with all of them—if he and Kuro were going to spend more time with Marie. She was making that obvious by bringing him and Kuro to this gathering.

"Duncan is also a key advisor to the consortium, not just the Darke Consortium specifically, but other regional consortiums who reach out with requests, too." Marie was placing a napkin across her lap.

Joe decided standing there, making Duncan also stand and wait, was worse than the risk of accepting the offered seat. He leapt into it and settled himself. That was when the magic twisted inside him.

Shape-changing, for him, was normally painless. He just smoothly changed from one form to the other in a surge of exhilarating magic. But with the hex, it was like someone reached into his chest, grabbed a handful of whatever, and twisted it. Being grabbed by a crocodile and taken into a death roll had to hurt less. When his vision cleared, he was human and seated at the table. Marie was looking at him with round doe eyes, her face puckered in concern.

After a moment, she said quietly, "Hi."

"Hey." His voice came out rough.

He glanced past her to Kuro. His partner gave him a small smile, there and gone again. Joe reached behind Marie's chair and Kuro grasped his hand. It was so damned reassuring, that contact.

"So this hex is pretty powerful," Thomas stated. He'd sat directly across from Kuro.

Ashke had his own seat on the table at the place across from Marie. Asamoah sat across from Joe.

"I did try a few things to attempt to negate it," Marie said.

While she was talking, Duncan removed the covers from the platters and everyone began helping themselves. Asamoah made eye contact with Joe and pushed a platter closer. Joe used the tongs to grab a sandwich for Marie, too.

"Thank you, Joe," Marie said. She gave Kuro similar thanks as he placed a small bowl of soup by her right hand.

"I wasn't aware you'd tried to remove the hex on us," Joe prompted her. He wanted to hear more.

"I probably should have asked permission," she admitted. "I just didn't want to get your hopes up. The chances of general spells working were pretty small."

Kuro pushed a bowl past Marie to Joe. He nodded at Marie so she knew he was listening and sniffed at the soup. There was the salty umami scent of miso and dashi, he thought, but the cloudy broth had squares of white and orange. The sandwiches looked like grilled cheese on home-baked bread, but they carried the complex aroma of curry.

"My home is already set up with the tools I need in place, so it was more about expressing my intent," Marie explained. "My intent is usually set for myself personally, so I took the time to focus on expanding that protection to the both of you."

There had been little dishes of salt in her apartment, Joe remembered. As she'd been bustling around in the morning, she'd poured out black salt flakes. He'd thought it had been for cooking. She'd also spent time tending her plants along her windows, especially the rosemary. She'd lit candles, too. He hadn't taken notice because she'd made it seem like everyday, practical puttering with things she loved, like cooking and plant maintenance. It hadn't seemed like any kind of ritual.

That had been a mistake on his part.

"It didn't work anyway." Marie's tone turned melancholy.

"You tried," Joe said quickly. "That matters."

He wanted to thank her, but he glanced warily at Duncan and Ashke.

Ashke laughed his bell-like laughter. "You can thank her around us, fox boy. We won't hold it against you."

Kuro leaned in close to Marie. "Thank you, Marie."

Joe snagged her left hand in his. "Yes. Thank you for trying, Marie."

"What's next?" Thomas asked. "You sure you won't come back to the island for the time being?"

Marie took a bite of her sandwich. The crunch sounded so satisfying, and Joe was impressed by the cheese stretch. His mouth watered as she closed her eyes and chewed for a moment before speaking. "The object we're investigating inside Socrates Industries is too powerful to just leave there, especially while human researchers are doing active experiments with it. It may seem like they're able to die and come back, easy peasy, but there are always consequences to this kind of thing. The chest plate looks Egyptian, and I'm not up to speed on how it was meant to be used. All I know for sure is that the blue lotus they've got on-site is the real deal. It's the variety used by ancient Egyptians in rituals, and it is psychoactive. Hallucinations and euphoria are the least of the effects when used in conjunction with an object that has that much power. I need to know more about what they're doing as quickly as possible. I can't just take my time researching and hope things will be fine as they are."

"We also need to appear to be working to acquire it for Babel," Joe pointed out.

Thomas growled.

Joe waved his sandwich like he was fending off the werewolf's threat. He didn't feel quite that confident, but the werewolf didn't need to know that. "The whole reason Babel hired a witch to do this to us was to give us a sense of urgency, and add a chaotic twist to the difficulty level of this job. It's what they do. What kind of soup is this, by the way?"

"Dashi miso soup with tofu and kabocha squash," Asamoah answered good-naturedly.

"It's good," Joe commented around a mouthful of grilled cheese. "A nice, soothing counterpoint to the scary werewolf."

Thomas glared daggers into him. Joe tried giving him a cheeky smile.

Thomas didn't lunge across the table to strangle him or rip him to pieces, which seemed like a good thing. Instead, he turned to Marie. "Ashke said the hex was done by a pain witch. I sincerely doubt it was a willing sacrifice."

"I'm not absolutely sure," Marie answered. If she had a theory, she didn't share it. Instead, she polished off the other half of her grilled cheese and reached for some fresh apple slices.

"Either way, it feels like this hex definitely inflicts harm," Thomas continued. "Goes against the 'harm none' rule, so I don't think the witches who cast it on your new...friends...would use personal sacrifices to gain the power necessary. Witches like that are definitely a danger to witches like you. They gain power a lot faster from torturing their sacrifices than you do drawing slowly from the life around you, no matter how many plants you grow in your apartment. You'd be safer and have access to more power in your more permanent residence, the current seat of your power."

Kuro set his spoon into his empty soup bowl with an audible click. "You're explaining a lot to the witch who already knows how her power works."

Silence fell around the table. Joe smirked. Kuro wasn't wrong. Asamoah wordlessly poked a platter piled high with grilled chicken legs at Thomas.

After a tense moment, Thomas grabbed the tongs and served himself several pieces of chicken. "You're not wrong. My apologies, Marie."

"Accepted," Marie responded. She didn't make a big thing about it, only offered him a bowl of soup, too.

Thomas took the bowl of soup. "I like these two. It makes me feel better that you're not alone. It's your call how you want to go after these objects. Just please, let us know how we can help. Even if we're spread too thin to be right there with you, we'll do our best to get to you if you want to take coordinated action."

"Glad we meet your approval," Joe said brightly. There was no sarcasm at all in his words. He was sure he kept it all out. Definitely not antagonizing the werewolf. Instead, Joe held up his third sandwich to Asamoah. "What exactly is in these grilled cheeses? They're amazing."

EIGHTEEN

MARIE

I still can't believe he uses butter on the outside of his grilled cheese sandwiches and not mayo." Joe was still ranting. "Obviously spreading a thin layer of mayo on the outside of your bread gives the best golden brown."

"Wouldn't work as well with the way he browns the curry powder," Marie countered.

"True," Joe admitted. "The browned curry powder on the outside of those grilled cheese sandwiches was so, so good."

She was extremely amused. Joe had dispelled the tension at the table after Thomas had eased up. Thomas was intense, and it showed he cared, but his nature drove him a little too hard, and he'd gotten out of hand. She and Punch both took turns pushing back with him, but Marie was glad Joe and Kuro weren't too intimidated to step up to the line with Thomas, too. Anyone she'd consider getting into a relationship with would need to be able to hold their own with the members of the Darke Consortium. They weren't just work colleagues. To her, they were family.

"So." Joe adjusted the straps on the dog backpack.

Kuro made a soft bark in response. Same as the evening before, Kuro had changed about an hour after Joe had turned back into a human. Marie ached for them. They'd been really great about meeting with the members of the Darke Consortium, but they'd missed out on time together while they were both in human form. She'd noticed they had taken the opportunity to hold hands behind her chair, and they'd both reached for her hand, too. Those little touches had been nice, really nice. She was learning that they were both tactile people, at least with each other and with her.

"Sew buttons?" Marie answered whimsically.

"Huh?" Joe blinked. A lock of hair fell across his forehead and across one eye. He didn't even have to try, and he had the cute but also incredibly hot K-pop idol vibe going.

Marie shook her head. "Sorry, my dad liked to make puns like that. Any time someone would prompt a conversation with *so* and leave it hanging like that."

Joe laughed. "*So*, I was wondering why we're in front of the Seattle Central Library in the middle of the night."

"Well, we might be coming back tomorrow when they're open." Marie pulled the extra-large tote bag she'd been carrying off her shoulder. "It all depends on Rensho."

"Who?" Joe asked.

Marie unzipped the top of the tote, murmuring the words to release the binding she'd had on it. Then she reached in and pulled out a scroll. The scroll immediately unrolled itself, hovering above her hand.

"I'm free!" The scroll tried to fly away and stopped, twisting itself as if its bottom was tethered to Marie's palm. "Ah. Sort of."

"Hello, Rensho," Marie said pleasantly.

"Witch," Rensho greeted her. They sounded cautiously genial.

"Joe, Kuro, this is Rensho." Marie thought introductions were the best way to start the evening. She also gathered Rensho in both hands, holding them as if she was showing the Japanese silk scroll painting to Joe.

"Kuro would know for sure, but that's a Japanese yōkai, isn't it?" Joe asked, using the term for supernatural beings and creatures from Japanese folklore and stepping close enough that his shoulder brushed hers. He was playing along quite nicely. It was unlikely anyone walking by would notice anything out of the ordinary.

"This yōkai is an ittan momen, thank you very much," Rensho said. They sounded significantly more irritated. "You can speak directly to me."

"I could," Joe agreed mildly. "But ittan momen have a reputation for being fairly malicious. Some of you have gathered a significant body count. So I figured I'd address the witch that was carrying you around. Especially since I like her, and I don't know you."

Rensho was silent for a moment. Then the silk of the scroll scrunched up like they were shrugging. "Fair."

"Rensho and I became acquainted not too long ago, when they were discovered as part of a collection of Japanese painted scrolls." Marie kept her attention on Rensho. They seemed to be playing nice, but they were tugging at the binding, testing her hold on them. "Since they had enough feeling poured into them over the years to gather enough power to become self-aware, I couldn't just put them away for safekeeping in the consortium archives. It seemed like that would be a form of torture."

"It would," Rensho agreed emphatically.

"I think I have a good solution to this problem, but I need more than a promise from you," Marie said. "I want a vow, witnessed and binding."

Rensho went still.

It wasn't a small thing she was demanding. Beings like Rensho took vows seriously. They were, after all, alive and self-aware because of the feelings and strength of will they had absorbed over time until they had achieved a life of their own. Plenty of objects of myth and magic exhibited a certain spark of will, but to be as completely self-aware as Rensho had become took a lot. Marie had had to research for days to figure out what an ittan momen was, then Rensho had filled in what her research hadn't turned up. They were actually quite knowledgeable, having passed from museum to museum for at least some of their long existence. They'd absorbed a certain amount of academic learning.

"What vow do you want from me, witch?" Rensho asked finally.

"This is the Seattle Central Library." Marie gestured to the complex geometric structure in front of them. "It's eleven stories of knowledge, with access to infinitely more if you learn to leverage the modern technology inside."

The ittan momen arched in her hands, and she wished they had features she could recognize as eyes, but that might also be creepy. It was just harder to talk to something without a face like it was a thinking, feeling being.

"What do I have to do?" Rensho asked finally.

"For the immediate future, I need your help researching a topic. I can't set up automated searches. I need a thinking, reasoning mind to do the queries and follow potentially useful leads." Marie hoped this would work. It would speed up her progress by a lot if it did. "I'll visit the library regularly. You meet with me discreetly and fill me in on what you've found."

"That's all?" Rensho sounded suspicious.

Well, they weren't wrong. There was more.

"You must not be discovered. Not by any human or supernatural. If you are, you must let me take you out of there." Marie didn't want to tell Rensho to do everything in their power to avoid discovery because there were too many ways to get around that. There were also circumstances beyond Rensho's control. "No suffocating people and definitely no killing. You must not harm anyone. You must remain within this specific building."

"Is that all?" Rensho had affected a bored tone now.

Marie pressed her lips together. She didn't believe what she was asking was of no consequence.

"Any time I need help with a new topic of research, you'll do your best to help me. Your sincere best." She needed to be able to trust them. "No lies, not even by omission."

"You're seriously going to set an ittan momen loose in a public building?" Joe whispered.

Rensho didn't say anything, maybe waiting to hear what she would say.

"This particular tsukumogami, with the vow I've specified, yes," Marie said evenly.

Tsukumogami were yōkai that resembled household items. They were once inanimate and had gained a life of their own over time, for whatever reason. Rensho had a passion for knowledge, like Marie did. It was why she thought Rensho would make this promise and allow themselves to be bound by it.

Rensho had a strong sense of pride, too. She was banking on them caring that she wouldn't set just any ittan momen or tsukumogami loose, even with restrictions. Besides, she wanted to trust them. This was the best solution she'd been able to come up with to give them happiness while still keeping them from harming anyone. It wasn't like they had a home they could safely go back to.

For many who'd lived for a long time, the safety of a place to call home changed over the passage of decades, and most couldn't ever go back to what used to be. She could empathize with that even if she hadn't lived half so long as Rensho had.

Anyone who'd been friends with Bennett would understand, at least a little bit. The vampire had lost a lot over the long years of his life. Marie was so very glad he'd found Punch.

"What do you say, yōkai?" Joe asked finally.

Marie was learning, of the two, it was Joe who tended to fill silences. Not a bad thing. She was getting too cold to stop her teeth from chattering as she waited out in the cold night for Rensho to make their decision. Her mask helped keep her face warm, but the chill autumn air was seeping through her pants and coat.

"Yes," Rensho responded. "I agree, witch."

Marie smiled. "Make your vow. My kitsune and gumiho companions will witness."

They didn't need an item to make the vow binding. Rensho simply repeated the terms she'd stated, vowing to abide by them. Magic hummed across Marie's skin and a few of the flowers in the landscaping around them leaned toward her to bear witness, too. It was as simple as speaking out loud for the wind to hear. That was the scary thing about binding oneself with a vow. All it took was intention. No spell. Magic did the rest for those with the talent to gather it.

When it was done, she walked to the book return slot. "First topic to research, Egyptian rituals using the amulet in this image." She showed Rensho the image on her phone. "Secondary topic, hexes and rituals used to bind shape-shifters."

"Interesting topics. I may actually enjoy this, witch," Rensho said, sounding cheerful now that the vow was made. "I'll get started right away."

Rensho changed in her hand, taking on the appearance of a novel. She glanced at the title and huffed out a laugh, then dropped them in the chute.

The Ink That Bleeds.

She returned to where Joe was standing with Kuro on the sidewalk. "Let's head back to my apartment, okay?"

Kuro let out a sharp bark. It sounded like agreement to her.

Joe just smiled and took her hand, interlocking their fingers and tucking them into his jacket pocket. "Is this okay?"

Warmth filled her, and not just from the contact. "It's nice."

Joe gave her hand a squeeze. "So, about these consortium meetings. Are you planning to introduce us to any other supernaturals? And is it too soon to hope you'll introduce us as your boyfriends?"

Before Marie could respond, Kuro nipped Joe's ear, and Joe yelped.

Startled, Marie regarded Kuro. "Does that mean you're against it?"

Kuro blinked, his fox face looking surprised to her, his ears up. He whined and shook his head.

"I'm not sure what dating is like for you"—Joe stopped and leaned in to brush his lips over her cheek—"but over the last couple of days, I've had a lot of time to talk with you and observe you. I already knew I was interested in you, and so did Kuro. This is, honestly, the slowest we've ever proceeded in a relationship when it came to...physicality."

"Ah." Marie breathed out the word. Joe's lips were so close. She only needed to tilt her face up the slightest bit and they would be kissing. "It's not because I don't want to...explore the physical attraction between us."

"The current situation is complicated, but I'm choosing to believe we'll figure out how to break the hex one way or the other." Joe's voice was deepening. He spoke against her lips. "In the meantime, how do you feel about exploring a little when we get back to your place? Kuro should be changing back in a few hours, too."

Both of them. Marie's body tightened at the suggestion. That would be amazing.

"I'd like that."

She'd get no sleep tonight, but honestly, it would be worth it.

Joe

It was a nice walk, all downhill and not that many blocks. Joe should have known it was going too well.

It was the cold chills that tipped him off. Marie's steps faltered next to him. He glanced at her and followed her gaze down the street and into the shadows of a wide alley not too far ahead of them. She had good eyes for a human witch. Fortunately, Joe was very familiar with this block. He'd been here just a few nights ago. The witch had brushed past him not too far from here, just around the corner.

Joe gently nudged Marie into the entryway of Haven House, between two planters with mini trees decorated with snowflakes and origami birds. With Kuro growling over his shoulder, he stood in the middle of the sidewalk and waited for the pain witch to come to him.

"Aren't the two of you adorable?" The man came to a stop in front of them, just out of arm's reach. "Are you dropping off another victim? Is she one of yours or did you pick up someone else's trash again?"

Joe scowled. "Stopping by to check on us?"

The man was white, scruffy, with gray stubble that was too long to be considered anything but unkempt, and gaunt. His eyes were mostly round with outer corners that drooped slightly, his irises a light brown, like light shining through colored glass. He wore a thick black overcoat with the collar turned up. There was a sort of harsh vigor about him. Not quite fear inspiring, just someone to watch with a certain amount of wariness.

"More or less." The man nodded. "Glad to see you two have figured out a way to stick together despite the...limitations imposed on you."

Joe clenched his jaw. He wanted to lunge at the witch, grab him by the collar and shake him until he lifted the hex. But that wouldn't help the situation.

"Oooh, your partner has quite the glare." The man grinned, displaying teeth that could do with a good cleaning. Joe suppressed a shudder. Ew. "I'm surprised neither of you has come at me."

"Why waste the energy?" Joe asked, keeping his voice light. He remembered Ashke and how unsettling a lilting tone could be. "You wouldn't be here to play with us if what you did was so easy to undo."

The other man's grin faltered at Joe's singsong tone. Good. Ashke would be proud.

"It can get worse," the man snapped. "Babel hired us to make certain you learned a lesson. Stay on task. Don't even think about wiggling your way out of this contract on a technicality. The thing about chaos is that it can come at any time, to anyone. You two aren't outside some imaginary splash zone. Show Babel you've made tangible progress in the next day or two, that you're serious about fulfilling your commitment, and maybe the next phase of the hex won't have to happen."

"And what's the next phase?" Joe had to ask. He did his best to sound unconcerned, for whatever good that would do.

The man practically cackled and Joe thought he actually spit a little. Creepy. "Maybe it'll be you, or maybe it'll be your partner. One of you will find the magic hour comes and you aren't able to change at all. Won't that be fun? Lived all your lives with two forms and soon, one of you could be limited to only one."

Only two forms, huh? He was misinformed. Joe rubbed his chin thoughtfully.

"What?" The man's face twisted into an ugly expression. "You think I'm bluffing? You two won't be able to get ahold of us. Each of you only knows one face. You don't know how many of us there are. As long as one of us is out here, you're trapped."

Joe raised his eyebrows. The less he said, the more the man gave them. Seemed to be a good strategy.

"It doesn't matter how many hearts or livers you eat, gumiho. You won't gather enough energy to break what we've done to you. Go do your job."

Joe simply nodded in acknowledgment. The man's face darkened with anger. Apparently, he craved Joe's response and the lack of one was enraging him.

Joe fluttered his eyelashes and lifted one hand, wiggling his fingers at him. "Message received. Ta!"

The man gnashed his teeth, turned on his heel, and stomped away.

Joe waited until he could hear the man's footsteps heading down the alleyway. Then he relaxed his posture. Kuro touched a cold nose to Joe's ear.

"That was insightful," Marie muttered from her spot in the entryway. "Among other things, he didn't acknowledge me at all."

"It's me and Kuro he wants," Joe said quietly. No need to project his voice.

"Mmm, it was like he knew you were with someone, but then I completely slipped his mind." Marie wasn't looking at Joe as she spoke.

Instead, she was studying the mini trees in the planters on either side of her. The entry to Haven was like a little alcove. The glass was tinted, and the lights inside the lobby were off. A person could hide in this sheltered spot until daylight. It was a wonder there were no vagrants trying to curl up here for the night. Then again, this was Haven House. A hungry soul wouldn't be left out in the cold.

Marie reached out to touch a tree with a fingertip. "Rosemary."

"You've lost me," Joe admitted.

"Practitioners plant it by doorways for protection," Marie responded quietly. "And it did, even without my will to guide it. I think it would protect anyone taking shelter in this doorway. Someone at Haven House casts very powerful, very subtle safeguards."

"We wouldn't have let him hurt you." A rush of emotion gave his statement vehemence. Kuro's growl resonated with his tone.

"Thank you," Marie whispered, her voice soothing. "I think standing in the shelter of Haven House gave me a measure of protection from anyone who intended harm."

Joe looked up at Haven House, then at Marie. "More witches?"

Marie shrugged. "Something like that. It was fortunate we were here when we noticed the pain witch. I think it would be safe for me to wait here while you take a look around, before we take separate routes back to my apartment."

Kuro let out a distressed whine. Joe shook his head. "I don't like leaving you alone."

"Better than them realizing you have an associate they can use against you," Marie pointed out.

That pricked Joe, a tiny stab right between the ribs. "An associate, huh?"

Marie reached out before he could step away, pinching his sleeve between thumb and forefinger. "We don't need to give anyone else a word that carries any more power than that."

But words meant something to him, too. Kuro probably felt the same way, even if he used fewer.

Marie tipped her head until she caught his gaze. "I'd like to meet you back at my place and resume the plan we had. I don't want to let that witch and his colleagues succeed in shaking us up."

It was a scare tactic. She was right. Joe hadn't had the chance to process the pain witch's threat. He wasn't sure he was ready to yet. At the moment, Marie was thinking clearer.

"Start a call on your phone," Joe instructed. "If we're going to separate, I want to at least have a live call going so we know how you're doing the whole way back."

Marie smiled and his heart expanded at least three times normal size. This witch. He watched as she took out her earbuds and slipped them in her ears. Then she tapped her phone and his own phone rang.

Looking directly into his eyes, she said softly over the call, "Hi."

Kuro

Kuro couldn't hear the phone call, but that was fine. He kept watch as Joe walked through the city streets, listening hard and testing the air for any sign of new dangers. Joe was taking them the long way back to Marie's apartment, going as far as the place they had been renting and slipping out a side door before returning to her building. She was already safely inside by the time they arrived and she let them into the building remotely via the app on her phone.

They were in the hallway when the alarm on Joe's phone went off, warning of Kuro's impending change. They'd set it after Joe's change that evening, estimating each of their magic hours to be just before sunrise or sunset respectively. Joe hurriedly pulled the backpack off his back and set it down.

Kuro had just wiggled free when the change wrenched through his body. He was just straightening to stand on two feet as Marie opened her door, blinking at the sight of the both of them.

She stepped back, letting them in, and they quickly removed their shoes. She squeezed past them to close the door and reset her wards. Then she was standing there looking at them, her back against the door.

"That was excellent timing," she breathed. "It's a good thing no one was in the hallway."

"Perfect, actually," Joe grinned. He held out a hand, palm up, and waited for her to take it. Then he tugged gently until she stepped into him. "I'd like to kiss you now."

She hesitated, watching Kuro. He kept eye contact, letting her follow his movement as he stepped behind her, placing a hand on her hip over Joe's. After a moment, she whispered, "Okay."

MARIE

Marie held her breath as Joe leaned in, brushing his lips over hers. She'd been waiting for them to arrive, slowly winding herself up in anticipation. It had been a while since she'd been intimate with someone, anyone. Not for any particular reason, just because she'd been busy. There'd been so much going on with the Darke Consortium and her own consulting business. And as Punch pointed out, Marie hadn't wanted complications from considering anyone she worked with in either aspect of her professional life.

Beyond all that, she had remembered the kisses she'd shared with Joe and Kuro, respectively. She'd daydreamed about them. And here they all were, taking a moment in the middle of everything to be with each other. Because as urgent as everything else was, this was important to them, too.

Joe nipped at her lower lip playfully, and she parted her lips in a quiet laugh. He smiled against her mouth, still kissing her softly, and his hands coasted over her upper arms in the barest of touches.

Kuro was a solid presence behind her and she leaned back into his chest, enjoying the feel of one of his hands settling at her waist. His other hand gently scooped her hair to one side, giving him access to her neck and shoulder. His mouth was hot against her skin when he started to trail a line of kisses from just behind her ear down to the juncture where her neck and shoulder met. She shuddered with how good it felt.

Joe felt her response and chuckled. "You like this, Marie?"

She nodded.

"Words," Kuro murmured in her ear. "We need words when we check in with you, so we can be sure."

That was a challenge. She pulled her completely singed and scattered thoughts together and tried for an actual sentence. "Yes, I like this."

Joe cupped her face in his hands and kissed her deeper, his tongue darting into her mouth and teasing hers until she reached for him. One of his hands dropped to cup one of her breasts, palming her and kneading lightly until she groaned. Kuro slid his free hand along her side, gripping her rib cage as he sucked at her shoulder. Then his hand came up to hold her other breast, giving her a firm squeeze.

Marie whimpered. Joe's kisses were intoxicating, Kuro's breath was hot against her skin, and their hands! Their hands were driving her to distraction in the best way. All she could do was arch her back and press her hips forward, trying for even more contact with the both of them.

Joe's hands lowered to her waistband, undoing her pants and tugging at them just enough for her to recognize his intent. "Okay?"

She had tilted her head to the side to give Kuro even more access, and he was brushing his thumb over her nipple through the fabric of her shirt and bra. She barely managed a response between gasps. "Yes."

Joe knelt as he pulled her pants down, helping her step out of them. He'd left her underwear in place and she was absolutely sure her panties were ruined already.

Looking down at him, with his cheeky smile, she managed to pull together enough strength to ask for something of her own. "If I lose a piece of clothing, each of you should, too."

Joe's face lit up with delight. "Happy to."

He reached up and over his back, pulling his shirt off. Then he made a show of holding it up for inspection and letting it drop to the floor. She wasn't paying attention to the shirt, though, not when she had the hard planes of his chest and defined abs to examine.

"He loves to be appreciated," Kuro whispered in her ear. It sounded like Kuro enjoyed it too, or rather, enjoyed Joe being appreciated.

She leaned forward, dropping soft kisses lightly across Joe's shoulder. She let her lips drift across his collarbone as her hands wandered over his chest and stomach.

"Fuck," Joe muttered, his hands coming up to cradle her elbows.

He wasn't trying to make her do anything, not even guide her in any particular way. It was like he just needed to be able to hold her as she continued to explore him.

Behind her, she heard Kuro undoing a zipper. Fabric rustled and she thought he had chosen to divest himself of his clothes. When he touched her again, his palms roamed over the curve of her behind and she pressed back into him. He'd definitely ditched his clothes.

He muttered something she didn't catch and turned one hand, his fingers reaching between her legs and lightly running over the damp gusset of her panties.

"I want to taste you, Marie," Kuro's voice was deep and coarse with need. "Can I?"

She palmed Joe's erection through the pants he was still wearing. She decided she had a question for them in return. "Can I taste you, Joe, while Kuro tastes me?"

Joe stared at her, his mouth open in an almost perfect O. Then he buried his fingers in his hair and tugged. "She's going to kill us. Seriously. Absolutely be the death of us, and neither of us has been inside her yet."

Kuro chuckled and scooped her up in his arms. She let out a squeak, completely unintentional. She didn't squeak. Or at least she normally wouldn't, but apparently for them she did. She wasn't even upset about it. Kuro strode farther into the apartment.

She looped her arms around Kuro's shoulders and let out a laugh as she caught sight of Joe following behind them, divesting himself of every stitch of clothing he'd been wearing.

Joe grinned at her. "I'm happy to save some time."

He was definitely happy. All of him. And he was beautifully endowed, very hard, and absolutely unabashed about walking naked through her apartment. As Kuro deposited her on her chaise longue, Joe took himself in hand and gave himself one long stroke. Marie licked her lips.

Kuro huffed out a laugh and gave Joe a kiss, quick, but extremely thorough. The two of them were very comfortable together. Then they both turned and looked at her. She swallowed, hard.

"Still okay, Marie?" Kuro rumbled.

She made sure to make eye contact with both of them, letting them see how hot they both made her feel. "Definitely, yes."

Joe held up a hand, mischief in his eyes. "Suggesting a slight change here. I really, really want to taste you, Marie. And I really want to see her sweet lips around your cock, Kuro. Since I'm the one who'll change if we lose track of time, can we indulge me here?"

Kuro's answer was to peel down his boxer briefs, releasing his equally impressive erection. Marie's breath caught. They were just both so indescribably tempting.

"No argument here," she breathed.

Kuro's lips curved in a slow smile and he moved to the end of the chaise close to where she was leaning. Which was good, because she wanted nothing more in this moment than to give his cock a kiss in heartfelt appreciation. Which she did, letting a drop of pre-ejaculate smear across her lips.

Joe knelt at the end of the chaise, muttering unintelligible compliments about the view. Then he lifted one of her legs, pressing a kiss to the inside of her ankle. She had no idea how she was going to keep the presence of mind to give Kuro proper attention, but she was definitely going to give it her best try. She opened her mouth and took Kuro in, sucking just a little.

Kuro let out a groan and braced his hands on the back of the chaise behind her head. She steadied his penis with her hand, and proceeded to lick and explore the length of him. He was smooth and incredibly soft and so, so hard.

Joe was trailing kisses along the inside of her thigh, spreading her legs open. He must have been watching her and Kuro, though, because he waited until she was just taking the length of Kuro into her mouth, then tasted her in a long, firm lick. She groaned around Kuro, drawing an answering grunt out of him. Joe feasted on her then, licking and suckling, exploring her while she tasted and worked her tongue along Kuro's shaft.

The sounds of all of them enjoying each other, the sensation of

Joe's mouth, of Kuro's hand in her hair, the feel of Kuro's cock in her mouth, all of it was amazing. The pleasure gathered inside her, swirling and tightening. Desperately, she took as much of Kuro as she could into her mouth, until the head of his cock bumped the back of her throat. Joe's tongue circled her clit wickedly. She swallowed against Kuro and he cursed, his hand tightening in her hair just as Joe's lips sealed over her clit and *sucked*.

Her entire body convulsed with the intensity of her orgasm as she cried out. She barely had the sense of mind to keep her jaw dropped to avoid hurting Kuro as she rode the waves of her orgasm, Joe licking her and drawing it out.

"Wow," Joe said reverently, looking up the length of her body at her. "You are glorious, Marie."

"Beautiful," Kuro murmured, pulling back and out of her mouth. He bent and gave her a deep kiss.

"Marie," Joe called softly. He ran a fingertip through her folds, drawing the moisture down and back, to delicately circle her anus. "Have you ever taken two men at once?"

Marie was still catching her breath. "Yes. It's been a while. But yes."

"Maybe best to let us prepare you, then," Joe suggested. "This first time, let's all stay within our comfort zones."

She wanted to argue, because the idea of the two of them inside her and filling her was incredibly tantalizing. But it *had* been a long time, and it would be smarter for all of them to work up to it. She caught her lower lip between her teeth and nodded in agreement.

Joe's gaze went up to Kuro.

"How do you want it?" Kuro asked, eyes locked on Joe.

Joe's gaze darted to Marie and she smiled. "This is your time. I'm enjoying this."

Joe smiled. "Oh, you two are spoiling me."

Then he reached for Kuro's hand and drew Kuro around until Kuro was standing behind him where he still knelt at the end of the chaise. Kuro chuckled, wrapping his hand around Joe's neck and giving him a kiss. Then he strode to the entryway and knelt to retrieve something from their backpack. As Kuro returned, Joe grasped Marie's hips and pulled her down, closer to him.

Kuro handed him a condom and Joe tore it open, unrolling it over his length. He reached down, wrapping his fingers around his sheathed cock, and dragged the tip through her folds. His gaze never left Marie's as he did. Her eyes fluttered at the sensation and she lifted her hips, wanting him. Oh, did she want the feel of him inside her.

"May I, Marie?" Joe asked. A few locks of hair had fallen over his eyes and his cheeks were flushed.

Only one answer occurred to Marie. "Yes."

He lined himself up and pressed inside her. She arched her back as he entered her, stretching her. They both moaned. He went slow and she was writhing by the time his hips met hers.

He held still then, panting. "So good. You're too good, Marie."

He flipped up her shirt, then, and pulled down the cups of her bra. His mouth closed over one nipple as his thumb brushed over the other and she moaned again. It felt so good.

She opened her eyes, looking for Kuro, and he was watching her and Joe. He had a condom on and one hand on Joe's hip. As Joe teased her nipples, refusing to move inside her, Kuro flipped open the cap on a small bottle of lube.

"Ready?" he asked.

Joe released her nipple with a wet pop. "Yes."

Kuro entered Joe, and Marie watched as Joe's eyes rolled up and back, his lips parted as he was caught between her and Kuro.

Marie realized this was what Joe had been waiting for. Kuro reached forward, catching her hand in his, their fingers intertwined, his other hand on Joe's hip. Joe had one hand on her waist and his other reaching back to grip Kuro's thigh. She felt so much a part of this, and they were about to go for one hell of a ride.

Kuro thrust his hips forward, pushing Joe into her. Marie called out, losing whatever coherence she had as the two of them set a pace that was slow and deep and mind-blowing.

Pleasure pooled and tightened in her again, fueled by Joe's fevered whispers against her collarbone and Kuro's deeper encouragements to both her and Joe. Their hands tightened on her and she reached for them. Every thrust pushed her closer and closer to the edge, until Joe let out a ragged cry and his hips jerked as he came, pushing her over the edge, too. Over top of them both, Kuro moved once, twice, and came, too.

Minutes went by as their hearts thundered and they gasped for breath, then both Kuro and Joe gingerly lifted off her.

They stood, looking at her, and she smiled up at them. She was completely and utterly wrecked. Their matching smirks proved it.

"Okay?" Kuro asked.

She let out an exhausted laugh. "Definitely, yes."

TWENTY

MARIE

"Three hours of sleep is not enough."

Marie lifted a steaming mug. "Which is why I'm drinking tea and not coffee. I want to wake up just enough for this outing and then come back and take a really long nap."

"All you've been doing since we started staying with you is catching quick naps," Kuro said. "Is this how you normally sleep?"

Marie sipped her tea thoughtfully. This was her favorite blend of Earl Grey. It was a loose tea mixed with flavors of vanilla and cream to take the sharp edge off the bergamot citrus notes that usually were present with traditional Earl Grey. She had taken the drink in an even creamier direction by making her version of a London fog, which was basically brewing a particularly strong mug of this blend and mixing it with heavy cream.

When she made this for herself in the afternoons, she also indulged in a little bit of rock sugar as a sweetener. In any case, this was a black tea blend, which meant it was high in caffeine, for tea. Just enough to kick-start her for what she planned this morning, then she could come back here and curl up for a solid three-hour nap.

"Honestly, I do like to take a nap in the afternoon." She wrapped both hands around her mug, taking comfort from the warmth seeping into her palms. A warm beverage in the morning was about more than just caffeine for her. “But it’s closer to normal for me to take a thirty-to-sixty-minute nap, not three hours like I have planned to make up for missed nights of sleep. I don’t really think we can risk me lying down for a whole night or whatever it would take to catch up with the sleep deficit, and I don’t think it would work even if we tried. I have a tendency to wake up after six or eight hours no matter how exhausted or sick or otherwise in need of rest I might be.”

Kuro studied her for a long time, then finally took a sip of the mug she had put together for him. “If we’re thinking ahead to planning naps, can you also let us know if there’s anything else we can provide to counteract the toll this is all taking on you?”

Just when she thought she was getting used to how good both Joe and Kuro made her feel, one or the other of them seemed to say or do something that made her heart expand another two or three sizes. She had never understood what some of her acquaintances or colleagues meant when they would gush over one of their partners doing something cute and proclaim that their “ovaries had exploded.” Now, she was kind of getting the reference.

“I’ll think about it.” She finished the rest of the tea in her mug, washed and rinsed it out in the sink, then placed it on the top rack inside her dishwasher to dry.

Foxtails brushed across the back of her legs and up over the curve of her behind as Joe wound himself around her calves like a cat. He tapped the dishwasher with a paw and gave her some pretty strong side-eye.

“Look,” she said. “Up until recently, I lived alone and wasn’t here more than a couple of days a week max. I didn’t use enough dishes to justify running an entire load. There’s not a whole lot of space on the counter, so why not use the rack inside the dishwasher for drying rather than taking up counter space? It makes sense.”

Kuro chuckled. He walked over to her, gently nudging her to one side with his hip so he could wash and rinse out his mug, and place it next to hers on the rack in the dishwasher. "Let's debate this some other time."

Right. Focus. Don't get distracted by the very attractive man who you already know can blow your mind. Marie turned with effort and walked to her entryway, taking her shoes off the shoe rack and slipping them on. Then she grabbed her mask off the hook on the doorframe and her keys. Lastly, she grabbed her light trench coat. It wouldn't be as cold during the day as it was last night, and it just made sense to her to change up what coat she was wearing when she was out. No need to catch anyone's attention by being consistently recognizable in the same outerwear.

Kuro and Joe both came with her this time, still unsettled by the encounter with the pain witch the night before. Kuro really did look attractive with Joe in a backpack on his back. In fox form, Joe passed for a dog more easily than Kuro's fox form did, but Marie wasn't going to say that to either of them.

It wasn't just that Joe had a lot of soft white fading into red across his face, and Kuro's face was a darker red with more black fur that resulted in a fiercer look. It was also the fact that Joe was just... fluffier. With Joe in the backpack, they got a lot more friendly smiles and a few compliments as they walked through Pike Place Market.

Marie led them into the main arcade and down the ramp to one of the lower levels. Tourists were only just starting to wander around the most well-known level of the marketplace where the fishmongers tossed fish, independent vendors set up booths in the crafts market, and the more iconic eateries were opening up for the day. It honestly took an act of willpower not to stop at her favorite crumpet shop.

"Have you two checked out what's here in Pike Place Market?" Marie asked as they headed for one of the lower levels.

"No," Kuro answered. "We've been in Seattle a year or two, but never had a reason to come into the market."

Ah. Marie wondered how many transient supernaturals moved through the Seattle area without becoming aware of the potential connections that could be made throughout the city. After all, she had been working with the Darke Consortium for ten years now, and there was still plenty she didn't know about the supernatural communities tucked away in pockets all around the city.

"I didn't realize there were this many levels to the marketplace," Kuro offered.

Marie laughed. "I didn't either for the first couple of years, but then again, the definition of what exactly is Pike Place Market has probably evolved over time, too. Some people don't necessarily consider the shops on 1st Avenue part of the market, or the shops up and down Post Alley. I think if someone were to check a map, they're all listed as part of the market along with an atrium and the mezzanine and even shops down Western Avenue. There's something like 450 or more individual stores here, and that makes it really convenient and easy for shops catering to the supernatural community to blend in as quirky antiques and oddities stores."

"Is that how you get supplies you need?" Kuro turned slightly as a passerby tried to pet Joe, covering it by murmuring a quiet thanks as they gushed about how cute he was.

Considering the appreciative glances and giggles, it was just as likely the compliment was intended for Kuro as it was for Joe. Even with Kuro wearing a mask in this crowded space. Take an incredibly attractive man and put a cute canine in a backpack on his back, and it was more attention than they actually wanted. But they were out and about now. They would just have to make the best of it.

Marie shrugged. "I grow most of the herbs I need and I have ways to forage for the rest. If I go on a shopping excursion, it's more in search of knowledge. When I first moved into my apartment, there was a shop selling crystals and herbs across the street from me, just a block away from the market. It was really popular with the tourists, while also having a lot of really useful supplies for my craft. But what was really the most valuable for me was chatting with the store owner, who had a lot of thoughts on creative ways to combine various herbs to make use of their magical properties. They also talked a lot about candle rituals and crystal properties that were more than the generic information one might encounter in other shops."

Kuro grunted. Marie held back a smile. She was learning that he ran out of words when he wasn't absolutely sure how to say what he wanted to say or was worried what he was thinking would come out in a way he wasn't intending.

"Here we are." She let them into an antique shop with shelves so full of items they had to walk slowly and carefully to avoid knocking anything out of place. They made their way through a veritable maze before they came to a counter at the back.

The man behind the counter stood waiting for them. He was tall and long-limbed with thinning hair and a salt-and-pepper scruff. He had a long, pointed nose and deep lines etched between his eyebrows and across his forehead. His eyelids folded over at the outside corners, giving him a look of perpetual squinting. His mouth curved in a frown, bracketed by more deep lines. Maybe once a upon a time those had been laugh lines, or maybe not, because everything she perceived was a glamour.

"Reinhardt, hello." Marie was careful to greet him with respect in her tone. Every time she interacted with him, she got the impression that he didn't mind her presence, which was a distinct improvement over the very clear irritation he projected toward most people who came into his store.

"Witch." That was Reinhardt's version of a greeting.

His gaze took in Kuro and Joe. "I have nothing in my store capable of freeing them."

Marie wondered suddenly how much Ashke had been able to sense the hex on Kuro and Joe when Reinhardt seemed to understand so much at a glance. It was hard to say, since there were so many kinds of fae, and they all had so many different types of abilities. The fae folk weren't exactly known for being forthcoming about what they were capable of, either. That included Duncan, Ashke, and Ellery, too.

"We're here to put in an order with your apprentice." Marie decided it was best not to say anything about the hex on Kuro and Joe. The less it was discussed, the less Reinhardt could interpret as a request.

"Hmm." Reinhardt pushed away from the counter. "Your request will not involve my apprentice in the business of pain witches."

He framed it as a statement. Marie decided to handle it as a question. "It has nothing to do with the pain witches who cast their work on my companions."

She was careful with her phrasing, because she really didn't know how many pain witches might be active in the area. She would've loved to know, but Reinhardt would make her pay for the intel, and might still not give her enough to be useful. If she was transparent and honest in her dealings with him, he'd proven in the past that he would drop important tidbits anyway, if only to make sure a customer he could actually tolerate interacting with would come back.

Reinhardt grunted and thumped the door behind the counter with the bottom of his fist twice.

"Yeah?" a sweet, high voice called from the other side.

"Customer is here to see you." Reinhardt didn't have to raise his voice, he just pitched it to carry right through the wall. It wasn't about volume, it was about resonance.

The door opened. A teen emerged, her black hair pulled into looped ponytails on either side and a little toward the back of her head. She had full lips and a wide mouth currently shaped in a pout. She wore minimal makeup, but had decided to do a dramatic eyeliner to accentuate her round, black eyes. Even in November her coppery skin had a healthy glow. Or maybe Marie was just jealous of the vitality of youth.

Jenna had tried to guess Marie's age once, and when she had found out exactly how old Marie was, her only comment was that Marie had good skin. So maybe Marie didn't have anything to be jealous of.

"Hey," Jenna greeted Marie. Then her gaze went past Marie to Kuro. "Well, hello, hottie."

"Rude," Marie stated.

"But also true," Jenna returned.

"Taken," Marie countered.

Jenna leaned back and crossed her arms over her chest, tucking her chin. Her eyebrows rose until they were hidden under her bangs. She regarded Marie with new respect. "Damn. You're good."

"You have no idea." Marie decided to shut this down because Jenna would offer to find out and Jenna was jailbait. Marie wasn't tempted in the least by anyone that young, no matter how much of a cougar she was. "Got a job for you. Do you want to keep drooling or do you want a new project?"

Jenna's lips parted and she ran her tongue over her teeth as she thought about it. "You always have interesting projects."

Marie smiled. "I've got a photo for you, and I need a reproduction. It needs to be good enough to fool a collector, but it doesn't need to fool an expert."

Jenna stepped toward the counter, hopping up so she could get a better look at the image Marie was holding on her phone. Marie was glad Jenna was willing to do that because Marie was not willing to lean over the counter herself. It was too damn tall, and she didn't fancy propping herself up so her feet hung inches off the ground. Let Jenna do it.

Jenna let out a low whistle. "That's intricate. Cool. What's the symbology for all this?"

Rensho had been quick, sending Marie a secure email with some preliminary information via the library's computers.

Marie zoomed in the image to the top part of the amulet. "To my understanding, the very top is a crescent moon cradling three figures. Horus is on one side with Set, or maybe Thoth, on the other side, and that's supposed to be Pharaoh in the middle."

"Which pharaoh?" Jenna asked.

Marie shrugged. "I'm not sure who it was intended to represent specifically. But the concept is about the balancing of the opposites, chaos and order. A need for both."

Marie didn't look at Kuro and Joe. Chaos wasn't her favorite concept at the moment, not when she knew what Babel had done to them.

"So is this the Eye of Horus?" Jenna asked. Reinhardt grunted and Jenna grinned. "I've been to a museum or two for school."

Marie tried to remember what she'd read of Rensho's notes. "It's the Eye of Horus, or possibly Ra. What's important is that it's bracketed by Wadjet snakes for protection. I think they're cobras with suns on their heads as a symbol of fierce protection."

"Protection from what?" Jenna asked.

"Sometimes a protective amulet is intended for general protection," Marie answered. That wasn't exclusive to Egyptian mythology. "Other times it's designed to be specific. But that's set by the intention of the person who made the amulet, and not necessarily something anyone else would know, not even the wearer."

"So what's this next level?" Jenna pointed, careful not to touch the screen of Marie's phone.

"The center is a scarab beetle, representing rebirth and dawn." Marie tilted her head. "Oh, I forgot those two upper tiers on top of this thing. That's supposed to be a solar boat, I think. The scarab is holding up the boat, lifting it up into the sky."

Rensho's notes had been incredibly helpful, and Marie was going to have to trust their interpretation, because she hadn't found any better explanations of the symbology, much less to this detail.

"So what's up with these wings on the side of the scarab?" Jenna was studying the image very closely. Her detail-oriented nature was part of why Marie liked to work with her.

"The scarab is apparently combined with some kind of bird, a hawk or a vulture." Marie paused to consider. "It's likely a vulture. Vultures are another traditional symbol of protection, representing...Nekhbet, I think? The vulture goddess. She's sometimes featured on a crown worn by Pharaoh or the queen, next to the snake."

"Huh." Jenna was more focused on the symbols than she was on the meaning behind them, as she continued to point at parts of the amulet. "What are the vulture's feet holding?"

"That's a shen symbol," Marie answered. "Papyrus held on one side and blue lotus from the other side. As a whole, the shen symbol represents eternity, or the place where all life emanates from."

Perhaps the dead man walking had been searching for eternal life. Humankind tended to attempt that on a regular basis throughout history. But generally, individual humans tried to find and keep it for themselves. Socrates Industries was in the business of selling the products of their research.

"So all this at the bottom is alternating papyrus and blue lotus." Jenna wiggled her fingertips at the bottom of the image. "Lots of protection and balance in the iconography here."

"Yes," Marie agreed, but her mind was processing Jenna's interpretation.

Eternal life wasn't a balanced thing. Looking at the scarab, maybe this was more about death and rebirth. After all, the next time they'd run into the scientist, he'd been alive and well. *Huh.*

"What materials are we talking about?" Jenna asked, reaching across the counter to slide her fingers across the phone and enlarge the image.

"Gold mostly. Some semiprecious stones like carnelian, lapis lazuli, and jasper," Marie answered. All of those were materials Reinhardt could acquire for his apprentice.

"This is different, though." Jenna tapped the center scarab.

"Ah, for that you're going to have to get creative," Marie stated. "From what I can tell that's not a material we want to re-create. Melt glass or something to look like it, but don't actually re-create it."

"So that's why you came to me and not an artificer." Jenna looked up at Marie through her long, dark eyelashes. Unfair what this teenager had to work with. She probably cut a swath through just about anybody at school and left a trail of broken hearts in her wake. Marie was glad Jenna had Reinhardt looking out for her.

"Correct. I want magically inert re-creation of it, not a magical replica."

Jenna threw back her head. "It's so boring being human. Imagine what I could make if I was an artificer, with the magic to enhance anything I can think of."

Marie was more inclined to be thankful for small blessings that Jenna had no magic. There were too many beings out there who would make a grab for her magic and care nothing for her artistry. They'd rip her magic out of her and the world would lose a bright young soul as well as an incredibly talented artisan.

"You're not just any human. Reinhardt wouldn't make just

anyone, supernatural or no, one of his apprentices. You have a talent that's much rarer." Marie wanted to say more, but also remembered what it was like when she was young and dissatisfied. Lectures got boring. So she satisfied herself with saying, "I like who you are, even if you're drooling over one of my boyfriends."

Marie instantly regretted letting that particular fact slip out.

Jenna's eyes widened and her mouth split into a huge grin. "Aw, Marie, I knew you were queer, but this is the first time you've given me evidence that you actually have a sizzling love life. Where's the other lover? Lovers?"

"Here," Marie answered simply.

"In the market?" Jenna asked.

Marie just shrugged. She wasn't going to explain. She'd promised Reinhardt she wouldn't involve Jenna with anything having to do with the pain witches, and explaining Joe's current form would break that promise.

"How soon can you have this piece ready for me?" Marie waved her phone.

Jenna sighed. "Send me the images you've got. I like that you've got other stuff in the pics to give me an idea of scale. I can have something for you by tomorrow."

That was why Reinhardt had taken over guardianship of Jenna. She didn't just create things with amazing craftsmanship, indescribably detailed. She managed it in record time. Like magic, only Jenna had none. She was a once-in-an-age talent.

"I'll pay you the cost of materials plus your usual hourly fee. Bonus if you never hit on any of my significant others ever again." Marie held out her hand in a loose fist.

Jenna reached out with her own fist and met her with a light fist bump. "So long as you know I'm never going to stop hitting on you."

"Not going to happen, Jenna."

"Not yet," Jenna insisted.

Someone save her. Marie glared at Jenna. "I refuse to entertain the idea."

"Because you're irrationally bound by overly strict societal rules," Jenna shot back.

"Because I am only attracted to mental, emotional, and physical maturity approaching my own," Marie clarified.

"I..."

"No. You're not."

Jenna tried to get assertive again. "Not yet."

Oh, but it would be a while before she was able to stand toe-to-toe with Marie. "I'm leaving now."

Reinhardt rumbled, "Safe travels home."

He might have been amused. He might have simply been glad they were leaving. Hard to say. But Marie rather thought Reinhardt enjoyed the back-and-forth. Thing was, the slightest mistake and Jenna could have her feelings hurt. Neither Marie nor Reinhardt wanted that. Reinhardt's reaction to that would definitively be bad for anyone involved.

Marie breathed out a sigh of relief as she left.

Kuro stepped to her side, offering his elbow, and Joe leaned close from his backpack to nuzzle her hair.

"Precocious." Kuro sounded amused.

"I'm lucky Reinhardt hasn't decided I'm a threat to her," Marie muttered.

"You handle her well," Kuro offered. "You like her."

Marie sighed. "No. She's still a kid. Obviously. Ew."

"Not that way." Kuro got that strained note in his voice, the way he did when he realized something he said hadn't come out the way he'd intended. "You think she's a person worth investing time in."

Oh. Marie gave his arm a squeeze. "Yes. She's bright and tough and deserves a chance at whatever future she wants. She's good for Reinhardt, too."

"They're not..."

"No. Reinhardt wouldn't, any more than I would. He's old. Very old. And he doesn't just have power, he *is* a Power among the fae. With supernaturals like him, it's mortal connections that anchor them to this modern world. Otherwise, he'd have no reason not to destroy everything."

That was a part of the reason Jenna was special. Because she could be found family for a being like Reinhardt, someone so very old and otherwise disconnected.

And that was also something humans as a whole shouldn't know. There were supernaturals in this world that could destroy it more thoroughly than nuclear war. The last thing anyone needed was whatever consequences would come out of humans being aware of and fearing the supernaturals among them.

TWENTY-ONE

KURO

Kuro followed Marie back into her apartment, considering the way she toed off her shoes with a sigh and gave up her jacket to him without a fuss. By the time he'd hung both their jackets in the hallway closet, she'd migrated to the kitchen and set mugs out on the counter. One for her, one for him, and an extra-wide one for Joe.

She didn't pull out tea bags this time. Instead, she pulled fresh ginger root out of her shopping bag and cut off a chunk about the length of her thumb. Then she gave it a quick wash and sliced it lengthwise. She dropped the slices into a glass teapot and filled it with hot water from her dispenser. That was it.

Joe joined them, walking to a position behind and to one side of Marie. His nine tails waved gently as he reared up on his hind legs and placed his paws on Marie's thigh. Then Joe looked at Kuro, head tilted in inquiry.

This was new. How could he talk to Joe without making Marie feel as if Kuro was talking about her while she was standing right there? Kuro had been chewing on his thoughts on the walk back from Pike Place Market, because he didn't want to say the wrong thing.

"The uses of herbalism in magic don't seem to be as well-documented as I thought they would be," Kuro said finally. He let the statement float out there, so it could be directed at Marie or Joe.

"There are reference books," Marie answered quietly.

Joe sneezed.

Marie huffed out a laugh. "I'm not going to say whether the reference books are accurate or not."

The tightness in Kuro's chest eased somewhat. Leave it to Joe to know how to lighten the mood without saying the wrong thing. Kuro had been able to accompany Marie, provide some support, but he needed Joe to help balance their mood.

She pulled a jar out of her shopping bag. It had been acquired in a last-minute stop before they'd headed home. Opening it, she dipped a teaspoon in and drizzled golden honey into the teapot with the ginger slices.

After she closed the jar again, she continued thoughtfully, "It's hard to sift through what's useful and what's not when it comes specifically to witchcraft. It depends on intent, the kind of witch you are, and other things. It's not straightforward."

"The responses you received from the acupuncturist and the herbalist were definitely not straightforward." Kuro had resisted grinding his teeth as he'd stood by Marie during those conversations. Both business owners had been human.

Marie sighed. "They were nice enough."

"You asked about the properties of certain herbs. They jumped to conclusions and started prescribing what they decided you needed instead of just giving you the answers." Kuro suppressed a growl of frustration.

Marie poured the ginger tea into the mugs and handed one to Kuro, then she took hers and the one for Joe over to the chaise and set them on the side table. She sat in the middle, leaving room for them on either side of her, if they chose. Kuro joined her and Joe hopped up on her other side.

"Honestly, I didn't expect a lot." Marie blew softly on her mug, then took a sip. "It's pretty easy to find out the properties of various herbs. Different parts of the lotus are used in Asian medicines and cuisine. The flower, the rhizome, the leaves, the stems, the seeds, the root. Just about every part has its distinct uses."

Joe sniffed his mug and cautiously dipped the tip of his tongue in for a taste. Kuro waited. Maybe it wasn't about saying the right thing. After the frustrating conversations where the humans had made assumptions and told her what they thought she ought to know, maybe she actually wanted space to speak...and be heard. Hesitantly, he placed his palm on her back and started to rub in light circles.

"The blue lotus, however, is a different plant. In fact, the samples I saw at Socrates Industries were mislabeled as the type from Asia." Marie leaned back into his touch. "But I'm familiar with those and could tell the difference right away. I thought I could get hints as to how the ancient Egyptians might have used the blue lotus in their rituals. All I learned from my research so far is that it's used somehow to help journey to the afterlife and back."

Joe leaned in, his ears twitching.

"Exactly," Marie said to him. "Seems like maybe our dead guy walking was a part of an experiment. Maybe they were intentionally trying to visit the afterlife and come back. There've been theories that one could bring back knowledge that way."

"Wasn't there a movie about medical students experimenting with near-death experiments where they took turns actually dying and being revived?" Kuro asked.

He and Joe had stayed in and watched a lot of movies over the years. It was one of their relaxing date night things to do together.

Didn't cost a lot and didn't involve having to be hypervigilant while they were out among people. He wondered if Marie liked movies.

Marie shuddered. "I think I know which movie you're talking about and I didn't watch it. I don't do well with horror movies in general."

Noted.

Marie wrapped her hands around her mug and took another sip. "Judging by the way Socrates Industries wants me to include blue lotus and papyrus in the garden concepts throughout their building, I don't think the plant is harmful just as it is. But there's a reason it isn't supposed to be grown outside of specific places in Egypt. Maybe someone wants it close to hand for experimental purposes and slipped it into the cuttings intended for interior garden design."

Joe barked softly, nudging her knee in what seemed like encouragement. Marie smiled and buried her fingers in the fur around his neck. Warmth bloomed in Kuro's chest as he kept petting Marie while she pet Joe.

"I've got a strong feeling the amulet the man was wearing has something to do with it." Marie tapped a fingertip against her mug. "It didn't seem like a fashion statement. I think there was a different and specific reason for him to wear it."

It sounded like she was on the cusp of connecting her thoughts and ideas together, but she just couldn't quite get there.

"Maybe I need to go back and actually work with the blue lotus samples," Marie muttered. "I can learn a lot about a plant the old-fashioned way, the way healers and green witches like me explored herbalism before the advent of modern medicine."

Joe sat up and stared at Kuro, his posture tense. Kuro sat forward too, slightly alarmed. "Why don't we explore a different alternative before you go into the heart of a corporation to mess with their magical plants that they definitely didn't want anyone to know were actual magic plants?" He took a deep breath once he got that out. That might be a record for the longest sentence he'd ever uttered.

Marie

Marie looked at Kuro, really looked at him for the first time since they'd left Pike Place Market. His brows were drawn together, and his gaze felt deeply earnest, like he was concerned about her. And bracketed as she was by him and Joe, she realized they both were.

She couldn't think of a time when anyone had been so attentive to her mood. It felt…really wonderful. She bit her lip.

Kuro's gaze dropped to her mouth then lifted back to make eye contact with her again. "I don't know what you're thinking."

It sounded like both an admission and a request.

She swallowed. "I realized you're both concerned for me. I like that."

His lips curved in a smile. The man could stop traffic with his looks. She wanted to let herself get distracted, but she also wanted to give him a full answer to his question.

"I also felt bad that I'm making you two worry."

That beautiful smile vanished, and she shrank into herself. She didn't want that.

Joe turned under her hand and took her fingertips gently between his teeth, almost nibbling. Kuro slipped his hand along her jaw, gently tilting her face back up so she would meet his gaze again.

"I think that's a shame cycle we have in common," he murmured. "Can I tell you what I tell myself?"

At a loss for words, she nodded.

Kuro smiled again and her heart throbbed hard in her chest. "It's okay to like someone caring for me, and instead of punishing myself for causing them worry, I think about how much I want to be just as considerate of them in return."

Marie chewed on her lower lip, thinking through what he'd said. "I'd like to think about that for a bit."

He nodded, accepting her words at face value.

"Thank you." That came out breathy because she was very aware of how close he'd leaned in as he'd spoken to her. He still had a light hold on her jaw. It was getting slightly awkward unless one of them closed the distance with a kiss.

He did close the distance then, brushing his lips over hers. Then he released her and pulled back. "I have another suggestion for you."

She cleared her throat, then looked at Joe. He was sitting with his jaw dropped open in a grin, almost like he was laughing at her a little. She wrinkled her nose and scratched behind his ear. He leaned into her hand happily.

"What's the suggestion?" she asked. She thought she sounded reasonably steady.

How did Kuro—and Joe—manage to unhinge her so thoroughly? She didn't even resent it. She just wasn't used to being off-balance. They only seemed to do it when she was heading into a spiral or was gnawing too much on a problem. It was, in a way, a relief to be derailed when she wasn't being constructive.

If Kuro was aware of his effect on her, he didn't show signs of it. He just continued to watch her steadily with that earnest regard. "Are you familiar with the concept of a mind palace?"

She stared at him, and her mouth shaped an O of surprise.

"Only as far as it was featured in a television show I watched forever ago," she admitted.

"It's a technique for recalling things you know." Kuro brushed a few strands of hair off her cheek. "In practice, a person creates a visual space inside their own mind. Pieces of information to be remembered are associated with specific physical locations in this mental space. So if your mind palace is a library, things you know are associated with books in the library."

"Okay," Marie said slowly. It sounded like an excellent memorization tool. "Does that work for things you don't know?"

Kuro hummed and tapped his temple with his index finger. "What I'm suggesting is more in line with connecting the dots between bits of knowledge you already have. I think you'd have better success in a different space than here or walking around the city to brainstorm. Especially with an environment that will respond to not just your conscious thought, but your subconscious, too."

Realization broke over her like a wave. "Your magic."

Kuro's smile widened and there was a spark of mischief in his eyes. "I'm going to make a pocket dimension for you."

"A what?" She sure was learning a lot about fox spirits these days. "Is this something you both can do?"

Joe shook his head.

"It's a power specific to kitsune," Kuro responded. "We're going to pick an object and fill it with my magic to create a space inside for you. It can't be moved while you're inside it and the pocket universe is active, and it's not a portal to someplace else, so you will always reenter this reality in the same place you entered the pocket universe. But the point is that my magic will create the space you need to brainstorm. It'll be your mind palace, and interactive in a physical way that might be more helpful to you."

Marie was fascinated. "I definitely want to experience this."

Kuro stood and held out his hand. "Let's choose an object."

It took them a few minutes, but eventually they landed on Marie's favorite book nook. It was a diorama of a miniature library built to slide between the actual books on her shelf. The effect was like another world in miniature tucked among the books. It was kind of perfect for what they intended to do.

Kuro studied the book nook, then pulled her to stand in front of him, his hands on her shoulders. He leaned close so his lips brushed the shell of her ear as he spoke. "Look straight into your book nook and walk forward, and believe you're walking right into it."

She stared at her book nook, at the tiny books inside. She imagined she could reach out and pick one up to flip through it and took a step forward, intending to do exactly that.

And stubbed her toe on the bottom of her bookcase. "Ow."

Kuro's arms wrapped around her from behind, pulling her back against him. "I'm sorry."

Joe was at her feet, sniffing her toe.

Heat rushed to her cheeks. "It's fine. You don't have to do that."

It was one thing when an actual dog or cat sniffed her feet. She felt uncomfortable with Joe or Kuro doing it. It felt a little like she was asking one of them to kiss her feet, even if Joe was the one who'd come to check on her stubbed toe.

She was being irrational. Probably to avoid the embarrassment of having walked into her own bookcase. Even worse, she was a witch and she'd just failed to follow simple instructions to do something magical.

"I wanted to give you the privacy of your own space," Kuro was saying, his tone contrite. "But you've never done this before and maybe there's more to it than keeping your intent in mind. I might not be explaining it right."

"Okay," Marie said slowly, trying to let go of her embarrassment. "What do you usually do with Joe?"

She was assuming they'd done this together before.

"Hmm." Kuro straightened and tucked her head under his chin. "I take him in with me. He's entered a space I created on his own before, but not before I'd taken him in at least once."

By the time he finished speaking, Kuro sounded a little embarrassed. He let his arms drop away from her and she immediately missed his warmth. Then he was stepping around her and offering his hand again. She smiled at him to let him know she wasn't upset and placed her hand in his. They could do this. She trusted him.

He gave her hand a tug, pulling her forward a step, and then she was standing inside a room. Maybe *room* wasn't the right word for it. A space.

Kuro was there, but he had fox ears and nine tails on his human form. "I'm going to leave now so I don't influence this space. It's yours. When you want to leave, just look behind you and you'll see the way out. If you don't, call me and I'll come get you. It's my pocket universe, so I'll hear you. I promise."

Marie nodded. He leaned in to brush his lips over hers in a swift kiss, then he walked past her and was gone. As she turned to watch him go, she saw a tiny hole in the space behind her. But she didn't intend to leave yet, so she faced forward again. The space around her was changing, gradually. The surface beneath her feet became smooth white marble streaked in gray. Columns rose up in a circle around her, wrapped in deep green ivy vines. In the circular room they formed, there were bubbles floating all around her, and suspended inside were different plants.

She stared at one and the bubble came to her, as if it realized it had her attention. As it came close, she reached out to touch it, and the bubble dissolved, allowing the plant specimen to fall lightly into her hand.

This one was a sample of dong quai, just like the plant she was growing in her apartment. As she turned it over in her hand, studying it, everything she knew about it flooded her mind.

"Dong quai, also known as Angelica root," she muttered. "Used for tonifying and replenishing in traditional Chinese medicine. It invigorates blood and relieves pain, stimulates the gastrointestinal tract and is used to treat irregular menstruation or amenorrhea. It's a warming herb, used to counter cold in the body and restore balance."

She knew how it was planted and grown, how it was harvested and preserved. Multiple ways to prepare it for consumption surfaced in her mind.

She blinked, so startled she dropped the plant, but it didn't fall. Instead, it simply floated back to where it had been and a bubble formed around it again.

"Wow." She hadn't even been aware she'd known that much about dong quai, and she cultivated it in her apartment.

A soft breeze flowed through the space, stirring the broad green leaves on the vines. It carried the earthy scent of deciduous trees and fallen leaves and the sharper scent of fresh cut grass drying in the sun. The forests of the Pacific Northwest didn't smell like this.

She remembered what this place resembled now. There'd been a battlefield near her hometown with a set of marble columns built at the edge of the battlefield to commemorate the historic spot. She used to sit in the circle of trees and columns, studying or reading. This place wasn't a replica of that place. That had been too open to the air and the battlefield. But this space had the same feel to it, the same peace that was both quiet and alive at the same time.

Even though Kuro had given her an idea of what this pocket universe was intended to be, it'd been too brief an explanation to really know what to expect. She turned slowly, taking in all of the plants suspended around and above her, the vaulted ceiling high enough to accommodate countless more floating specimens. Every plant she had ever encountered, ever studied, ever even heard about was here.

When she let her gaze wander back to the floor, a stone counter materialized in front of her with space underneath for a wood burning fire. There was a huge wok set into a recess in the stone, directly over the flames, and another small charcoal stove sat on top of the counter with a small teapot ready to be placed on it to heat. There was a thick cutting board nearby with a selection of knives and a drying rack for herbs.

The trickling sound of water caught her attention, and she looked to the right to find a waterfall between two columns that hadn't been there before. It wasn't the rushing sort—this was freshwater seeping through a cliff face, naturally filtered and trickling down a crevice of its own making into a small pool lined with smooth, flat stones and green moss. Suddenly, her small space felt like it was nestled inside a cozy cave with an opening above letting natural light filter in.

This was the kind of space she dreamed about. A place to brew and experiment, test different portions of plants to understand their properties. She could research their medicinal properties, but she had no recipe book, no teachings passed down from witch to witch to instruct her on how to combine plants in her spells to work magic guided by her intentions.

She wasn't a hereditary witch or a witch brought into a coven, taught the ways of witchcraft learned over generations. She had no grimoire, no book of spells. She simply had intuition, learned through trial and error, and had memorized what worked for her.

Now, Kuro's magic had given that pieced-together knowledge and experience a physical form. This space was a tangible expression of what she knew and the perfect place for her to build on it. And it made her indescribably happy.

Tears streamed down her face, even though she was grinning. She bounced on the balls of her feet once, then looked around, hoping there were specimens of both the Egyptian blue lotus and the lotus she was more familiar with from Asia. Two bubbles started floating toward her and she grinned even wider.

Perfect.

TWENTY-TWO

JOE

Joe sat up from where he'd been curled up on the bed as Marie emerged from the book nook Kuro had used to create her pocket universe. She'd been in there since Kuro had taken her in a couple of hours ago.

She let out a heavy sigh and climbed on the bed to curl around Joe. He snuggled against her, wiggling in her arms and letting out a happy whine. He could tell she was deep in thought, but the alarm had gone off, letting them know he was going to change soon, and he was looking forward to holding her in his arms as a human.

Kuro came into the room, having stepped away to get a glass of water. He set it down on the nightstand and joined them on the bed, lying down behind Marie and wrapping an arm around her waist.

"Making progress?" Kuro asked.

Marie sighed. "Yes, but not enough."

Joe prodded her cheek with his nose.

Marie let out a soft laugh and snuggled her face in the fur at his shoulder. "The space you set up for me is amazing, Kuro. It's like a literal mind palace, which is something I was never really able to grasp when I read about them. But the magic is amazing, because it lets me recall all the things I didn't even know that I knew. So

I was able to find a lot about that Egyptian chest plate and what is depicted on it. I was able to track down things I didn't remember reading about what the symbolism might mean. I was even able to pinpoint the medicinal purposes and growing habits of the Blue Lotus. But it can't help me with what I don't know. I don't know what I need to fill in the missing pieces of how Socrates Industries is doing what they're doing and what the ramifications are."

"You're worried that if we take away the amulet and the plants, the people who've been using them will suffer," Kuro said quietly.

"Exactly." Marie's arms tightened around Joe. "All we know is that they're sometimes dead and then they're alive again. We don't know if they need the amulet to sustain life or if they'd be completely fine never coming into contact with it again. Would we be responsible for their deaths if they can't live without contact with the amulet? I need more information. Nothing Rensho has given me so far has helped answer those questions. They did find me a documentary on rituals using the blue lotus, though."

Joe studied Marie, struggling with a mess of conflicting emotions. He wanted to do anything in his power to help her, of course he did. And it was within his power to help her. But there was a risk associated with it, and he didn't think it was worth it or the knowledge he could give her. He didn't want to do anything that could hurt her.

The hex took hold of him and he rolled away from her, not wanting to expose her to any more of it than she already had been. It probably wouldn't affect her, but when it was active like this he didn't want to take any chances. When he could finally open his eyes and breathe again, he was taking up half her bed.

He turned his head and there was Marie with Kuro looking over her shoulder. Her lovely lips were curved in a smile and she had that soft look in her eyes that she had for him and Kuro that he hadn't seen her give anyone else.

He couldn't deny her anything, he realized. And it was entirely possible she would be incredibly angry with him if she ever found out that he had withheld information just because he thought it was for her own good. That wasn't the way to respect Marie.

"What if there was a way to give you the answers you can't get anywhere else? But you would risk your life getting them." The words came tumbling out. "For every moment you spend seeking knowledge, you pay for it in life energy. Would it still be worth it to you?"

Kuro stiffened behind her and Joe saw his hand tighten on her wrist. But he didn't say anything, didn't argue, didn't even glare at Joe. Joe was torn between being relieved and disappointed, because he kind of wanted Kuro to stop him from offering this to Marie. Marie was looking at him, her gaze moving over his face and taking in his entire body, his posture.

"How?" she asked softly. "Exactly how does it work?"

Joe buried both his hands in his hair before sitting up straight and meeting her gaze directly. "I would give you my fox bead. While it's inside you, it will draw your life essence from you. But there's an exchange that takes place. Concentrate clearly on what it is you want to know and my magic will give you the knowledge. It will give you what you want to know, and depending on how long you hold on, it will also give you what you *need* to know—sometimes it can give you everything. But don't do it, don't look up to the sky and try to understand the universe, because there isn't enough time in your life to hold all of that knowledge."

"You can take it back before it's too late," Kuro said, talking to Joe.

"But what if he takes it back too soon and I don't get what I need?" asked Marie. "If we're going to take the risk, I should control when to stop, shouldn't I?"

"You can," Joe answered. "Your will is definitely strong enough. But Kuro's right. I can also stop you, take back my fox bead at any point."

"It doesn't sound like you want to do this at all," Marie whispered.

"I really don't," he whispered back. "But I have the power to give this to you, and it's the right thing to do to tell you that I can."

He loved her, he realized. It was too soon to say it out loud. He wasn't ready, and he didn't know if Kuro was ready to hear it, and he definitely didn't know if Marie was ready to hear it. But he did.

He loved the way she moved through the world, unafraid to take up space, making space for other people. He loved the way she could move among supernaturals who could kill her as easily as breathing and yet trust them, having earned their trust and respect in return. He loved how expressive her face was and how many different smiles she had just for him and Kuro.

He loved the sound of her laughter, and he wanted to keep learning every sound she could make when he was giving her pleasure. He loved how driven she was in her quest to find out all there was to know about each thing she dedicated her time to. She was so thorough, so detail oriented, and so careful to make considerate decisions.

She reached out and laid a hand against his cheek. He leaned into the warmth of her palm against his skin. He'd become infatuated with her months ago. In the space of just these few days and nights, she had become someone so incredibly precious to him, he couldn't bear for her to ever be disappointed in who he was. She made him want to be a better person.

"It's worth it. If we can avoid killing people by accident, out of ignorance, it's worth it," Marie said quietly. "Please tell me what I have to do."

Joe choked on a laugh, or a sob, he wasn't really sure which one it was. He'd known that would be her answer. Marie? Say no to the chance to find the answers she was seeking? Never.

He took the hand she held against his face in his own and gently pulled it away, leaning over her so that she laid back on the bed. He looked up at Kuro, into his lover's eyes, and begged him, "Don't let me kill her."

Because he could.

"You won't," Kuro said, and the conviction in his voice steadied Joe.

Joe dredged up some sass from somewhere deep inside and gave Kuro a smirk, then he looked down into Marie's eyes. "Think about what it is you want to know. Hold onto it, love."

Then he lowered his lips to hers and kissed her.

There was a moment between them when the kiss was just a kiss, and yet it was everything at the same time. She was so sweet, so trusting. He ran the tip of his tongue along the seam of her lips, coaxing her to open for him, and she did. He took a deeper taste of her, sliding his hand along the side of her neck and gripping her at the nape. He helped her tilt her head for him, allowing him to kiss her even more deeply, and then he released his yeowoo guseul, his fox bead, into her.

Twenty-Three

Marie

Kissing Joe was wonderful. The feel of his lips moving over hers, the slide of his tongue against hers. She could keep kissing him for as long as he'd let her. As he deepened their kiss, her senses overloaded.

She was standing on the banks of a river. Lush vegetation grew along either side, tall reeds growing in stands and leaning out over the water. They were a shape she'd never seen in person before, a triangular shape, topped with thin leaves spreading out like starbursts. Somehow she knew she was looking at papyrus. She knew how to use the reeds to make paper, to build mats or boats or even shelter. She knew how to press the flowers and what essential oils drawn from the flowers smelled like.

Then she was looking into the water next to the land, aware of how the roots of a particular plant dug deep into the mud. She watched as the blue lotus rose up above the surface of the water and bloomed with the rising of the sun and closed with the sunset. She knew its pleasant smell and how it could change the state of the mind and enhance sexual vigor. She knew how it had been consumed over the centuries, how its scent had been inhaled, how it had been soaked in wine, brewed in tea, or even smoked, how it had been absorbed through the skin as an oil. She saw depictions on the walls of Egyptian tombs of rituals and moments from the past in which people used the blue lotus. Her mind was filled with the ways it had been used as medicine, in magic and rituals, and in celebrations of life, death, and life again.

Far in the distance, on the horizon, she saw a shooting star, a meteor, fall to earth. She heard the unimaginable sound of impact, felt the deadly searing heat as it literally melted the desert sands around it. She felt the sand cool and reform in ways it never would again in this world.

There was more. She knew if she looked up to the sky, she would learn more. She would see past the blue of day and clouds to the stars and universe beyond. All she needed to do was hold on and look.

She hesitated. She had promised, hadn't she? Not to look up at the sky.

She sifted through all of the new information, held on to the vivid images and tucked them carefully away. She thought back to the conversations that had brought her here. Her magic pulsed as she did. She hadn't promised. But she had listened as someone had warned her. The sky and land and people faded, and she became aware of hot tears running down her cheeks, of a mouth pressed desperately against hers. She resisted the temptation to swallow as a burning sensation was pulled up from deep inside her. Then Joe was whispering her name against her lips. She pressed a kiss of her own against his, and he gasped.

He pulled back then, and both his and Kuro's faces came into her view. She felt so, so tired. Drained. And she guessed she had been.

Moving even her lips felt like a huge effort, but she smiled for them anyway. "Hi."

Joe buried his face in the curve of her neck and shuddered. He was crying, she realized. She summoned more energy from nowhere and curved her arm so she could pat his hair.

Kuro leaned close and kissed away the tears Joe had cried on her cheek. "You cut it close."

"Ah." She knew. But she had the information she wanted, and if she could understand what she had seen and heard and felt, the knowledge she needed, too. "I didn't look at the sky, though."

"We're glad you didn't," Kuro said softly.

She nuzzled against him. She could sleep for a while. But she should probably eat first.

"Let him take care of you tonight," Kuro whispered. "I'm about to change, and I'll be here, but ask him for the things you need so he can care for you."

"All right," Marie whispered.

Kuro kissed her then. His kiss was firm and she gave him full credit for taking the lead between them. It was like he called sparks from some previously untapped reservoir inside her, and she thought maybe she had just enough energy to do something about the heat he was awakening inside her. But then he was backing away, the small smile playing across his lips saying he totally knew what he'd done to her. Then he was changing, and where he'd been kneeling on the bed was his fox self. He crossed the bottom of the bed and swept his nine tails over Joe's back.

Joe pushed himself up and scrubbed his face with his hands. He took a ragged breath and shook himself all over, as if he was still in fox form. Then he gave her a shaky smile. "How about some ramen?"

"Yes." She gave him her best saucy look. "And also yes the other way it could be interpreted."

His eyes widened slightly as he stared at her and then he threw back his head and laughed. "Luckily for you I can actually manage to cook packaged ramen. It won't look as nice as the stuff that you put together, but I bet it'll taste good. I'll even make the chicken flavor if you like."

She shook her head. "How about the shrimp flavor?"

He grinned. "Whatever you want, love."

He backed off the side of the bed then, running his hand down Kuro's back in a quick caress as he did. Then he scooped up Marie with one arm behind her back and another under her knees. Once he straightened, he tossed her into the air just a little to resettle her in his arms and carried her into the living area. "I figure it'll be easier for you to eat out here on your chaise with the side table, and this way I can still see you while I'm cooking."

She caught her lip between her teeth and watched him move around her kitchen. He moved with grace and she suddenly wondered what it would be like to be with him in a club, moving with him to the music.

"Still processing everything?" Joe called from the counter as he opened packages of ramen.

Her head felt full and images kept flashing through her mind. "Yes."

"Do you want to talk about it? Or would it help to let it all run in the background and talk about something else?" Joe sounded unconcerned.

But then, it seemed like he always kept conversation on the light side. It wasn't that he didn't take things seriously. He was always ready to take action when necessary, and he gave accurate feedback in discussions. It was that he kept it all from getting too heavy to bear.

"I think I'd like to talk about something else," Marie answered slowly.

It wasn't that she didn't want to talk about what she'd learned. It was that she wasn't ready yet. Sometimes, unpacking everything might take hours or days, even weeks. She didn't have that much time, but she could give her mind the amount of time it took to eat something.

"After all this is resolved, will you let me and Kuro take you out on a date?" Joe looked over his shoulder at her with that smile of his that revealed a hint of dimple.

Be still her beating heart. It was almost not fair how charming he was. "What did you have in mind?"

He tipped his head up, thinking. "Our invite to boba tea still stands. We never did make it. But I think for an actual date, Kuro might want to take you out for a more involved meal. Dinner?"

They both looked at Kuro, who was curled up at the foot of the chaise with his nose tucked into his tails. He opened his eyes sleepily, nodded, then snuggled back down. Well, he hadn't been getting much sleep, either.

"Dinner it is," Joe said cheerfully. "I'm betting he'll have a restaurant in mind. I'm the one to ask about delicious street food and quick eats in any city. He's the one who makes it a point to know the fine dining establishments. That way, we always know a place to go that fits whatever our mood is."

"I like it." Marie settled into the chaise, reaching for a throw blanket from the basket nearby.

It took a lot of effort, and she had to admit that it wasn't just Joe's good looks and charm responsible for her elevated heart rate. She leaned on the side arm and nestled into the blanket. Sitting upright was taking a little more energy than she had at the moment. And this was how it felt when Joe hadn't been intentionally feeding on her energy. Wow.

"Joe." Even her voice sounded a little unsteady to her.

He turned to face her, his attention completely focused on her. "What can I do for you?"

So earnest. She did her best to project a reassuring expression.

"While the water is boiling for the ramen, could you put on a second pot of water for ginger tea? I need something to chase the cold out of my body. I'll talk you through how to make it."

"Okay." He grabbed a medium-sized saucepan from her cabinets. "This good?"

"Yeah." She took a minute to sort through the mess of thoughts and images in her head. "In the cabinet above the counter, right next to the fridge, there are a couple of sealed bags. Pull out the ones labeled jujube dates and goji berries. We'll just need a few of each."

"Got 'em," Joe said in less time than it had taken her to give the instructions.

She tried not to be irked that he hadn't needed the step stool she had sitting nearby to reach the upper shelves. She was taller than Punch and definitely average height for women in the United States, but top shelves still eluded her.

"There should be a glass canister of brown sugar, too. We only need maybe a tablespoon, but keep it out so you can add more if you want it sweeter."

"Yup."

"In the refrigerator, in the crisper drawer, there should be ginger root. It should be the only thing that looks like a root in that drawer right now."

"This?" Joe waved a tightly wrapped bundle at her and she could see through the plastic wrap.

"Yes."

"Okay, what next?" Joe was unwrapping the ginger and sniffing it.

Of the ingredients, the scent and taste of the ginger were what she wanted most. "Give the ginger a rinse and pat it dry. Then get a knife off the magnetic strip on the backsplash there and cut thin slices off it. Don't worry about peeling."

"How many slices?" Joe asked, pulling the cutting board off a hook.

"About this much." Marie held up her thumb and pointed with her other hand to the first knuckle.

Joe chuckled. "Okay, Asian Auntie."

"Hey, you were just talking about taking me on a date." It was funny, because she'd never minded being called that by some of her old college classmates, way back when. She'd always been a sort of old soul.

Joe finished slicing the ginger and started wrapping up what was left. "You're right. How about noona? I like watching noona romances on streaming video, anyway."

She opened her mouth, then closed it, unable to think of a comeback.

Kuro let out a fox laugh. Marie honestly hadn't ever heard a fox laugh before, but it was a singular sound.

"Water's boiling," Joe called.

"Just drop all of it in and let it boil. It'll be done about the same time as the noodles." Marie sighed. She didn't have the energy to continue to match wits with him. Instead, she pet Kuro's head.

"Got it." Joe put all the items back in their respective spots and returned to cooking the noodles. "So, back to this date. Do you like to go dancing, Marie?"

She thought about that. "There was a time when I liked to dance."

"Seattle is a great dance town," Joe commented.

She nodded, then spoke up when she realized his attention was on the stovetop. "I used to love going to clubs once in a while, not every night, but a couple of times a month for sure."

"What kind?"

"Different kinds." She looked out the window over the city

below. "In college, most of my friends liked the dance clubs with hip-hop and R&B and whatever had a fun beat. Later, I got into West Coast Swing, and a few friends introduced me to Blues Fusion. I had a coworker talk me into trying out a few tango classes with her, too. I've been a bridesmaid in a few weddings and I might've been the only person in the bridal party to enjoy the ballroom classes when the bride asked everyone to take them."

"Sounds like you've got a knack for dancing." Joe sounded pleased.

"I'm not amazing, but I definitely enjoy all different kinds of dance." She sighed.

"That's what's important. Why do you talk about it like you don't do it anymore?" Joe's question was posed lightly as ever, but he was more insightful than most people would notice right away.

She gave him a sideways glance and smiled when he met her gaze. He knew he was digging deeper under the surface than she usually let people go. With him and Kuro, she didn't mind. "You might have noticed, but I don't really interact with anyone on a daily basis. The closest friends I have are the members of the Darke Consortium."

Joe was getting out bowls and utensils. "Hard to believe it's only been a few days, but yeah, you don't have many people checking in on you."

"True." Marie huffed out a laugh and maybe it had a bitter note to it. "Not like anyone I used to call friend would have checked in anyway. About a year or so ago, I had a moment of honesty with a few people I used to think of as friends. There were specific situations with each of them, but in general it was all variations of them only coming to me when they needed something from me and not really giving anything to our friendship in return."

"That sucks." Joe brought her a mug. Fragrant steam rose up from it, sweet and spicy.

"Thank you. Yeah." She wrapped her hands around the mug, caught up in the flow of memories. "For example, they would ask me to go clubbing with them on nights that were only convenient for them, regardless of whether I had early meetings the next day. They'd bring me just to attract the attention of people at the club. Which sounds conceited when I listen to myself say it, but that's what would happen. They'd latch on to whoever had caught their eye for the night, and I'd be left to dance alone on the dance floor, fending off the advances of people I wasn't interested in. Those friends would leave with whoever, and it was always the same thing, 'You're good to get home by yourself, right?' I got tired of it."

"So maybe taking you dancing after dinner is a bad idea." Joe returned with a bowl of noodles, chopsticks balanced across the top.

Marie shook her head. "Actually, I think I'd like going dancing with you and Kuro. Replace those bitter memories with positive experiences."

His lips curved into a slow smirk. "We can do that."

She thought that assurance was a promise of more than just fun at a club. Or maybe it was a lot of fun at a club.

Heat flushed her cheeks. "I look forward to it."

"Eat. Then nap. Then we steal an ancient Egyptian artifact and a whole lot of mystic blue water lilies from a modern corporate research facility. Then date."

Marie gave him a matching smile in return. "Sounds like a plan."

TWENTY-FOUR

JOE

The night air was warmer than the last two nights. Seattle weather could be like that. Joe looked up into the sky, unable to make out many stars because of the lights in the city. The view wasn't half bad, despite that. He'd left Kuro to watch over Marie as she slept and come out to walk off some energy. The pain witches had issued their warning the other night, so the chances they'd be out here, breathing down his neck, were slim to none. Babel still wanted him and Kuro to do the job, after all.

He didn't know how long he walked and didn't care how far. He'd even gone over to some of the steps leading down from 1st Avenue to the waterfront and come back up them again. More than once. It took a lot to wear himself out physically, a fact he liked to smirk about any other time.

Fine. He could smirk about it now, too.

But he was still angry. Angry with the pain witches who had hexed him and his lover. Angry with Babel for hiring those damned supernaturals to make things more difficult. Yeah sure, the main goal of Babel was creating chaos. Fine. Adding it into their lives wasn't something Joe had expected, and he was realizing just how terrible it had been for him and Kuro to be a part of doing this kind of thing to others. And it could have been worse. Could still *get* worse. Which made him angrier.

He was even slightly angry with Marie for asking for knowledge from him. Not that she didn't have good reason. She at least wasn't completely selfish in wanting to know more. At least a major part of what drove her was consideration for others, worrying about what the consequences would be for the people involved.

He used to think people didn't appreciate the truth in the phrase *ignorance is bliss*. Now, he still thought it was a thing people should embrace more often than not. But having met Marie, he also realized it was a privilege to choose ignorance.

He couldn't keep going through life, taking contracts from Babel, and not realize how much harm came with the kind of chaos Babel incited as an organization. So here he was, angry because a person he was falling in love with had chosen the exact opposite of ignorance and it had been within his power to give her what she sought.

It had been a truth only acknowledged between himself and Kuro that Joe didn't have the best control. He had never experienced fear like watching the pallor take over Marie's complexion as his yeowoo guseul, his fox bead, had been inside her. He'd tried not to absorb her life energy, and when he couldn't stop it, tried to slow the process as much as possible.

Still, he could have killed her. If she hadn't had such a strong will, if she hadn't been such a gifted witch, if she hadn't been surrounded by her plants and in one of her places of power, she wouldn't have survived him.

Worse, he couldn't even control when to take his fox bead back. Because she needed the knowledge, and it was her choice. So all he could do was respect her wishes and be ready, be alert for when he sensed her begin to push him out. Then he'd taken his fox bead from her as fast as he could. The waiting had been torture. The longer it had drawn out, the harder it had been to hold back from consuming her life energy.

His phone vibrated in his pocket, the alarm giving him advance notice of the hour when Kuro would change back. Joe blew out his breath long and slow. He should head back. He turned and looked up at the high-rise that was Marie's apartment building. She was on one of the middle floors, not particularly high, but still a floor that could overlook any of the immediately surrounding buildings. He wondered if he could pick out her apartment, with row after row of plants in the window. He searched for it and failed. Of course. She was a clever witch and her wards probably hid her in more ways than just magical detection.

She really didn't need him.

At least Kuro had been helping her during the day with the investigation. He'd also created the pocket universe for her to use as her own think tank. Yes, Joe had given her knowledge she couldn't have acquired for herself, but he'd almost killed her to do it. She might feel it was worth it, but he sure as hell didn't agree. He couldn't even control his own form to be reliably there for her at any time, day or night. There was precious little he had control over in his life right now and he couldn't remember a time when he had been so miserable, despite being so in love.

There wasn't much he could do, but he could still make good decisions, right? Each one would lead to something better. It had to. Because there were two people waiting at home for him, even if he didn't think he had much to offer them right now. So he could take one step at a time to be more, be better, for each of them. And he'd better get his ass back to Marie's apartment before she and Kuro worried.

"Joseph Choe. Nine-tailed. Gumiho." A familiar voice raised all the fine hairs on the back of Joe's neck. "I warned you things could get worse."

Joe turned to face the pain witch. "Are you kidding me? It's only been a couple of days. What kind of results is Babel expecting?"

The pain witch laughed and it was an ugly sound. "Oh, this isn't because orders came in from Babel. I just don't like your attitude."

Well, damn. This wouldn't be the first time Joe's sparkling personality pissed somebody off.

"You fox demons just popped up out of nowhere. You take contracts and you operate like you're too good for any of the other supernaturals in the city." The pain witch grimaced. "When you come to the offices, you don't acknowledge us. It's like every time is the first time you've ever met me or my colleagues."

Joe raised his eyebrows. "*Have* we met?"

"Fuck you."

Joe held up his hands, palms out. "No seriously, I'm standing right here looking straight at you and if someone asked me to describe you, I don't think I could."

The man sputtered. "Well, of course not. We're out in public, on the city streets. Precautions are necessary to prevent eyewitnesses."

"Ohhh!" Joe drew his exclamation out, nodding. "I wondered why I could never quite remember what you looked like. Not when you brushed past me the first time and not when you threatened me the other night. Oh, I'm sorry, was that one of your associates and not you? It's really not fair to hold that against me, if your magic is performing as designed. Really, me not recognizing you is just confirmation of a working feature, not a bug."

The man's hands were curving into claws, like he wanted to reach out and strangle Joe. That was okay. It was a common sentiment. He probably shouldn't be antagonizing the pain witch, but he'd been spinning his wheels mentally and emotionally with no outlet for his anger. He needed to mess with somebody. Maybe if he riled this guy up enough, the witch would let something slip and Joe could gain an advantage.

He sneered at the man, tossing his head so his hair flipped back just so. "But really, what can I do to help you feel better? I could recommend a great pho place that serves the freshest liver—cooked, of course. Have a bowl on me."

"Gumiho can give preternatural knowledge."

The memory of Marie's face, becoming more drawn, paler by the moment, floated in Joe's mind. "We can."

Rage was boiling up inside him until he could barely see past it. This was his nature as a gumiho. He was all rage and bloodthirst and he wanted to rip out this man's heart and liver for daring to even mention the gift Joe could give.

"Share your knowledge, give me something to have an edge on the other witches in my coven, and I'll think about delaying the next consequence for you and your lover boy."

The pain witches must have formed a coven within the shelter of Babel. Of course. It would change the balance the established coven of hereditary witches had maintained. Babel was all about chaos. Solitary witches like Marie would be in danger.

Well, that was information he could give to Marie without sucking the life out of her.

Joe chuckled and he knew the sound of it was different, darker. He reached for something to pull him back from the dark abyss. He focused on this man's face, only he couldn't quite register details. No memorable characteristics. Joe recalled what he'd been thinking earlier—when he was determined to be a better person—about Marie's wards. He hadn't really thought about how Marie had been going around the city as striking as she was and not being noticed by these pain witches. Must be a witchcraft thing. But he and Kuro had been able to recognize her. Why? Witchcraft was about intent, Marie had said. She set her wards with intention. Even if she hadn't realized it, Marie hadn't intended to hide from him and Kuro.

Joe smiled.

"Well? Are you going to give it to me or do more bad things need to happen?" The pain witch sounded like a cat hissing and spitting.

Joe sauntered over to the man. "I'll give you the knowledge you seek."

This close, Joe could at least tell where the man's gaze was going. It worked the way it always worked.

"I want to mess up that pretty face of yours."

Joe pouted. "Oh, but then how would I give you my yeowoo guseul? It's not personal. Just say ah."

The man muttered a curse, then opened his mouth.

Joe tilted his head forward enough to seal their mouths together. This time, he let his yeowoo guseul into the man and deliberately drew as much life essence as he could, as fast as he could. There was a long minute when the man stood, lost in the knowledge he was gaining, probably observing the lands within his inner being, then the people. Who knew what horrors a person like him, who had visited terrible acts on other lives, would learn? But then the man choked. Joe raised his hands, grasping either side of the pain witch's head, keeping him from jerking away. Joe reached out his tongue, pushing his yeowoo guseul far down the man's throat. Finally, he reflexively swallowed it, and Joe let him go.

"What? How?"

"Did you look up at the sky?" Joe asked. He'd never done this. Exhilaration left him giddy. This was on a whole new level from what he'd experienced in his past feedings.

"What are you talking about? No. There was just dark." The pain witch put a hand over his chest. "What did you do?"

"You mean what am I doing?" Joe sneered. He could be ugly, too. This was a part of his nature. With this person, he wasn't sorry.

"That's enough." A new voice came from behind him.

Joe shifted his stance to face the newcomer, but before he could do anything the newcomer raised his hand and pointed. Shadows wrapped around Joe and then there was nothing.

TWENTY-FIVE

KURO

Something was wrong. Kuro paced the length of Marie's apartment, still trapped in his fox form. Joe hadn't come back yet. It was almost dawn, when they would have a single precious hour together in the forms of their choice, then Joe would be trapped as a fox for the entire day.

Joe was the more outgoing of the two of them, with the better people skills and more genial personality in general, but it didn't erase the deep rage that came with Joe's nature as a gumiho. Even if it had been at Marie's request, it had torn something inside Joe to know what he had done to her as the price to be paid for the knowledge she sought. She was still asleep, exhausted and recovering.

Kuro had let Joe go out, knowing his lover would need to burn off some of that rage in order to make room for any chance at forgiveness. It wasn't Marie, or even Kuro, who had to do the forgiving. It was Joe who needed to give himself grace.

It'd been hours and Kuro had hoped Joe would come back, so he could see how quickly Marie was recovering. Her plants were drooping a bit, but none of them had completely wilted. They were all still green and alive, and she was regaining color. She was replenishing her life force far faster than a human could.

Warmth touched Kuro's fur and spread until it heated his skin, growing progressively hotter until he was burning. He curled on his side, the pain of the spell releasing him from his fox form more intense this time. This time he wanted to scream as his bones lengthened and his joints dislocated to realign in a human configuration. His muzzle and cheekbones broke in multiple places, then fused back together as a human face.

It was over in minutes, but the agony of it left him panting on the floor, curled up in the fetal position. As soon as he could move, he reached into his pants pocket for his phone. Maybe Joe had sent a text message before finding a bolt-hole somewhere to wait out the day.

"Kuro? Joe?" Marie called from her bedroom.

Kuro opened his mouth to answer, but anger and fear constricted his throat. Nothing came out.

Blankets rustled, followed by soft footsteps. Then Marie was there, kneeling on the floor beside him. Her touch was cool against the back of his hand as he clenched his phone.

"What is it? Are you okay?" Marie's voice was full of worry, her face drawn with concern. "Where's Joe?"

Kuro turned his phone so she could read the text message on the screen. "Babel has him. They're holding him as collateral. I'm supposed to fulfill the contract on my own, or the curse will get worse for the both of us."

Anger was boiling up inside him. He might be the quieter one between himself and Joe, but his self-control came from the stability of their relationship. The only thing stopping Kuro from going on a rampage was the featherlight pressure of Marie's fingertips on his skin. Otherwise, Kuro would do everything and anything he had to in order to get Joe back, and there was a high chance he'd leave carnage in his wake.

"Ah." Marie sat back on her heels, her touch never leaving the back of his hand. "We're out of time, then. No more research."

Kuro searched Marie's face. He felt himself stumble back from the edge of insensible rage as he looked at her. Her expression was calm, almost carved from something as warm as wood and hard as stone. He'd never realized how sharp her gaze could be. This was the corporate version of Marie. The consultant who could silence a boardroom just by staring and waiting. No magic required.

She caught him in her gaze and said with absolute confidence, "My plan isn't fully baked, but it's what we've got to go with. We're going to need to gather a couple of people to make this work."

Checking in at the front desk of Socrates Industries was easy. Both Marie and Kuro had been there before, and the receptionist didn't even take a new photo of Kuro. They only printed up a new temporary visitor pass and handed it to him, instructing him to keep it clipped to his clothing in a visible spot.

The security checkpoint on the research level felt like it took longer than it had in the past. Kuro stood in the tight space with her, his solid warmth at her back and his heartbeat steady. How he could be so calm was a mystery to her.

She wasn't usually the person in the thick of things when the Darke Consortium moved to take an object of myth and magic into custody. That was usually Bennett or Thomas. They were the heavy hitters of the group. She guessed that Duncan could match either of them for physical advantage, but the sidhe rarely chose to. She was usually an investigator in advance, or she provided support during an actual operation.

But this time, she had plans for the item they were targeting, and there wasn't time to discuss it with the few members of the Darke Consortium who were available. This was one of those instances when she thought it would be better to ask for forgiveness, rather asking for permission and potentially being denied.

So here she was, trying to look harmless and innocent while walking into a research facility to take what was certain to be one of the company's most valued research items. At least she wasn't alone.

"Which is the one you want me to carry?" Kuro asked as they ducked into the storage room. They removed their coats and hung them up the way they had the last time they'd been here. It'd look weird if they kept their coats on walking through the research area.

"This one." Marie tapped the side of one of the buckets. "But put this on first."

Opening her shoulder bag, she pulled out an apron and handed it to him, then retrieved one for herself and pulled it over her head. "I wear these when I'm doing planting. It'll make more sense for us to be carrying around cuttings with these on."

Kuro grunted in what sounded like an affirmative. She allowed herself a small smile, pleased he didn't seem to have any reservations about following instructions. No arguments, not even insisting she explain her plan. He'd simply come with her and done whatever he could to expedite their activities.

Speaking of which, they needed to get moving. It was early enough in the morning that Toby probably hadn't come into the office yet. She was hoping most of the researchers hadn't yet, either. She picked up a flat of smaller seedlings.

The two of them left the storage room and headed toward the research and development area. They stopped in a break area, placing seedlings in glass terrariums on shelves lining a corner nook, planned for that purpose. Then they continued deeper into the section. They made it all the way to the cubicle area, and it was mostly empty. That was a good thing.

Except it was so quiet, she was almost certain a normal human could have heard her heart pounding in her chest. Which meant Kuro definitely could.

"Excuse me," a familiar voice called. "You can't be here."

Marie jumped in spite of herself and almost dropped her flat of seedlings. Damn it. She'd been expecting something like this. Hoping for it, even. She needed to pull herself together.

She plastered her sweetest smile on her face and turned to face the speaker, their dead man walking, but not dead anymore, research scientist. Much better than Leslie, the very sharp research lead in this place.

"Hi." Marie walked directly to him. "We were hoping to find someone in this early. I'm so glad you're here."

The best way to mislead someone was to only speak the truth. She'd learned that from hanging around supernaturals. Vampires and werewolves could sense a lie from hearing a person's heart rate and smelling their scent. So could several other supernaturals she'd encountered in the past.

The man tugged self-consciously at his lab coat as she got close. She noticed Kuro was following, but staying back a step or two so as not to crowd their target. Perfect. It was too bad the scientist wasn't wearing the amulet again. That would've been too easy, wouldn't it?

"We've been cataloging the absolutely fantastic range of plants the company wants me to incorporate into the urban gardens throughout the building," she began.

The scientist barely made eye contact before his gaze darted away and landed on the bucket in Kuro's hands. "You can't just take those plants out of the storage room. There's no garden planned for this department."

Good. Stay focused on the blue lotus in the bucket.

"Some micro gardens were planned for the break rooms." Marie kept her tone cheerful and earnest. "Oh, and we found something that I think might've been stored with the plants by mistake."

She carefully balanced the flat of seedlings on one arm and reached into her apron pocket with the other, retrieving what looked like a very old scroll of papyrus. The scientist's eyes widened.

"There were samples of plain papyrus. Probably to incorporate into a display," Marie continued. "But this one has writing on it. Artwork, really. I thought maybe it got placed in the storage room by mistake."

"That shouldn't have been in the storage room." The scientist leaned forward to look at the scroll in her hand.

"I thought so." Marie pulled the scroll close to her chest. "Thank you for confirming. I really should turn this in to Mr. Mancini. We'll just get going now."

She turned and starting walking away with purposeful strides. Kuro followed, the bucket in his hands sloshing slightly.

"Careful with that." The scientist sounded flustered. "Miss, wait!"

She shouldn't smile. But Punch would be so proud of her acting. Ashke would've been so amused. So would Joe.

Suddenly serious, she turned to the scientist again, all wide eyes and polite expression.

"You can't hand that to Mancini," the scientist said. His voice had risen a little at the end.

Marie drew her brows together in a troubled expression. "Oh, but he's the person who gave me access to the storage room. I specifically heard Leslie—your supervisor, right? Leslie wasn't happy with Mr. Mancini for taking over one of the storage rooms on this level."

"You can hand it over to me." The scientist held out his hand. "There's only one research and development department in this building."

"No," Marie said regretfully, shaking her head. "I really don't feel right just handing it off to someone without being sure where it's supposed to be. Anything I find in the storage room should be reported to Mr. Mancini. I'm sure he'll find out which department it goes to."

As she spoke, she stepped closer to Kuro and the back of her hand brushed the petals of the blue lotus. She held her breath, watching as the man stepped closer, obviously wanting to take the scroll but not quite willing to literally grab it out of her hand. His eyes dilated as he took in a breath, then inhaled deeper.

Excellent. Normally, the blue lotus would need to be processed and imbibed, but her magic boosted its psychoactive properties without the need for consumption.

"It'd be different if it was part of a collection and obviously had a place it belonged," Marie murmured. Just a suggestion. Super obvious. But the man wasn't exactly thinking clearly anymore. He was a little more open to suggestion.

"Of course." He looked affronted. "Come with me."

He led them past the cubicles to another hallway. He badged into a room and through a set of doors that seemed almost like an airlock. This was one of the most eclectic lab areas she'd ever seen, and that included movies and television shows.

The first thing to catch her attention was the hospital bed on one side of the room. There were all sorts of devices for monitoring biometrics. She definitely recognized a crash cart. On the wall behind the hospital bed was a carved slab of stone she recognized from the research Rensho had sent her about ancient Egypt.

"Is that Egyptian?" she asked, walking toward it. "Wow."

"It's a false door." The scientist moved to get between her and the stone slab. "It's an ancient Egyptian threshold between the worlds of the living and the dead."

If she remembered correctly from the information Rensho had found, she'd bet the false door was hung on a west-facing wall.

Nearby was a table covered in scrolls and right next to them was the amulet. No pedestal or display case. Not even a glass plate. The amulet should have at least been in a museum and instead, here it was lying on a table in a lab waiting for the next experiment.

She didn't spare the amulet more than a glance. Instead she held up the scroll. "I guess this really does belong here."

She extended the scroll toward the scientist, offering it to him.

He stared at the scroll and her outstretched hand for a long second before he seemed to process what she'd said. "Of course. I told you."

He took it and placed it with the others on the table. While he did, Marie approached the false door.

"Careful, don't touch that." The scientist moved toward her.

At the same time, Kuro stepped past her and put the bucket down on the hospital bed with a slosh.

"Hey!" The scientist redirected to grab the bucket and shove it back into Kuro's arms, heedless of the water that now splashed onto Kuro.

"That's why I had us wear aprons," Marie said to Kuro. "It's always a good idea when carrying water containers around. It's not like the plants are kept in crystal clear water, you know. They always create an aquatic microbiome with beneficial bacteria. It's fascinating, especially for aquatic gardeners and aquarium enthusiasts, but generally a bad day to end up soaked in if an accident happened. Like this."

As she spoke, she rushed to grab paper towels from a dispenser near the door and came back to try to brush water off the front of Kuro's apron.

"What are you doing? It's all over the floor, too." The scientist went to get more paper towels.

Marie risked a glance at the table just in time to see Rensho in his scroll disguise wrap around the amulet. A moment later, they unwrapped themselves and an amulet was on the table. Just not the real one.

Marie had to give credit to Jenna. The girl's replica looked just like the real one.

"We're so sorry." Marie straightened and grabbed the paper towels from the scientist. "I'll take these with us and dispose of them. Let me just get my seedlings."

She rushed back over to retrieve the flat she'd put down when she'd gone to help clean up all the water. As she passed close to the table, Rensho tipped into her apron pocket and changed their appearance to match the paper towels.

"Yes, yes. The sooner you two get out, the better," the scientist grumbled. "Seriously. A pair of walking accidents just waiting to happen."

The scientist stopped short when he realized Kuro was looking directly at him. He cleared his throat and gave Kuro a nervous nod.

Marie didn't want the scientist to remember too much about Kuro. She rushed to the door. "Okay, well, bye!"

It took everything she had in her to walk past the storage room and through the security checkpoint to one of the planned garden areas on a different floor. This one had a water feature and she made a show of placing several lotus plants in the shallow pool. The blue lotuses remained in the bucket with her and Kuro. The rest of the seedlings went into tiny pockets at intervals on a green wall behind the pool, where drip irrigation would nurture them.

Mancini never showed up to check on her. No irate scientist came after them. Security didn't come down on their heads. Her heart was just pounding through her chest the whole time.

She placed the last seedling and murmured to Kuro, "I think we can go now."

He nodded.

They headed straight for the storage room and emerged without the aprons. At the front desk, a security guard stopped them and asked to check Marie's shoulder bag. She handed it over without comment, detaching the large umbrella she had hanging off the bag and leaning it against the front desk. The security guard then patted each of them down.

It confirmed that security had been watching them the whole time. She'd guessed that might be the case. The comedy of errors they'd enacted had been as much to distract security surveillance as it had been the scientist in the room.

"We'd intended to be here longer, but my assistant got splashed with water and it got into his shoes," she explained to the receptionist. "Kind of made a mess in one of the research rooms, and the scientist in there told us to get out. I figured it would be best to leave the premises until Mr. Mancini has a chance to smooth things out with that department before I try to resume work down on that level."

"Hmm? Yeah, maybe," the receptionist responded, staring across the lobby. "Mancini and the lead down there don't get along."

"Nothing on them," the security guard reported. Then the guard focused on the receptionist. "What?"

The receptionist blinked a few times. "Nothing. I just… I thought I saw an umbrella moving across the floor, but there's nothing there."

The security guard turned to look. "You mean someone knocked one over and it went rolling? That happens all the time. I keep telling them to get better umbrella stands to leave by the front doors."

"Speaking of which, my assistant forgot to bring one and mine is too small for two people to share. Mind if we grab one on the way out?" Marie asked.

The receptionist rubbed his eyes. "Sure. This time of year, you never know if it's going to rain."

Marie nodded. "Thanks."

She took her shoulder bag from the security guard with a nod, grabbed her umbrella, and headed toward the front door with Kuro. As they passed the umbrella stand, Kuro pulled an umbrella free and carried it out with them.

They said nothing for most of the walk to the public library.

"Go to level three," Rensho whispered.

Marie and Kuro followed their quiet directions without giving any sign of having heard. In minutes, they were among the book stacks next to a mural of a hidden cephalopod.

Rensho popped up out of the umbrella in Kuro's hand. "That was fun!"

Kuro put the now-empty umbrella down and it hopped up and down in place. Its appearance changed from a nondescript black umbrella to one of the traditional Chinese-style oiled-paper umbrellas. The handle changed into a single leg balancing on a bony foot. A lone, large eye appeared and rolled at them playfully.

Kuro scowled at them. "Maybe don't go running across the lobby in plain sight next time. I thought that was it for us."

The umbrella, a Japanese yōkai called a karakasa kozō, only lolled its very long tongue at them. Then it spat out several firm, light brown, bare lotus roots. What was left of the blue lotus plants from Socrates Industries.

Marie sighed, gathering up the roots and stuffing them in her shoulder bag. "If someone looks at the security footage, I don't think they'll be able to tell I brought in two umbrellas and only had one when the security guard stopped us."

"Ah, security can't be vigilant all the time." Rensho chortled. "Besides, humans always explain away what they witness. They don't believe their own eyes most of the time."

Rensho levitated in the air in his scroll form, approaching Marie. She held out her hand and he deposited the amulet into her palm. It was bigger than her hand. Hefty.

"This was fun, Marie," Rensho said. "I'm going to get back to my manga now. Let me know when you want to invite me on another adventure."

Marie shook her head. "Hopefully more research in the future. Less crime."

Twenty-Six

Kuro

"Are you sure you want to be here with me?" Kuro asked. He kept his voice low, for Marie only. There were no other supernaturals close enough to overhear.

"Absolutely." There so much determination packed into the word Marie uttered, he couldn't help but smile just a little bit. He wouldn't dare argue with her. No one should.

They walked side by side into the boardroom currently occupied by Babel. For the time being, the organization had tucked themselves into corporate office space in one of the newest buildings in downtown Seattle, but not the newest. It was a high-rise, but not the tallest. The building itself housed a combination of office space, retail space, and residential units. It was easy to overlook in the long list of other companies leasing space in the building. And they were leasing. At any time, Babel could be gone from these offices without a trace.

But they did like their luxury.

The boardroom was immaculately decorated in a luxe but minimalist decor. It was a clever blend of just enough technology for its human leadership and not enough to interfere with any of its supernatural representatives. At the moment, there were a handful of individuals in the room, all human.

"Ah, Kuro," Eamon greeted him. "This is the first time you've completed a contract for us and had to do a formal debriefing. But then again, it's a good idea to observe such formalities, considering the way the last contract went, isn't it?"

Kuro didn't answer. There hadn't been a question. He only studied Eamon. To date, he and Joe had only interacted with Eamon over secure video call. He appeared to be a white man, not too far from Kuro's age, early-to-mid thirties. He had a long, oval-shaped face and a slightly upturned nose. His hazel eyes were bright, picking up the light in the room, and the look Kuro found there was voracious. The black suit Eamon was wearing was impeccably tailored, but it still looked like he was dressed to go to his own funeral. Kuro was inclined to revise his initial impression about it being just humans representing Babel in the boardroom today.

"Where is our partner?" Kuro asked.

Eamon smiled. "What a lovely companion you have here. I wasn't aware that there was a witch operating in the area who wasn't at least in our asset database. It is a pleasure to make your acquaintance, my dear."

The smile Marie returned to Eamon was cool and professionally pleasant. She held her head high, accentuating the long line of her neck. She was, more than Kuro, absolutely at ease in a setting like this. "We have successfully acquired an item from the research and development department of Socrates Industries. It is our understanding that this is an item of interest to you and your associates. I believe a trade is in order."

Eamon laughed, then all pretense of mirth left his face. "I don't like you."

"You don't have to," Marie answered, her voice the exact same pleasant pitch as before.

"Please don't tell me you all hid the chest plate someplace. I'll just have to take another one of you hostage and leave the remaining one to go off and fetch it." Eamon tapped the glass tabletop impatiently.

"Don't tell us you will consider the contract fulfilled without both Kuro and Joe present," Marie countered.

Kuro was happy to give her the speaking role. She was better suited to verbally spar. He was ready to counter the other two people in the room and any guards who might enter.

"Ah, you have a point, my dear." Eamon raised his hand and one of the other men took out a phone.

Moments later, three pain witches entered and one of them carried Joe, stuffed in a pet carrier bound with magical chains. That was something Kuro had never encountered before, and he didn't like it.

"Your gumiho is impressively strong," Eamon admitted. "It's quite difficult to bind a fox spirit while it remains aware and active. Do keep in mind that this was a courtesy. We would have had a much easier time rendering him unconscious to keep him safely contained."

Marie waved her hand, and the magical chains fell away from the pet carrier. Joe burst out on his own, darting to her other side.

"Interesting." Eamon sounded both irritated and amused, if that was possible.

"The hex was supposed to be removed upon completion of the contract," Kuro said.

He wasn't comfortable with Eamon's attention on Marie for this long, and that discomfort had increased exponentially now that the pain witches were aware of her. She was done with being discreet, which meant he and Joe needed to be ready to watch her back.

Eamon sighed. "Come now, it is tiring for you to assume we would lift the measures we put in place to keep you and your partner in check before you actually fulfilled your contract."

Kuro pulled the slender satchel he'd worn slung across his body over his head and placed it on the end of the conference table closest to him. Watching everyone in the room as best he could, he opened the bag and pulled out the amulet. But he didn't place it on the table. He kept it securely in his grip. "One item safely acquired from Socrates Industries and brought here. It is unique and confirmed to have been used in rituals for traversing to the afterlife and returning alive."

Eamon sat forward, steepling his fingers as he rested his elbows on the table. "Excellent. Once your hex has been lifted, you can place that on the table and leave. I'm sure your witch can confirm it has been dispelled. Do you see how simple it can be to complete contracts with us? There really is no need to worry, so long as you fulfill them."

Eamon gestured with one hand again.

One of the pain witches held up both hands. "Wait. Before we let them go—"

"That is not within the bounds of this contract nor the contract between Babel and your coven," snarled Eamon.

"We're not lifting that hex until the gumiho undoes whatever he's done to Ruben."

"He's not going to undo anything while he's still locked in fox form," Kuro countered.

Marie added, "This is not a part of any contract. It seems like a problem to take outside, after you fulfill the contracts to Babel."

"Shut up, white witch," snapped one of the pain witches, who was apparently not Ruben. "You're all alone. You should watch yourself around us."

"Not alone," Kuro growled.

"Not white." Marie shrugged.

"Don't talk back to us!" shouted the pain witch.

Marie tilted her head, then walked—no, glided—down the length of the boardroom table to the nearest empty seat to Eamon. She placed the fingertips of one hand on the table surface, and addressed him. "I'm not talking to anyone but you. Finish the contract, then we'll take all the background noise out of your office."

"Bitch!" The pain witch pointed at Marie. Kuro didn't see anything, but Marie flew backward and smacked into the glass window hard enough for her to immediately crumple to the floor.

Kuro and Joe both darted to her side. Joe let out a bark that sounded more like a scream.

"How dare you!" Eamon's raised voice lashed out as he surged to his feet.

More guards entered the room, taking hold of the pain witches. One of the humans rose from the conference room table and approached Marie. Both Kuro and Joe snarled at her.

"She's dead, assholes." The pain witch was red in the face. "She was too stupid and too slow to even try to dodge that death spell."

Eamon moved too quickly for him to be human. He was suddenly behind the pain witch with his arms wrapped around his upper body, pinning the witch's hands across his chest. He spoke so close to the pain witch's ear, his lips brushing the outer shell, but he wasn't whispering. "You will honor contracts made with Babel."

A wet stain formed on the front of the pain witch's pants and the acrid scent of urine tinged the air. Hurriedly, the other pain witch, the one not clutching his chest, took out two photographs bound in string. He began unwinding one, and Kuro felt constrictions he hadn't been aware of falling away. The witch tossed both the string and the physical photograph on the conference room table. It was a picture of Kuro, taken at a distance. The pain witch repeated the process with the other photograph of Joe.

Joe instantly changed to human form.

"Marie," he whispered, immediately bending over her and carefully touching her body.

Kuro stalked forward and took the photographs and string. He shoved them into his satchel, slinging it across his body. Then he placed the Egyptian amulet on the table.

"Business is completed," the human woman stated, retrieving the amulet and returning to her seat.

"Well, Kuro and Joe, you two may leave with the body of your witch. I do apologize for the unforeseen tragedy. I will see to it that a bonus is included in your payout as compensation," Eamon said, back to his pleasant and professional self.

"Y—"

Kuro shook his head at Joe. Joe met his gaze and choked back his rage. Instead, he rose to his feet and charged the pain witches. Before anyone could stop him—Eamon simply didn't bother, his expression mildly curious—Joe took Ruben's face between his hands. Joe didn't kiss the man, instead holding Ruben until Ruben's eyes opened wide and he started to scream. Joe's yeowoo guseul ripped its way through the man's throat, leaving him gurgling blood as Joe took it back in his own mouth. He released Ruben and the man fell to his knees, clutching his throat.

"Her life was too precious for an exchange," Joe growled.

Leaving the man kneeling in the growing pool of his own blood, Joe gathered Marie's unmoving body in his arms. Kuro ushered the both of them out.

As they left the conference room, a young man in a shirt and tie met them. "We have a car downstairs waiting to take you to whatever destination you wish. It can take you to an emergency room, if there's a chance for your, uh, friend. Or it can drop you anywhere discreetly. This way to the private elevator."

Of course. Babel was thorough that way.

After they exited the building, Kuro and Joe rushed to the waiting vehicle. "Pier 66," Kuro said. "Hurry."

Twenty-Seven

Marie

For Marie, it felt like she was swimming through fluid thicker than water, reaching for the surface. Other times, she struggled as if she was wrapped in layers of blankets. Regardless, she worked hard to take long, deep breaths, certain that more air and more oxygen would help her.

But sometimes those deep breaths lulled her right back into dreaming again.

She was aware of quiet voices simmering with anger. Then she dreamed of cold evenings whale watching with her family near the Thousand Islands, listening for the calls of whales and seals and seabirds. She came back a little bit more, to the clean evergreen smells of the woods around the Darke Consortium manor and heard more murmured arguments.

Really, did no one get along well enough to let a person have a good nap?

But then she dreamed of wandering through a nightclub, trying to find the humans who used to be her friends. She fought her way through packed dance floors of people just standing, not moving to the music, and crowded tables of people scowling at each other, talking about business deals. All she could think of was finding a place to enjoy the music, with people actually using a dance floor for what it was intended, and having fun. Couldn't she leave the people she'd come with behind and go find a place where she fit in better?

The scent of frankincense and eucalyptus opened up her sinuses and cleared away the fog of sleep. She didn't want to dream anymore, especially not frustrating dreams that left her heart pounding, and her chest burning with frustration.

When she attempted to open her eyes, her eyelids felt slightly stuck together. She must have slept for a lot longer than usual. She lifted her hands after some effort and rubbed the sleep from her eyes before looking around. A celestial sky greeted her. Wisteria vines rose up in curving, woven columns to form a circular space around her. The clustered flowers hung in curtains from column to column, enclosing her in the airy sanctuary. It was like one of the magic hours either just after sunset or just before dawn, when the light was uncertain, and both her loves were with her. But where were they?

She lurched upright.

"Hey! Whoa, whoa, whoa." Joe's voice was quiet but full of surprise. He rolled up from where he'd been lying on the floor nearby, kneeling so he could be at eye level with her. "You're safe. Take it easy."

The blankets rustled next to her, and Kuro's arms came around her. "We're inside one of my pocket universes. The Darke Consortium is waiting outside, when you're ready."

"Only when you're ready." Joe scowled. "We brought you here because they were full of questions and there was no way they were going to leave you alone until you woke up on your own. We didn't want to hide from them, but we also didn't want to deal with them if they weren't going to believe us. So here we are."

Marie stared at Joe and a growing sense of horror warred with the urge to giggle maniacally. Whatever had transpired between everyone while she'd been out of it—she really didn't want to think of it as having been dead, even though technically, she'd been dead—there was probably a significant amount of damage control required to get everyone even remotely back into the realm of friendship.

"Exactly what did you use as the entrance to this pocket universe?" she asked.

Kuro shrugged and she felt the motion across her back and shoulders. "One of the book dioramas you had on your shelf inside your cabin."

Her thoughts turned over at high speed. Some of the fragments of her dream lingered, and she was guessing she'd risen close enough to consciousness to absorb some of what had been going on around her. "So you brought me to Pier 66, and Duncan brought us all here."

Joe nodded. "Yup, exactly like last time. They were all waiting at the dock, too. The werewolf just about lost his shit."

Never a good thing for Thomas to lose control. He was a reasonably old werewolf. He wouldn't have survived in this world if he hadn't had his more volatile tendencies leashed. She hadn't anticipated a situation involving her would push his limits, even if they were friends. He wasn't exactly good at feelings, but then again neither was Bennett. Or Duncan, for that matter. To be fair, of the three of them, only Thomas ever had human feelings to begin with.

"But I sent them messages in advance," Marie sputtered. That should count for something. "And you told him too, didn't you?"

"It's one thing to read a message and know you'd seem like you were dead, and another for every sense and instinct he had telling him you were dead," Joe explained. "I was freaking out, too. But Kuro talked me through it, and I trust Kuro."

Ah. That was it, wasn't it? "And Thomas doesn't know the two of you, despite whatever I texted him."

"He didn't hear it directly from you," Kuro rumbled.

It took more than introductions and a meal for Thomas, or any of the Darke Consortium, to get to know someone. Marie felt the same way, so she could understand their reticence.

Kuro's voice was comforting. His warmth felt good at her back, too. Joe was holding her hands now, his thumbs brushing over the backs of her wrists.

"He and Ashke were asking us to prove it was you who sent the messages and not us using your phone." Joe tilted his head and looked up. "Which is valid, when I think about it from their perspective. I just wasn't inclined to be reasonable while we still had you in our arms and not settled in a safe place until you could wake up."

Chances were that there had been more demanding than asking, but she appreciated Joe attempting to be diplomatic.

"So I didn't walk around while dead." Whew. Relief spread through her like cool water. She hadn't been tense before, but she'd been the kind of stiff that came from waking after lying in an awkward position for a long time. Now she felt like she could get up and get some blood flow going.

"No," Kuro confirmed. He let his arms drop from her, and Joe's grasp tightened as he pulled her up to standing. "You were right that they were using the blue lotus in too concentrated a dose. The way you held the fresh flower and breathed it in with intention before approaching Babel was sufficient to prepare you for the amulet's power to be activated."

She nodded. Kuro stepped off the large bed behind her as Joe steadied her from the front. The floor was cool marble. There were tatami mats and blankets scattered around the space, with plenty of pillows in various sizes. It was all inviting without feeling messy. One could lounge just about anywhere on the floor here. Delicate gauze curtains hung between the columns of wisteria, stirring gently in the barest of breezes.

"So this is our space?" A pocket universe inspired by the desires of the three of their hearts combined.

"Yes," Kuro answered. "Now that you are awake, you can influence it more intentionally."

Of course. Magic, in all its forms, was guided by intent.

Her stomach growled and completely ruined the vibe the three of them had going. She clutched her belly and groaned.

Joe chuckled. "I guess one of us should have thought to make breakfast. I don't suppose one of your friends would have while they were waiting out there?"

"Did either of you explain to them what you were doing before you disappeared in here with me?" Marie asked.

Silence. Probably not, then.

She sighed. "You two are going to need to learn to play better with others. I'm going out first. Give me to a count of thirty before the two of you pop out or they might attack you on principle."

She walked over to where bookshelves stretched in the space between two columns. Among the books, there was one shining with its own light. This was the way she could look out into the real world. Or the dimension she came from. Whatever anyone wanted to call it. She was getting better at using the pocket dimensions Kuro created and that was what mattered. She reached for the diorama, through it, and out into the space beyond.

"If you destroy it, you could destroy Marie," Ashke was saying.

"Did anyone make breakfast?" she asked.

Thomas and Ashke were facing off directly in front of her. Duncan and Asamoah stood a few steps back. Thomas started to lunge at her, but she held up a hand to stall him. He froze.

It wasn't that she thought he'd hurt her. He wouldn't. None of them would on purpose, unless she gave them a reason to. She knew this. But Thomas, in particular, was susceptible to strong emotions and he'd been kept waiting for hours already. Besides, she had to keep in mind what Joe and Kuro had said about Thomas almost losing it earlier.

She did some mental math. Kuro and she had gone to Babel midafternoon, and it would have taken a few hours to get from Seattle to the little island the Darke Consortium used as a center of operations. Regardless, the way the amulet worked, she wouldn't have woken until dawn. So all of these people, her colleagues—no, her friends—had been waiting all night with only the word of two fox spirits to go by. Thomas, in particular, had to be at the very end of his ability to temper his reactions. He'd feel terrible if he accidentally hurt her with a touch, even if he'd only intended to check and confirm she was okay.

So no touchy-touchy.

"I'm okay," she said to all of them. "This was what we hoped would happen."

"About that." Ashke did a slow pass around her head before coming to hover in front of her. "The whole 'dead but not really dead' thing is a disturbing concept. Also, the possibility of you walking around dead. You know it didn't make any sense to ask us not to kill you when you were already dead, but also not really dead. I'm not sure that word means what—"

She cut in. "It makes sense with context, so yes, the word does mean what you think it means. How about everyone here promises not to harm my boyfriends and you can all sit down while I explain."

Duncan and Asamoah said nothing, but they did sit at the small table in her breakfast nook. That was probably as close as she was going to get to a High Court Sidhe promising her anything in such a casual situation. After all, she hadn't actually died and was obviously standing and talking and holding off irate werewolves. Look at her, being all sorts of spunky in the morning.

Thomas stared at her. Two puffs of magic burst behind her and suddenly Joe and Kuro were standing on either side of her. Soft fur brushed her wrist and she looked to her left to find Joe with fox ears instead of human ones. His nine tails waved gently behind him. She turned her head to her right and found Kuro similarly in human form, with his fox ears and all nine tails. This was how she'd met them, and she realized, neither of them had been able to control their forms enough to appear like this together while they'd been under the hex.

She smiled. It was really good to be reassured the hex was truly lifted.

"Wolf," Kuro greeted Thomas.

"See? We tried to tell you she'd wake up in the morning." Joe's voice was a tenor counterpoint to Kuro's deep rumble, but no less a challenge to Thomas.

Her stomach growled louder than any of them.

"Please, nobody take a swing at anyone inside my cabin." She walked straight over to her refrigerator.

"What are you doing?" Thomas asked.

"Making breakfast," she responded, grabbing things out of various drawers. "My stomach is upset."

"We heard," Duncan commented dryly.

Asamoah chuckled.

"If you are willing to listen, I'll give you all a recap while I'm cooking," she promised. "If you're still here by the time the rice is done, you can eat, too."

No one said anything. No one left, either. Asamoah usually did the cooking up at the manor, but he had come by once in a while to have a meal in her small space. It was nice to be able to cook and have her food appreciated by someone who she thought of as an incredible cook himself.

She placed her armful of fresh ingredients on the counter, then pulled her rice container out from under the counter. It took a minute to scoop the rice and rinse it, setting aside the rice water to give to her plants later. It'd been a few days and surely some of them could do with hydration.

"The pain witches took Joe," Marie started. She pushed the start button on her rice cooker and waited for the short song to finish playing before continuing. "So there was no time to do more research or develop a complicated plan."

Joe growled. "I didn't expect them to take me, but I figured if they'd come to talk to me, it couldn't be a good thing."

She picked up the head of napa cabbage and started pulling off the large outer leaves, stacking them on a cutting board. "I'm kind of mad at you, now that I'm remembering it. That was really upsetting to find out about."

She paused, snuck a glance at Thomas and the rest of the Darke Consortium members. She also remembered Joe, in fox form, trapped in a pet carrier, having to see her go flying across a room. "But this is pot calling kettle. So, moving on. Kuro and I threw together a plan to take an Egyptian amulet and some very specific variants of blue water lilies out of Socrates Industries. They're going to report them stolen."

"Reinhardt mentioned to me that you requested a replica be made," Duncan said.

Marie washed the cabbage leaves in the sink and gave them a firm shake to get rid of excess water. "Yeah, that was part of my initial plan which completely got rearranged in the rush. I had to improvise and fortunately, Jenna was able to make a second replica in even less time than she made the first."

"I want to know why any plan included you being prepared to be harmed in any way," growled Thomas. "Let alone dead."

"Only mostly dead." Marie delivered that line with a deadpan expression and at least Asamoah chuckled.

For the rest of them, the reference might have been too recent. She glanced at Joe and Kuro.

Considering the source material before their time kind of stung a bit, but she might as well get used to that and just start making a list of movies to ask them to watch with her. Maybe they could listen to audio books together, too.

Before Thomas could get more irritated, Marie starting layering thinly sliced pork belly with the leaves of cabbage. It helped her calmly continue. "It really wasn't part of the plan. It was more of a precaution. We were walking into a place where we were reasonably certain Kuro had a measure of protection as a subcontractor arriving to fulfill a contract. He couldn't go in alone—it was too risky to go in without backup—not when he needed to both finish the contract and negotiate the release of Joe. Too many variables. Me going in as a wild card was good, but I'm also aware of how tempting a target I make. That was going to work to our advantage in a couple of ways. Still, I'm physically vulnerable. We had the amulet anyway, so I performed the initial stages of the ritual before we arrived at Babel's offices."

It was a mistake for the pain witches to consider her weaker simply because she drew her power more slowly from her sources. A witch's talent and their capacity to manage a reservoir of power varied. It wasn't limited by the kind of witch they were. Marie had formidable talent and the ability to maintain a massive reservoir of power. It was to her advantage to only make herself known in moments of acute need. It was also preferable to have as few witnesses as possible. Eamon and his two associates were aware of her now, and likely were sensitive enough to recognize the type of magic she had wielded in that room.

They would know she wasn't a pain witch and that she hadn't had the power of a coven behind her. If they were particularly sensitive, they might know she drew her power from the life energy of growing things. That was too much information, as far as she was concerned.

"It was a good thing I did, too." She took a breath, thinking carefully. It was best for the members of the Darke Consortium to know what might be a threat to her, and through her, them. "I did reveal myself as a witch in that room. And while the pain witches are probably in no shape to come after me, if any of them survived, there were three Babel representatives present who now know what I am. It might be good if they think I'm dead for a while. I'd rather stay out of sight and out of mind, if at all possible."

She reached for a large kitchen knife and cut the layered cabbage and pork belly into sections, then arranged the stacks in a pot in a circular shape, leaving space in the center. She quickly chopped an onion into large chunks and dropped those in the center, then added sliced ginger and a handful of dried mushrooms. Normally, she would have soaked those in a bit of boiling water and used both them and the water in this dish, but it'd be just about the same to put them in and cook it this way. She filled a large measuring cup with boiling water from her electric hot water dispenser and added dashi powder to make a quick stock then poured it over everything.

"You didn't have time to call any of us?" Thomas's voice was quieter and the growl had left it.

Marie put a lid on the pot and placed it on the stove to come to a boil. She turned to completely face Thomas. "We're spread thin as it is, and I honestly wanted to limit the number of us coming directly into contact with Babel. Right now, they're an organization competing with us to acquire objects. I didn't want it to start evolving into an actual rivalry."

"It may come to that, regardless," Thomas replied.

"Maybe." Marie looked to either side. She didn't know if Kuro and Joe would continue to freelance for Babel. After all, the pain witches who had kidnapped Joe had acted outside the terms of their contract with Babel. "But Babel is obviously hiring supernaturals. There will be more occasions when we encounter people working for them. There's no need to start anything on a large scale anytime soon."

Thomas shrugged. Asamoah and Duncan continued to listen without comment. The two of them were a bit more distant from anything having to do with direct interaction with humans. They were advisors to the Darke Consortium and they believed in taking objects of power out of human possession to prevent mass harm. It was like being morally against genocide and taking action to prevent it. The right thing to do, but without a personal investment in the cause.

Like Bennett, up until recently, neither Asamoah or Duncan had direct relationships with humans to make them personally invested in the day-to-day interactions of mortals. Unless Marie counted. As a witch, she was essentially human, but gifted and longer lived than most.

She sighed and cleaned off her counter, then added a couple of splashes of soy sauce and a splash of mirin to her pot. "In any case, I was wearing the amulet under my clothes because it seemed like the best place to hide it while Kuro held the second replica. We needed the feel of the amulet's magic in the room, but until we actually handed the replica over, no one should have been able to tell that the one he was showing them was a dupe and didn't hold any actual power. Doing the ritual beforehand was mostly an added safety precaution, and if that pain witch hadn't lashed out at me, it never would have had to be activated at all. I would've just walked out of there and had to wait for the blue lotus to leave my system."

"What are the properties of the food you're cooking, Marie?" Asamoah asked quietly.

Marie was glad to have a different line of conversation to pursue. She had offered the last bit of information because it was good to be thorough in her explanation, but mostly to fill the heavy quiet in the room. "Pork belly layered with napa cabbage. The pork belly is a healing protein source and a comfort food. It's particularly good for maintaining stomach health and can help the spleen, too. The cabbage goes well with it, decreasing inflammation and bloating. Shiitake mushrooms are good for immune system and liver health and supporting the cardiovascular system. Ginger is also really good for digestion and is a magical catalyst and accelerator. Since I'm coming back from the dead, I figured it would be important to eat restorative foods."

"Your intuition is your greatest strength," Asamoah said. "Much of the knowledge you've gained has been through following your intuition as you choose courses of study and lines of research. This was a complicated situation, and I am glad you came through it alive and well."

"Even if it did take the dawn to bring you back to life," Ashke added.

A corner of Duncan's mouth might have twitched. Thomas grunted. Marie huffed out a breath and stacked bowls next to her rice cooker, then placed a handful of long-handled spoons next to them. Her rice cooker sang as it finished steaming the rice. Her pork belly and cabbage had come to a boil, and she lowered the flame to allow it to simmer. She lifted the lid and gave the broth a quick taste, then added a touch of fish sauce before nodding. She grabbed herself a bowl, scooped some rice, then used another serving spoon to help herself to pork belly and cabbage with a scattering of the now-tender mushrooms.

"Help yourselves."

Joe and Kuro waited until the others stood and made their way to the bowls. Asamoah and Duncan each handed a bowl to Kuro and Joe, respectively. Thomas didn't growl. Marie smiled behind her spoon and figured that was about as good as she could hope for.

Twenty-Eight

Joe

"We have returned!" Joe announced, letting himself and Kuro into Marie's apartment. No, their apartment. They'd decided to share this space, with a few subtle alterations.

Marie leaned back from the kitchen counter. "Excellent timing. I was just making dinner."

He and Kuro took their shoes off. Joe grinned as he slid his feet into his slippers, not the thin disposable slippers Marie kept around for guests, but his own pair of cushioned house slippers sized to his feet. Being with Marie added a different dimension to the way he and Kuro were living and so far, he was enjoying every bit of it. Even the little things. Especially the little things.

Marie had a tablet propped up next to her as she continued her cooking. It had two windows open side by side, with annotations on the text in one.

"All work and no play makes Marie a naughty girl," Joe sang into Marie's ear, setting his hands on her hips.

She leaned back into him, laughing softly. "I dropped by the Seattle Central Library to pick up the research Rensho has been doing for us. It's promising, so I wanted to review it as soon as possible. Rensho and I think we might have an answer. No eclipse required."

Joe turned his head and traded glances with Kuro. Nope. No idea why she was chuckling to herself.

She twisted her upper body so she could crane her neck and look from him to Kuro and back again. "She's a hawk by day, he's a wolf by night. Never can the two touch. Seriously, did neither of you boys watch that movie?"

Joe lifted his hands and shrugged. "No idea what you're talking about."

Marie groaned and blew out a breath, the puff of air lifting a stray lock of her hair from her forehead. "Honestly, moments like this are the only times our age gap seems to be an issue."

He took hold of her hips as she reached for her tablet, possibly to bring up some app to show them whatever it was she was talking about. All in the name of helping them understand the context of her research findings that day. Her focus was formidable.

"I am unreasonably turned on by your work ethic." Joe let a playful growl add texture to his voice. "What do you think, Kuro?"

His—their—lover's hands settled on Joe's hips, and Kuro's voice rumbled against his back. "I think if I don't distract you from distracting her, dinner isn't going to be ready anytime soon."

Joe pouted and nipped at Marie's ear. "But that would leave our love here to cook while we're having fun. Doesn't seem fair."

Kuro set his teeth into Joe's shoulder, making Joe gasp, then licked the same spot. "It'll give her incentive to finish so she can join us. This way, she'll give her eyes a rest from screen time, too."

Kuro gently pressed his hips into Joe, which pressed Joe and his very apparent hard-on into the curve of Marie's behind. Both Joe and Marie groaned.

"Rude," Marie muttered.

"Frustrated?" Kuro asked, chuckling.

"Maybe," Marie responded. "Happy you're both back. And

I was hoping you'd share how your afternoon went, but if you'd rather get distracted without me, I'll understand."

"I'm all for continuing to distract you." Joe licked her ear and started to nuzzle his way down her neck, filling his senses with her.

Kuro reached around him, pulling Marie closer to them both. Obviously, Kuro agreed with him. Any resistance there might have been in Marie's body was quickly melting away.

The rice cooker sang at that moment, and Marie pushed back enough to dislodge them both. "There. Rice is done and I have a clear soup simmering in the pot, with spicy cucumbers on the side and kimchijeon already made. Dinner is ready whenever we are."

Kuro reached over to the stove and turned off the burner under the soup. "It'll keep."

"Agreed." Joe lunged at Marie and she dodged back with a cute squeal. Joe froze, lifting his eyebrows. "What was that?"

Kuro darted past him, catching Marie around the waist, earning a matching squeal for himself.

Then Marie laughed. "It's just a lot, you two. This is the first time you've both come at me at once, with this much enthusiasm."

There was no fear in her voice. Any tension in her posture seemed more about awareness of them both, not hesitation. As Kuro carried Marie into the sleeping area, Joe grasped the sliding door, then paused. "It's okay, you know."

Marie and Kuro both stilled on the bed, looking at him.

Joe dragged his fingers through his hair, chuckling to himself. How was he the one with the most self-control right now? This relationship dynamic was bringing out new things in all of them.

He met Marie's gaze. "It's okay to ask us to slow down, or stop, even. You don't have to let us sweep you off your feet if that's not what you want."

Kuro nodded, easing his grip on Marie to give her space. "True."

Marie smiled that slow, beautiful smile of hers that she had for them and no one else. The one that made Joe's heart expand almost painfully inside his chest.

"I know," she said softly. "Thank you for checking in with me. I honestly was just surprised and excited all at the same time and that's what came out."

Joe smirked at her and pulled the sliding door closed. "Well, then…"

Then he jumped on the bed with both his lovers, prompting another squeal from her. How was she this cute?

"All of us have too much clothing on." He followed up his statement with action, stripping down until he only wore his boxer briefs.

Kuro pinned him with a look and proceeded to take off every stitch of clothing he was wearing.

Joe ran his fingers through his hair again and chuckled. "Fine, then. Marie, will you help me, love?"

"Mmm." Marie turned to him and drifted soft kisses over his chest and down his abdomen. She paused to nibble at the inside of his hip.

He jerked, caught between being ticklish and wanting to press against any part of her. She finally hooked her fingers in the waistband of his boxer briefs and started to pull them down.

Kuro leaned over her shoulder and wrapped his mouth around Joe's cock.

Joe threw his head back, gasping in surprise. He started to lose himself in the sensation of Kuro's hot mouth, tongue working against his shaft, when Marie giggled.

"I'd get you completely naked, but I'm stuck under here," she said.

Kuro chuckled, the vibrations against the head of Joe's cock pulling a groan from him. Then Kuro pushed himself up without letting go, continuing to suck and work up and down with his tongue.

Marie shimmied out from under Kuro, still giggling, and finally pulled Joe's boxer briefs the rest of the way down his legs. Joe opened his eyes and watched her appreciatively as she slipped her own clothes off. Her face was flushed as she watched him watch her.

"Do you like watching us, Marie?" he asked. He knew the answer. He just liked how she blushed even more.

"Yes," she whispered.

He reached out a hand to her, and she took it, rejoining them on the bed. He pulled her to him until he could kiss her, reveling in the softness of her lips.

Kuro let go of him and Marie gasped into Joe's mouth. Joe smiled and nipped her lower lip. "We like the taste of you, Marie."

She whimpered and Joe looked past her shoulder to find his lover's head angled to feast between her legs.

"Tell me," Joe whispered into Marie's ear. "What is our lover doing to you?"

Marie panted. "He's...he's licking me."

Joe caressed her breasts, rubbed the pad of his thumb over a taut nipple. "Oh, I think you can be more specific than that."

A strangled whine worked its way out of her throat. "He's sucking on my labia and licking at my clit."

Firm lips and heat surrounded Joe's erection again. Joe groaned. "Now he's sucking my cock. His tongue is so fucking talented."

Marie nodded, dropping her head to his chest. "He put his finger inside me."

This was so hot. Joe loved getting her to tell him what they were doing to her. He loved the way her voice changed pitch mid-word. He loved her gasps and the way her voice lifted into a higher register as she lost herself.

Joe put his hands on Marie's hips and tipped her to the side carefully, giving Kuro time to adjust so neither of them hurt her. Kuro straightened up on his knees, the lower half of his face wet from his attentions to both Marie and Joe.

Joe climbed to his knees and leaned into Kuro for a kiss, tasting Marie on Kuro's tongue.

Then they both turned and looked at Marie lying on the bed between them.

"What do you want right now?" Joe asked.

Marie caught her lower lip between her teeth, looking between the two of them. "Both of you inside me, please. Not in my mouth. One in front and one behind me."

Joe smiled. He loved that she felt comfortable enough to tell them. Not just what she wanted, but what she didn't want in that particular moment. But she needed to get more specific. They had plenty of time to work up to that.

"Why don't you show us?" he suggested gently.

Next to him, Kuro nodded.

Marie sat up and reached for Kuro, tugging him down to lie on the bed flat on his back. She gave him a quick kiss on the lips, then climbed over him. Kuro set his hands on her hips to steady her and she turned to pull Joe close.

"Behind me," she whispered.

Joe wrapped a hand around his aching cock. "You want both of us at the same time. Are you sure you can take us?"

They'd done a little anal play, so she wasn't completely unprepared, but this would be a first for the three of them.

She nodded. "I want to know how it feels to be that close to both of you at the same time."

He looked at Kuro, and the hungry expression on his lover's face was enough for Joe to know Kuro was all for it.

Joe smiled. "Sounds fantastic."

He reached between Marie's legs to grasp the base of Kuro's

cock, positioning Kuro for Marie. As she lowered herself on him, both of them moaned. It took her a minute and more to take his full length inside her. Joe sat back and admired the two of them.

Muscles rippled under Kuro's skin as he raised his hips up to meet Marie, the two of them slowly fucking each other. Marie was a vision and he drank in the sight of her. The curve of her lower back. The soft fall of her hair over her shoulders.

He reached into the nightstand drawer and pulled out the tube of lubricant, a condom, and a small washcloth. Carried them with him as he knelt behind her, straddling Kuro's legs. He dragged his fingers along the outside of Kuro's thigh, giving his lover's ass a brief squeeze as he reached up with his other hand to cup his other lover's breast. They both sighed.

He pressed a kiss to Marie's shoulder, right at the juncture where her shoulder met her neck. Then he set his teeth against the same spot and bit down gently. She whimpered.

"You're so good," he whispered in her ear. "So responsive. So perfect for us."

Her breath quickened and he gently pressed a hand between her shoulder blades, encouraging her to lean forward over Kuro. There was a sucking sound and she called out. Kuro must be enjoying her breasts. Good. Joe trailed kisses down her spine.

He straightened finally and rolled the condom over his length. Then he squeezed a generous amount of lube into his palm, making sure his erection was thoroughly coated. Finally, he used his fingers to spread more lube over Marie's hole.

"Joe." She whispered his name like a prayer.

"Hmm?" He pressed a fingertip against her, adding pressure until he breached the ring of muscle.

"Feels so..." She gasped. "You both feel so good. Need more of ...you."

Kuro was keeping a steady, slow, deep pace with her. His eyes met Joe's over Marie's shoulder, half-lidded and so damned sexy. Joe grinned and reached down with his free hand, teasing the delicate skin under Kuro's balls as he continued to stretch Marie with the fingers of his other hand. Kuro's eyes rolled up briefly and Marie gasped as he thrust deeper into her.

"No more teasing," Kuro ground out.

That was fine with Joe. He was so hard at this point it hurt. The two of them were glorious, and he was desperate to join them.

Joe pulled his hands away and wiped his fingers on the washcloth before dropping it to one side. He palmed Marie's ass with one hand and lined himself up with her using the other. Another moan tore itself from Marie as Joe pressed into her slowly. Kuro paused, giving her time to adjust to the sensation. Joe eased himself into her with slow, shallow thrusts.

"I can feel you." Kuro forced the words out through gritted teeth. "It's so good. I won't last long."

Joe swallowed and nodded. She was so tight, so good. He wasn't going to last long, either. Finally, he was seated fully inside her. He held still, listening to Marie pant and feeling her body tremble as she was caught up in the sensation of having them both inside her at the same time.

"Marie, love, you okay?" Joe asked.

She nodded. "Yes."

Kuro reached up and caressed her face. "Take your time. We've got you."

Her breathing steadied and the tremors eased, her body relaxing into the both of them.

"This is…so full." She laughed, a little shaky, but still a laugh. "It's so intense."

Joe huffed out a laugh as Kuro chuckled.

"You can move now," she said. She flexed her hips experimentally. "I want you to move."

Kuro placed a hand over Joe's where he held her hip. Their eyes met over her shoulder and Kuro nodded.

Joe withdrew slowly. At the same time, Kuro pressed inside her. Then Joe slid into her as Kuro pulled back. They continued that way, slow and careful. They were all moaning now, groaning and sighing. The pleasure built and Joe savored every sound, every sensation.

Marie tightened around him and Kuro groaned, so she must be doing the same around Kuro, too. She called out, her head tossing back and her back curving even further.

"*Fuck*." Kuro's hips jerked as he came inside her.

The movement inside Marie pressed against Joe and he couldn't hold himself back. He reached around to press his fingertips against Marie's clit and managed one more thrust before he came apart too, spending himself inside Marie as she wailed through her own climax.

MARIE

Joe brought her tablet into the bedroom after they'd all managed to recover, settling himself beside her and Kuro. "Okay, show us what you and Rensho found."

Marie pressed a kiss on Joe's cheek, then settled the tablet in her lap so he and Kuro could both see the screen easily. "The hex was actually fairly complicated. It took a lot of power—drawn from the excruciating torture of multiple sacrifices, in this case—and a lot of preparation to ensure it could be cast successfully without some sort of object to attach to each of you as anchors to the spell. We honestly couldn't find enough information to re-create the spell. The knowledge for the exact steps might be something only those pain witches know, unless it was a part of a family spell book or grimoire. Not something we're going to find in any library system or archive."

Joe sagged next to her. "Not reassuring."

Kuro tightened his arm around her shoulders. "Go on."

"The thing any cook or baker or pharmaceutical researcher will tell you is that that can work in our favor."

Joe lifted his head, face scrunched up in confusion. "I wouldn't have ever related those professions in the same sentence. Please tell me how all of them would agree on a thing?"

Marie shrugged. "There's always a recipe, in a manner of speaking, and the way to keep a recipe a secret is to make sure only a very limited number of people know exactly what the steps are. The more steps, the more complicated the recipe, the harder it is to replicate. This applies in cooking, in baking, and in drug development. Trust me, I've had a few clients in the pharmaceutical field, and you pick things up as you design urban garden spaces for them."

Kuro chuckled. "And for you, all knowledge is valuable."

Marie shot him a sideways glance and allowed herself a smirk of her own. "Font of random information here. You never know when a piece of trivia is going to come in handy."

Joe wrapped a hand around her thigh. "Okay, so this works in our favor how?"

Marie tapped on the window with her notes of the various components for the spell. "Anything this complicated, with this many steps, has points of failure. A lot of them. Instead of trying to replicate the spell, Rensho and I figured out a way to consistently disrupt the hex at the point where it would be cast on the targets. It should be possible to incorporate into my wards and any wearable item you choose. We can make sure the spell won't be cast on either of you again."

"A ring," Kuro said quietly.

"Hmm?" Marie had to turn her head and tip her face up to look into Kuro's. "Is that what you'd like to wear?"

He leaned into her until he nose-booped her. "One for each of us. Yes."

Joe's hand tightened on her thigh. "Would you like that, Marie? Will you go choose a set of rings with the two of us?"

Her heart kicked into high gear. "I'm thinking there's a lot going unsaid in this moment, and I'm really, really afraid to read into this too deeply, because it could be very awkward. Could you both give me a little more clarity here? This feels like more than a thing to carry around a protective warding spell."

Kuro's gaze lifted and she looked between the two of them, watching something unspoken pass between them before Joe spoke again. "Rings, specifically, that we choose for each other. We don't want to rush you, and we don't have to get them, but I'd personally like a symbol of what's between us."

"I would too," Kuro added. "A promise, if not an engagement."

Oh. This was definitely what she was hoping it was. Her chest tightened, and emotions swirled without any place to go. Her eyes burned hot as tears welled up.

Joe pushed himself up to his knees, his brows drawing together in concern. "Hey, hey, hey. Please don't cry. We didn't mean to push you too fast. It's only been a short time, we know. It's just, we want you to know how serious we are about this relationship and about you. We want to give this thing between us a real commitment."

"No more moving around," Kuro said. "No more freelancing for Babel."

"Or any other shady contractors," Joe added. "Your friend, Thomas, connected us with one of the fixer teams who work with your consortium. We won't be a part of your cool ki—er, specific organization, but we'll be working with a group here specializing in damage control whenever there's spillover from supernatural events witnessed by humans."

"We'll be starting with the team that's going to follow up on Socrates Industries," Kuro continued. "They don't have the real amulet anymore, and you made sure the only lotuses left in the storage room were the Asian kind and not the Egyptian, so they won't be able to successfully carry out the ritual."

"It was a good thing you decided to leave the second replica at Socrates Industries," Joe said. "Because your teenage talent had to rush, it was actually identifiable as a fake. So no one had to die for the research team to realize the ritual wouldn't work anymore."

That had been weighing on Marie's mind.

"The fixer team managed to infiltrate that super secret security team we saw scoop up our walking dead guy in the first place," Joe continued. "So they've been able to confirm no other mythic items in the research lab. Just a couple of collectors' items from a pharaoh's tomb. Lots of symbology, but no real magic."

"Were we right about what they were trying to do?" Marie asked. "Were they trying to go into the afterlife to bring knowledge back to this life?"

Kuro nodded. "Yes. Death and rebirth. They were trying to make breakthroughs in medicine using experiences gleaned from going through the false door and wandering the worlds beyond, which weren't always the Egyptian afterlife. The blue lotus helped them travel through the false door and wearing the amulet brought the subject back into balance by ensuring the soul returned to the body with the dawn."

"Huh." Marie considered all of that. "The fixer team shared a lot of information with you."

"We provided a lot of intel to them first," Joe pointed out.

Marie smiled. "So we're all working together now."

"Not directly," Joe said quickly.

"No more conflict of interest." Kuro sounded pleased with the solution.

"And probably steadier work than freelancing anyway." Joe reached forward and wiped a stray tear from her cheek. "Is that okay? Is that what made you upset?"

She shook her head.

"Then what is it?" Joe asked, his confidence cracking as his hand dropped away from her face.

All those feelings started to well up inside her again, a fresh wave to overwhelm her. She caught his hand and reached for Kuro's with her other hand. "I just… Promise or proposal, or whatever, it just made me so happy I didn't know what to say. All the feelings boiled up and I…I don't… What are words, even?"

Joe stared at her, wide-eyed.

Kuro started chuckling.

Then Joe's surprise morphed into a bright grin, mischief sparking in his eyes. "We rendered you speechless. And it didn't even take an orgasm."

"Joe!" She tried to yank her hand back so she could whack him across the shoulder, but he kept hold of her hand and pressed his lips to the inside of her wrist.

"Rings, then," Kuro said as he tightened his arms around her. He started trailing kisses along her shoulder, toward her neck. "For all of us."

"Yes," she whispered.

"Good." Joe pressed a kiss on her leg, just above her knee. "Because you're ours now, witch."

She buried her fingers into Joe's hair as he continued to kiss a path up the inside of her thigh and reached for Kuro with her other hand, cradling his head as he found the sensitive spot just behind her ear. This felt right, so right.

She sighed happily. "And you're both mine."

Field Notes on the Supernatural and the Paranormal

Observations by Members of the Consortium Community

Greater Fae

Found in: All regions of the world

Category: Sentient

Details: Among the fae, Greater Fae are the most difficult to discern. The term Greater comes not from physical size or geographic origin, but from power. Whatever the permutation and expression of magical power, Greater Fae manifest their abilities on an order of magnitude above and beyond the overwhelming majority of other fae. While no fae will ever provide enough data to accurately measure their power, it is generally believed that Greater Fae have power comparable to the impact of a natural disaster.

Fae demonstrate broad variation in phenotypic presentation. While many are bipedal and generally resemble humans, many others may be quadrupedal, be significantly larger or smaller than the average human, or exhibit anthropomorphic characteristics. Further uncertainty regarding fae forms exists due to the ability of many fae to use glamours to change their appearances to the human eye. As a result, many Greater Fae are able to blend seamlessly into human populations or hide completely from them.

It is advisable to avoid interacting with Greater Fae. Fae are not human and do not experience emotions in the same way humans do. Similarly, they have differing priorities and values. Thus, there are many opportunities for misunderstanding, which can lead to disastrous consequences for the individual. Furthermore, Greater Fae are usually immortal, and consequences of their ire could fall on not only the human who upset them, but the human's friends and family, including future generations for an undetermined portion of eternity.

GUMIHO

Found in: Korea and all regions of the world

Category: Sentient

Details: Gumiho are fox spirits originating from Korea and the surrounding regions. Like other types of nine-tailed foxes, gumiho possess paranormal abilities such as shape-shifting.

A distinctive feature of the gumiho is the yeowoo guseul or fox bead. This mystical item is created by the gumiho at birth and is essential to the gumiho's survival. The yeowoo guseul can provide knowledge to a chosen host. The gumiho sends their yeowoo guseul into a human by means of a deep kiss. While the human hosts the fox bead in their body, the human is given knowledge while the fox bead draws on the human's life force in exchange. The person is purported to witness "land, people, and sky," during which each observation gives the person knowledge beyond what can be obtained by mundane means. In many folktales, the human fails to observe the final phase of the experience, the sky. As a result, the human gains special information, but not the most important.

Beyond this method of obtaining life-sustaining energy, gumiho are suspected to be bloodthirsty. They crave human flesh, particularly the heart and liver, through which life energy flows.

While gumiho are portrayed to have more carnal appetites than other nine-tailed fox spirits, they are also represented in lore as fierce guardians and allies.

Ittan Momen

Found in: Kagoshima prefecture, Japan

Category: Sentient

Details: Ittan momen are a type of Japanese yōkai, or supernatural creatures or phenomena described in Japanese folklore. In particular, ittan momen resemble long, narrow sheets of cloth, which were common household items in Japan for a time. Yōkai that have the appearance of household items are sometimes referred to as tsukumogami. Therefore, one could classify ittan momen as Japanese yōkai, with a further specification as tsukumogami.

While ittan momen are generally described as being 1 tan in surface area (approximately 10.6 meters/35 feet in length and 30 centimeters/12 inches wide), they have demonstrated the ability to change shape and appearance to a certain extent in order to appear as aged scrolls or even books. Ittan momen are also able to move on their own, and are occasionally witnessed flying through night skies.

Ittan momen have been known to attack humans, wrapping their length around the victim's face and shoulders until the victim is suffocated. Other accounts indicate an ittan momen could wrap around a victim and carry the victim off into the night. It is not confirmed that ittan momen attack humans as prey. Rather, such occurrences seem prompted as an act of self-defense or driven by anger or vengeance.

It is possible to converse with ittan momen, if they allow it. In most cases an agreement can be reached, and on rare occasions some ittan momen have entered magical contracts with other supernaturals. They are, however, beings of mischief, and will actively explore loopholes in any agreement that is not specific enough.

Kinnaree

Found in: Himmaphan Forest

Category: Sentient

Details: Kinnaree are quite possibly the loveliest of the Himmaphan beings, certainly capable of flight should they decide to leave the deep forests and mountains of their home. Descriptions vary from region to region, claiming these beings appear human in the upper half of the body with a human head, torso, and arms, yet below the waist, they have the body, tail, and legs of a swan.

However, many versions of the legend of Suthon and Manora describe seven kinnaree sisters—bird princesses—flying down from the forests of the Himmaphan to a lake in human lands. These sisters cast off their wings and tails to play in the waters of the lake under the light of the full moon. It is reasonable to conclude that in the absence of wings and tail at least some kinnaree appear wholly human with head, torso, arms, and legs. How these magical beings remove their wings and tails is unclear from the various renditions of the legend.

Perhaps there is a difference in phenotypic characteristics among kinnaree. A hereditary trait?

While kinnaree seem to have an affinity for air and water, the full extent of their abilities or powers are unknown. They are not natural predators of humankind but are capable of defending their territory if human civilization encroaches on the forests of the Himmaphan. At present, the Himmaphan has not been discovered by humankind as a whole, though it is possible individuals or small groups have ventured into these forests.

KITSUNE

Found in: Japan and all regions of the world

Category: Sentient

Details: Kitsune are a type of Japanese yōkai, purported to be spirit foxes or fox spirits who have amassed enough magic and wisdom to possess paranormal abilities. Theoretically, as a kitsune ages and becomes wiser, their power increases. The more tails a kitsune has, the more powerful and influential a kitsune has become. However, instances of Japanese diaspora, descendants of kitsune and human, have been known to have as many as nine tails by adulthood. This is an extremely short period of time and may indicate the number of tails is more an expression of magic potential or a measure of power, rather than wisdom.

Kitsune are known tricksters with the ability to shape change, shifting from fox to human form as well as a hybrid of the two. Some folklore indicates kitsune shape-shifting to other forms as well. While they do use this ability to trick others, there are an equal number of accounts portraying kitsune as loyal allies, friends, and lovers.

In many stories, kitsune are frequently known to impersonate attractive people and are known for seduction. This may be a result of the need for kitsune to feed on life energy by means of intimate contact.

Kitsune are also able to generate pocket universes. Very little is known about this aspect of kitsune abilities, but it has been established that once an object is used to create a pocket universe, it cannot be moved. The shape and appearance of the pocket universe is determined by the people inside it. Also, the size of the pocket universe is limited by the amount of magic the kitsune possesses.

SIDHE

Found in: All regions of the world

Category: Sentient

Details: Often referred to as "The Fair Folk," the sidhe are featured in many tales in western European folklore. Care is taken to avoid angering or insulting sidhe, and any humans who encounter one should proceed with caution in their dealings with these powerful individuals. In particular, one should never thank fae as this can be perceived as a dismissal of the effort or work done. Sincerity and thoughtful response is much better received.

Sidhe are generally described as essentially human in appearance with features that vary as much as humans around the world, though they are almost universally faster and stronger. Many have been described as exceedingly attractive, inhumanly so. It is posited that most sidhe use glamour to tone down or completely alter their appearance in order to pass for human.

Though two major factions exist within fae culture, the Seelie and Unseelie Courts, many fae are unaffiliated or far removed from the politics of either court. Some human scholars interpreted these factions to indicate good or evil nature, but further research indicates all fae are morally ambiguous regardless of faction and it is better to proceed with caution, regardless.

Cold iron is believed to repel or harm the fae, and direct contact to skin can burn the individual. Large amounts of iron can impede a fae's use of magic. The age and power of the fae may offer some resistance to the effect of cold iron.

While sidhe are not usually predators of humans, they can be considered competitors for the same territory and resources. On the other hand, evidence exists indicating sidhe can be allies and develop mutually beneficial relationships with humans. Sidhe are immortal and reproduce very rarely. There are instances in recorded history of sidhe abducting humans to bolster their population.

VAMPIRE

Found in: All regions of the world

Category: Sentient

Details: Vampires resemble humans and are able to pass as human at night. During the day, vampires are inanimate and can be mistaken for a lifeless corpse. They vary in appearance, most often described as exceedingly attractive. While vampires are stronger and faster than humans, they can exhibit a variety of other supernatural abilities. Such abilities may include flight, shape change, affinity to animals, forms of necromancy, and more. Age may increase power over time, but there is insufficient evidence to validate this theory.

Vampires are natural predators of humans. While vampires can feed off other beings or creatures, humans are their prey of choice and provide the most sustenance. Because of this and their supernatural abilities, they can be considered extremely dangerous to humans.

There are multiple types of vampire propagation. The most prevalent belief holds that a vampire bite can change a human to a vampire. This is an oversimplified misconception in that a vampire must first bite, then drain a human to the brink of death, then offer vampiric blood in return. This exchange provides the mortally wounded human the chance of rising after death as a vampire. It is uncertain what the success rate is for this method of propagation. Vampires are also able to reproduce amongst themselves or with humans. Offspring of vampires and humans can potentially be vampires, dhampir, or fully human in a 25% to 50% to 25% chance, respectively.

Vampires are immortal, in that they do not age and can continue existing indefinitely. They are not, however, invulnerable. Vampires can and have been hunted by humans. The most effective method of destroying a vampire has been to trap them in the open and expose them to sunlight. Another method is to sever the head from the body and burn both with fire. A wooden stake to the heart has been found effective against younger or less powerful vampires, but older vampires can survive. Holy water and other religious objects have not been proven to be a reliable weapon. Young vampires may starve until they crumble to dust. Older vampires may fall into a type of torpor and can be revived with sufficient fresh blood.

WINGED FAE

Found in: All regions of the world

Category: Sentient

Details: Sometimes referred to as fairies, sylph, or pixies, it is unclear whether any of these names are correct. Winged fae appear to be miniature humans with wings resembling those of a butterfly or moth or dragonfly. They are mischievous and rarely give direct answers when questioned about their nature. Like many of the fae in general, winged fae do not lie, but they are skilled in speaking partial truths and allowing the listener to make assumptions or come to inaccurate conclusions.

Because winged fae are significantly smaller than humans, averaging between twenty to twenty-five centimeters in height, some humans have perceived these fae to be childlike even when the winged fae in question is a fully mature adult. In addition to flight, winged fae have the ability to wield magic such as glamour. Their glamour is so powerful that they are often indistinguishable from butterflies or other winged insects, and may go undetected when hiding among flowers.

Fairy dust is associated with winged fae, though it is uncertain how they produce this substance. Any humans coming into contact with fairy dust are blessed (cursed?) with a kind of sixth sense for the supernatural.

Winged fae have an affinity with growing things, particularly flowering plant life. They can both encourage such plant life to grow and bloom and derive sustenance from these plants. Arches of flowering vines and hedges seemingly occurring naturally are often the work of winged fae, as are mushroom circles.

As delightful as their appearances might be, a human would be well-advised to remain alert and cautious. Winged fae have a great love of mischief at best and can be frighteningly malicious at their worst. Many have made the mistake of underestimating these beings.

WITCH

Found in: All regions of the world

Category: Sentient

Details: Witches can be found among the human population of every continent. The practice of witchcraft takes many forms and draws from many traditions. Though many humans claim to be or have been accused of being witches, for the purposes of these field notes, observations will be focused on witches who manifest supernatural abilities.

Witches are generally mortal, though the use of magic may grant them long lives, depending on how they practice their craft. The types of magic witches might manifest are not intrinsically good or evil; however, the purpose with which such power is used may fall across a broad spectrum of benevolent to malicious intent.

Witches may draw their power from a variety of sources. The most common are the natural world, sacrifice, and personal reservoirs. Accounts exist of a single witch drawing power from a coven or other gathering of witches supplying their magic either willingly or without informed consent. Some witches exhibit the rare ability to draw magic from an object or naturally occurring power reservoir, such as a ley line.

Though witches are human, there is no known genetic marker for who will become a witch. While entire family lines have been known to exhibit the supernatural trait, witches have been born with no previous record of the ability in their family history.

Karakasa Kozō

Found in: Older, traditional households in Japan

Category: Non-sentient ???

Details: Also known as kasa obake or karakasa obake, karakasa kozō are oiled-paper umbrellas that have transformed into Japanese yōkai. As such, they have gained a single eye, hop around on one leg, and have a rather long and protruding tongue.

The tongue is of particular note as karakasa kozō enjoy sneaking up on humans and surprising them with a large, wet lick of said tongue. While not particularly dangerous or physically harmful, it could be fairly traumatic for the recipient.

Karakasa kozō are rather playful spirits and very amenable to cohabitation within a household. There are other umbrella yōkai that are not as harmless or benevolent as the karakasa kozō, so caution is advised when identifying exactly which yōkai a particular animated umbrella might be.

Karin Puksa

Found in: Himmaphan Forest

Category: Non-sentient

Details: The Himmaphan Forest is perhaps one of the few places it is possible to observe an elephant-like creature fly. The Karin Puksa resembles a member of the Elephantidae family with smooth, black skin and the wings and tail of a bird sporting bloodred plumage. The wingspan of the Karin Puksa is quite impressive, at least twice as wide as its body length, and despite its bulk, this creature can fly at great speed over significant distances.

The tusks of the Karin Puksa are used for digging in search of water or roots, for debarking or marking trees, and even for lifting and moving vegetation or obstacles from their path. In fights, the tusks are used in both attack and defense.

It is currently thought that Karin Puksa are herbivores and generally peaceful unless attacked.

Kraisorn Rajasri

Found in: Himmaphan Forest

Category: Non-sentient

Details: These impressive predators resemble white lions. Their coloring is strikingly contrasted with deep red mane and tail tip, red paws, and red markings around their mouths. They have broad skulls, implying high intelligence, and heavily muscled hindquarters. Their hunting habits include both stalking and ambush, and it is theorized that their preferred prey are large hoofed ruminant mammals such as deer.

Kraisorn rajasri are thought to be solitary, seeking out others of their kind only during mating season. As they are nocturnal, one might hear a variety of sounds to warn of the proximity of a kraisorn rajasri, including roars or grunts. These may be territorial in nature and intended to warn others off before a direct confrontation occurs.

TSURUBEBI

Found in: Coniferous forests, mainly on Kyushu and Shikoku in Japan

Category: Non-sentient ???

Details: These small tree spirits appear as balls of blue-white flames bobbing among the branches of coniferous trees deep in the forest. The bobbing motion resembles the way a bucket swings back and forth in a well. Occasionally, one can get close enough to perceive facial features in the flames. Eyewitness accounts are inconsistent as to whether the face resembles a human or an animal.

These spirits are generally uninterested in humans and seem benign, for the most part. However, some scholars suggest that the tsurubebi is related to another yōkai, or supernatural creature of Japanese folklore, called a tsurube otoshi. The tsurube otoshi is found in the same habitats, but is quite dangerous. It would be advisable to approach with caution unless one is certain they have accurately identified this creature. Even then, it is best to observe and leave it be.

Will-o'-the-Wisp

Found in: United Kingdom and Europe

Category: Non-sentient

Details: A will-o'-the-wisp is a ghost light appearing at night, flickering and glowing like a candlelight within a lantern. They are most often encountered over bogs, swamps, marshes, or cemeteries. Will-o'-the-wisps do not inflict direct harm on those who encounter them, but one should still exercise caution as these spirits are often mischievous and may lead humans deeper into mists or fog until they are lost or fall victim to the dangers of the environment. They are not always malicious and may instead lead a lost wanderer back to well-travelled roads or lead searchers to a lost child.

The difficulty in choice for one encountering a will-o'-the-wisp is deciding whether it will lead you to hope or to harm.

Bluebeard's Key

Region of Origin: Western Europe

Category: Inanimate

Details: One of a set of keys, purported to open a forbidden door within a legendary chateau. The actual location of the chateau is currently unknown. The chateau belonged to Bluebeard, a noble man of great power and wealth. Bluebeard was known to have married many times, and all of his brides disappeared under dubious circumstances.

The key has magical properties, with the ability to unlock any door under specific circumstances. When exposed to blood, the key's more damning properties are activated, potentially revealing a holder as guilty of transgression or betrayal while also inflicting vivid visions of murder on the holder. Some believe activating these latent powers will curse the holder, resulting in their own death by the hand of a loved one.

It is worth noting that where the most popular French tale of Bluebeard and his wives depicts the heroine as a damsel in distress, having used the key out of greed and waiting for her brothers to rescue her, older folktales and stories told among the proletariat portray the heroine as having used the key out of curiosity, then being clever and cunning enough to rescue herself.

Breastplate of Tutankhamun

Region of Origin: Egypt

Category: Inanimate

Details: Found in the tomb of Tutankhamun, this breastplate was originally identified as a pectoral that would be worn by the pharaoh across his chest. A prominent feature of this particular breastplate is the unique gemstone used to form the central scarab.

The gemstone was originally thought to be chalcedony, a common variety of quartz. However, later study revealed the gemstone to be a type of desert glass consisting of almost pure silicon dioxide with traces of very unusual elements, including iridium—one of the rarest minerals on Earth—and reidite, an exceedingly rare mineral that only forms under very high pressure, such as that which occurs during massive meteorite impacts.

While the breastplate contains a great amount of iconography which could grant mystical attributes, the central gemstone likely grants a significant boost to the magical properties of this object.

Noose of the Phayanak

Region of Origin: Kamchanod Forest

Category: Inanimate

Details: First record of the noose of the phayanak indicates this item was given as a gift from a phayanak to a human after the human had saved the phayanak's life. The human had requested this item with the intent to capture a kinnaree. In addition to giving the human the noose, the phayanak also taught the human how to use it effectively.

When dormant, the item resembles a lasso or lariat—a length of rope with a loop at one end, designed to be thrown around a target and tightened when pulled. Once the noose binds its victim, the remaining length wraps around the victim like the coils of a serpent. The harder a victim struggles, the tighter the coils of the noose bind them. The noose is also impervious to being cut or burned and is essentially indestructible by mundane means.

The Red Shoes

Region of Origin: Northern Europe

Category: Inanimate

Details: Cursed items, the red shoes were created by humans. The exact origin of the curse is unconfirmed but is potentially of human origin as well.

The shoes become active the first time a human dances in them. The wearer is then compelled to continue to dance, unable to stop. Eventually, the wearer dies, either from exhaustion or from some mishap as they are forced to continue dancing without surcease.

The shoes appear to be made of red satin and have changed style over time. Descriptions vary across incidents in which the red shoes have been confirmed to have been involved. The nature of the shoes is to be attractive to potential victims. It is possible the shoes themselves compel victims to put them on. The area of effect when the shoes are not worn or are contained within some type of packaging is uncertain, but it is thought that the shoes have greater effect with proximity and visual exposure.

Beings of supernatural or paranormal nature and humans under the influence of magic may have some resistance to the curse of the red shoes. Though folktales and lore surrounding the red shoes indicate religious elements to the nature of the curse, it is theorized that these shoes became cursed first and then became incorporated into religious teachings as time passed in various regions.

Acknowledgments

Mythwoven continues to be the series in which I redefine myself and who I am as a writer.

Thank you to K Tempest Bradford and Alethea Kontis for almost a month in Egypt, exploring pyramids and tombs, breakfasting along the Nile, and wandering through museums. I drew so much inspiration from the experiences we shared and so much encouragement from both of you as writers.

Thank you to Mary Altman, my editor, for loving this story and for telling me how much you enjoyed it. Your feedback, both encouraging and critical, has been exactly what I needed to bring this story to life.

Thank you to Courtney Miller-Callihan, my agent, for continuing to believe in me as a writer and recognizing how much I needed my dual careers in publishing and in life sciences to continue to excel in both.

Thank you to Matthew, my love, for being my sounding board. You've always been happy to brainstorm with me and take a step back when my thoughts needed to wander. The most important question you taught me to ask myself has been, "Am I enjoying this?"

Finally, thank you to my readers. I appreciate you so, so much!

About the Author

Piper J. Drake is a bestselling author of romantic suspense, paranormal romance, science fiction, and fantasy. Foodie. Wanderer. Usually not lost. She lives in Seattle with her husband and beloved corgi.

Website: piperjdrake.com
Facebook: AuthorPiperJDrake
Instagram: @piperjdrake